THE GHOST BOOK
SIXTEEN STORIES OF THE UNCANNY

LADY CYNTHIA ASQUITH

WFP
WORDFIRE PRESS

The Ghost Book, edited by Lady Cynthia Asquith

The Ghost Book, first published in 1926.
This work is in the public domain.
Foreword © 2023 Kevin J. Anderson.
This edition edited by Jessica Guernsey

EBook ISBN: 978-1-68057-520-0
Trade Paperback ISBN: 978-1-68057-521-7
Hardcover ISBN: 978-1-68057-522-4

Cover design by Allyson Longueira, Katie E. Nelson, and Jessica Guernsey
Cover artwork image © Ana | Adobe Stock
Photo: National Portrait Gallery London
Published by WordFire Press, LLC PO Box 1840 Monument CO 80132
Kevin J. Anderson & Rebecca Moesta, Publishers
WordFire Press Edition 2023

Join our WordFire Press Readers Group for sneak previews, updates, new projects, and giveaways. Sign up at wordfirepress.com

THE GHOST BOOK

CONTENTS

FOREWORD

KEVIN J. ANDERSON

If you're a fan of ghost stories, you owe much of your reading to *The Ghost Book*. This influential anthology redefined the genre, set a high bar, and crystallized the modern psychological ghost tale.

First published in 1926, *The Ghost Book* was a groundbreaking collection of literary ghost stories assembled by socialite Lady Cynthia Asquith, focusing on atmospheric and cerebral aspects of the chilling supernatural story, rather than the more garish and shocking tales published in penny dreadfuls.

The Ghost Book contains sixteen stories (seventeen, actually, since Oliver Onions throws in two of them), written by some of the most well-known and well-respected authors of the day. By bringing in works from such significant literary figures, Asquith raised the ghost story to a new level.

Many of these tales hold up remarkably well almost a century later. The authors took their time and used the words they needed, working with meticulous care to build a sense of dread to extraordinary creepiness. Aficionados of ghost stories can truly savor the experience, feel the chill grow and goose-flesh crawl. Often times, a significant part of the story is spent simply establishing the narrator and his situation, until his mysterious and haunted guest could sit in front of a fire, sip a brandy, and begin with, "Here, let me tell you a tale..."

Reading these entries, you will recognize many standard twists and tricks and surprise endings—and many of these tropes were first introduced here in *The Ghost Book*. Some of the authors are no longer known by modern readers, but many are well known in the pantheon of weird and supernatural fiction. *The Ghost Book* contains works by masters such as Algernon Blackwood (one of the most prolific ghost story writers of his day), Arthur Machen (best known for *The Great God Pan* and *The Three Impostors*), Hugh Walpole, Walter de la Mare, Oliver Onions (*Widdershins* and the horror classic "The Beckoning Fair One"), May Sinclair, and Enid Bagnold (author of *National Velvet*). The most well-known story in the anthology is "The Rocking Horse Winner," a riveting tale by D. H. Lawrence (best known for *Lady Chatterly's Lover*), which was made into a 1949 film and two subsequent films.

These authors and stories were hugely influential on the next generations of supernatural writers, from H. P. Lovecraft to Stephen King. You'll find much here to give you a chill.

I have a personal connection to this book, and when I saw that it was being reissued in a fine new edition from WordFire Press, as a project for the graduate program in Publishing for Western Colorado University, I happily offered to write the foreword. This book had a great impact on me, both as a writer and an appreciator of fine supernatural fiction.

I was about ten years old, a kid with an overactive imagination, who already had dreams of being a writer someday. I loved to watch classic black-and-white horror movies whenever I managed to stay up late for the Friday night Creature Features.

One Christmas morning, amongst other gifts, I tore off the wrapping paper of what was obviously a book, to find the 1970 Pan paperback reissue of *The Ghost Book*, with tiny print and a compelling cover photograph of a cobweb-bedecked candelabra and rats nosing among long-abandoned plates from a haunted banquet. The next gifts I unwrapped were *The Second Ghost Book* and *The Third Ghost Book*, also edited by Lady Cynthia Asquith, then *The Fourth Ghost Book*, edited by James Turner.

What a great Christmas! My parents certainly knew my interest, and I had a fictional feast before me. I loved those books, turning page after page, fascinated by the hauntings and the murders and the dark secrets of vengeful spirits. These anthologies whetted my appetite as a boy and fired my imagination. I began to write ghost stories of my own—mostly terrible ones, but I got better.

It was a delight to reread this book now, reminded of these great stories. "The Rocking Horse Winner" by D. H. Lawrence remains particularly powerful, and Hugh Walpole's "Mrs. Lunt" gave me a chill. The lavish descriptions of Arthur Machen's "Munitions of War" make the story quite memorable, and "Twelve O'Clock" has a perfect twist, but perhaps the story I most enjoyed was "The Lost Tragedy," in which Shakespeare's ghost desperately tries to prevent an antiquarian book collector from publishing an abysmal first draft of one of the Bard's lost plays. There are other amusing stories here in contrast to the creepiness, such as "Mr. Tallent's Ghost" by Mary Webb and "Two Trifles" by Oliver Onions.

This is an important collection, make no mistake about it.

You know many of the stories, at least tangentially (they've been mimicked by so many other authors). Now read them again.

Lady Cynthia Asquith was a socialite in England, popular in literary circles in the early 20th century. She was the personal secretary of J. M. Barrie, author of *Peter Pan*, from 1918 until his death in 1937. She knew many other writers, participated in literary salons, hobnobbed with the most respected authors of the day. Through her connections, she managed to get original fiction, as well as select reprints, for *The Ghost Book*.

Asquith wrote essays, short stories of her own (including one of the stories in *The Ghost Book*, "The Corner Shop," under a pen name), and edited several anthologies including influential supernatural collections *Shudders* (1929) and *When Churchyards Yawn* (1931), as well as children's anthologies.

Even though *The Ghost Book* was a success, Asquith did not return to the series for more than a quarter of a century until she released *The Second Ghost Book* in 1952, followed by *The Third Ghost Book* in 1955. After Asquith's death in 1960, James Turner revived the series in 1965, followed by Rosemary Timperley, and then others—at least thirteen *Ghost Book* volumes under varying titles and alternate titles.

But none had the impact of the very first *Ghost Book*.

I hope you enjoy this fine new edition of the original classic. WordFire Press is pleased to bring these ghosts out of the dusty corners of time so they can haunt readers' imaginations again. Enjoy!

THE VILLA DESIREE

MAY SINCLAIR

I

He had arranged it all for her. She was to stay a week in Cannes with her aunt and then to go on to Roquebrune by herself, and he was to follow her there. She, Mildred Eve, supposed he could follow her anywhere, since they were engaged now.

There had been difficulties, but Louis Carson had got over all of them by lending her the Villa Désirée. She would be all right there, he said. The caretakers, Narcisse and Armandine, would look after her: Armandine was an excellent cook; and she wouldn't be five hundred yards from her friends, the Derings. It was so like him to think of it, to plan it all out for her. And when he came down? Oh, when he came down, he would go to the Cap Martin Hotel, of course. He understood everything without any tiresome explaining. She couldn't afford the hotels at Cap Martin and Monte Carlo; and though the Derings had asked her to stay with them, she really couldn't dump herself down on them like that, almost in the middle of their honeymoon.

Their honeymoon; she could have bitten her tongue out for saying it, for not remembering. It was awful of her to go talking to Louis Carson about honeymoons, after the appalling tragedy of his.

There were things she hadn't been told, that she hadn't liked to ask: Where it had happened? And how? And how long ago? She only knew it was on his wedding night, that he had gone in to the poor little girl of a bride and found her dead there, in the bed.

They said she had died in a sort of fit.

You had only to look at him to see that something terrible had happened to him some time. You saw it when his face was doing nothing: a queer, agonized look that made him strange to her while it lasted. It was more than suffering; it was almost as if he could be cruel, only he never was, he never could be. *People* were cruel, if you liked; they said his face put them off. Mildred could see what they meant. It might have put her off, perhaps, if she hadn't known what he had gone through. But the first time she had met him he had been pointed out to her as the man to whom just that appalling thing had happened. So, far from putting her off, that was what had drawn her to him from the beginning, made her pity him first, then love him. Their engagement had come quick, in the third week of their acquaintance.

When she asked herself, "After all, what do I know about him?" she had her answer, "I know *that*." She felt that already she had entered into a mystical union with him through compassion. She liked the strangeness that kept other people away and left him to her altogether. He was more her own that way.

There was (Mildred Eve didn't deny it) his personal magic, the fascination of his almost abnormal beauty. His black, white, and blue. The intensely blue eyes under the straight black bars of the eyebrows, the perfect, pure, white face suddenly masked by the black moustache and small, black, pointed beard. And the rich vivid smile he had for her, the lighting up of the blue, the flash of white teeth in the black mask.

He had smiled then at her embarrassment as the awful word leaped out at him. He had taken it from her and turned the sharp edge of it.

"It would never do," he had said, "to spoil the *honeymoon*. You'd much better have my villa. Some day, quite soon, it'll be yours, too. You know I like anticipating things."

That was always the excuse he made for his generosities. He had said it again when he engaged her seat in the *train de luxe* from Paris and wouldn't let her pay for it. (She had wanted to travel third class.) He was only anticipating, he said.

He was seeing her off now at the Gare de Lyons, standing on the platform with a great sheaf of blush roses in his arms. She, on the high step of the railway carriage, stood above him, swinging in the open doorway. His face was on a level with her feet; they gleamed white through the fine black stockings. Suddenly he thrust his face forwards and kissed her feet. As the train moved, he ran beside it and tossed the roses into her lap.

And then she sat in the hurrying train, holding the great sheaf of blush roses in her lap, and smiling at them as she dreamed. She was in the Riviera Express, the Riviera Express. Next week she would be in Roquebrune, at the Villa Désirée. She read the three letters woven into the edges of the grey cloth cushions: PLM: Paris-Lyons-Mediterranée, Paris-Lyons-Mediterranée, over and over again. They sang themselves to the rhythm of the wheels; they wove their pattern into her dream. Every now and then, when the other passengers weren't looking, she lifted the roses to her face and kissed them.

She hardly knew how she dragged herself through the long dull week with her aunt at Cannes.

And now it was over and she was by herself at Roquebrune.

The steep narrow lane went past the Derings' house and up the face of the hill. It led up into a little olive wood, and above the wood she saw the garden terraces. The sunlight beat in and out of their golden-yellow walls. Tier above tier, the blazing terraces rose, holding up their ranks of spindle-stemmed lemon and orange trees. On the topmost terrace the Villa Désirée stood white and hushed between two palms, two tall poles each topped by a head of dark-green, curving, sharp-pointed blades. A grey scrub of olive trees straggled up the hill behind it and on each side.

Rolf and Martha Dering waited for her with Narcisse and Armandine on the steps of the verandah.

"Why on earth didn't you come to us?" they said.

"I didn't want to spoil your honeymoon."

"Honeymoon, what rot! We've got over *that* silliness. Anyhow, it's our third week of it."

They were detached and cool in their happiness.

She went in with them, led by Narcisse and Armandine.

The caretakers, subservient to Mildred Eve and visibly inimical to the Derings, left them together in the salon. It was very bright and French and fragile and worn; all faded grey and old greenish gilt; the gilt chairs and settees carved like picture frames round the gilded cane. The hot light beat in through the long windows open to the terrace, drawing up a faint powdery smell from the old floor.

Rolf Dering stared at the room, sniffing, with fine nostrils in a sort of bleak disgust.

"You'd much better have come to us," he said.

"Oh, but—it's charming."

"Do you *think* so?" Martha said. She was looking at her intently.

Mildred saw that they expected her to feel something, she wasn't sure what, something that they felt. They were subtle and fastidious.

"It does look a little queer and—unlived in," she said, straining for the precise impression.

"I should say," said Martha, "it had been too much lived in, if you ask me."

"Oh no. That's only dust you smell. I think, perhaps, the windows haven't been open very long."

She resented this criticism of Louis's villa.

Armandine appeared at the doorway. Her little, slant eyes were screwed up and smiling. She wanted to know if Madame wouldn't like to go up and look at her room.

"We'll all go up and look at it," said Rolf.

They followed Armandine up the steep, slender, curling staircase. A closed door faced them on the landing. Armandine opened it, and the hot golden light streamed out to them again.

The room was all golden white; it was like a great white tank filled with blond water where things shimmered, submerged in the stream; the white-painted chairs and dressing table, the high, white-painted bed, the pink-and-white striped ottoman at its foot; all vivid and still, yet quivering in the stillness, with the hot throb, throb of the light.

"*Voilà*, madame," said Armandine.

They didn't answer. They stood, fixed in the room, held by the stillness, staring, all three of them, at the high white bed that rose up, enormous, with its piled mattresses and pillows, the long white counterpane hanging straight and steep, like a curtain, to the floor.

Rolf turned to Armandine.

"Why have you given Madame this room?"

Armandine shrugged her fat shoulders. Her small eyes blinked at him, slanting, inimical.

"Monsieur's orders, monsieur. It is the best room in the house. It was Madame's room."

"I know. That's *why*—"

"But no, monsieur. Nobody would dislike to sleep in Madame's room. The poor little thing, she was so pretty, so sweet, so young, monsieur. Surely Madame will not dislike the room."

"Who *was*—Madame?"

"But, Monsieur's wife, madame. Madame Carson. Poor Monsieur, it was so sad—"

"Rolf," said Mildred, "did he bring her here—on their honeymoon?"

"Yes."

"Yes, madame. She died here. It was so sad. Is there anything I can do for madame?"

"No, thank you, Armandine."

"Then I will get ready the tea."

She turned again in the doorway, crooning in her thick, Provencal voice, "*Madame* does not dislike her room?"

"No, Armandine. No. It's a beautiful room."

The door closed on Armandine. Martha opened it again to see whether she were listening on the landing. Then she broke out:

"Mildred—you know you loathe it. It's beastly. The whole place is beastly."

"You can't stay in it," said Rolf.

"Why not? Do you mean because of Madame?"

Martha and Rolf were looking at each other, as if they were both asking what they should say. They said nothing. "Oh, her poor little ghost won't hurt me, if that's what you mean."

"Nonsense," Martha said. "Of course it isn't."

"What is it, then?"

"It's so beastly lonely, Mildred," said Rolf.

"Not with Narcisse and Armandine."

"Well, I wouldn't sleep a night in the place," Martha said, "if there wasn't any other on the Riviera. I don't like the look of it."

Mildred went to the open lattice, turning her back on the high, rather frightening bed. Down there below the terraces she saw the grey flicker of the olive woods and, beyond them, the sea. Martha was wrong. The place was beautiful; it was adorable. She wasn't going to be afraid of poor little Madame. Louis had loved her. He loved the place. That was why he had lent it to her.

She turned. Rolf had gone down again. She was alone with Martha. Martha was saying something.

"Mildred—where's Mr. Carson?"

"In Paris. Why?"

"I thought he was coming here."

"So he is, later on."

"To the villa?"

"No. Of course not. To Cap Martin." She laughed. "So *that's* what you're thinking of, is it?"

She could understand her friend's fear of haunted houses, but not these previsions of impropriety.

Martha looked shy and ashamed.

"Yes," she said. "I suppose so."

"How horrid of you! You might have trusted me."

"I do trust you." Martha held her a minute with her clear loving eyes. "Are you sure you can trust *him*?"

"Trust him? Do you trust Rolf?"

"Ah—if it was like that, Mildred—"

"It *is* like that."

"You're really not afraid?"

"What is there to be afraid of? Poor little Madame?"

"I didn't mean Madame. I meant Monsieur."

"Oh—wait till you've seen him."

"Is he *very* beautiful?"

"Yes, but it isn't *that*, Martha. I can't tell you what it is."

They went downstairs, hand in hand, in the streaming light. Rolf waited for them on the verandah. They were taking Mildred back to dine with them.

"Won't you let me tell Armandine you're stopping the night?" he said.

"No, I won't. I don't want Armandine to think I'm frightened."

She meant she didn't want Louis to think she was frightened. Besides, she was not frightened.

"Well, if you find you don't like it, you must come to us," he said.

And they showed her the little spare-room next to theirs, with its camp-bed made up, the bedclothes turned back, all ready for her, any time of the night, in case she changed her mind. The front door was on the latch.

"You've only to open it, and creep in here and be safe," Rolf said.

II

Armandine—subservient and no longer inimical, now that the Derings were not there,—Armandine had put the candle and matches on the night-table and the bell which, she said, would summon her if Madame wanted anything in the night. And she had left her.

As the door closed softly behind Armandine, Mildred drew in her breath with a light gasp. Her face in the looking glass, between the tall lighted candles, showed its mouth half-open, and she was aware that her heart shook slightly in its beating. She was angry with the face in the glass with its foolish mouth gaping. She said to herself. *Is it possible I'm frightened?* It was not possible. Rolf and Martha had made her walk too fast up the hill, that was all. Her heart always did that when she walked too fast uphill, and she supposed that her mouth always gaped when it did it.

She clenched her teeth and let her heart choke her till it stopped shaking.

She was quiet now. But the test would come when she had blown out the candles and had to cross the room in the dark to the bed.

The flame bent backwards before the light puff she gave, and righted itself. She blew harder, twice, with a sense of spinning out the time. The flame writhed and went out. She extinguished the other candle at one breath. The red point of the wick pricked the darkness for a second and died, too, with a small crackling sound. At the far end of the room the high bed glimmered. She thought, *Martha was right. The bed* is *awful.*

She could feel her mouth set in a hard grin of defiance as she went to it, slowly, too proud to be frightened. And then suddenly, halfway, she thought about Madame.

The awful thing was climbing into that high funeral bed that Madame had died in. Your back felt so undefended. But once she was safe between the bedclothes it would be all right. It would be all right so long as she didn't think about Madame. Very well, then, she wouldn't think about her. You could frighten yourself into anything by thinking.

Deliberately, by an intense effort of her will, she turned the sad image of Madame out of her mind and found herself thinking about Louis Carson.

This was Louis's house, the place he used to come to when

he wanted to be happy. She made out that he had sent her there because he wanted to be happy in it again. She was there to drive away the unhappiness, the memory of poor little Madame. Or, perhaps, because the place was sacred to him; because they were both so sacred, she and the young dead bride who hadn't been his wife. Perhaps he didn't think about her as dead at all; he didn't want her to be driven away. The room she had died in was not awful to him. He had the faithfulness for which death doesn't exist. She wouldn't have loved him if he hadn't been faithful. You could be faithful and yet marry again.

She was convinced that whatever she was there for, it was for some beautiful reason. Anything that Louis did, anything he thought or felt or wanted, would be beautiful. She thought of Louis standing on the platform in the Paris station, his beautiful face looking up at her; its sudden darting forward to kiss her feet. She drifted again into her happy hypnotizing dream, and was fast asleep before midnight.

She woke with a sense of intolerable compulsion, as if she were being dragged violently up out of her sleep. The room was grey in the twilight of the unrisen moon.

And she was not alone.

She knew that there was something there. Something that gave up the secret of the room and made it frightful and obscene. The greyness was frightful and obscene. It gathered itself together; it became the containing shell of the horror.

The thing that had waked her was there with her in the room.

For she knew she was awake. Apart from her supernatural certainty, one physical sense, detached from the horror, was alert. It heard the ticking of the clock on the chimney-piece, the hard sharp shirring of the palm leaves outside as the wind rubbed their knife-blades together. These sounds were witnesses to the fact that she was awake, and that therefore the thing that was going to happen would be real. At the first sight of the greyness she had shut her eyes again, afraid to look into the room, because she knew that what she would see there was real. But she had no more power over her eyelids than she had had over her sleep. They opened under the same intolerable compulsion. And the supernatural thing forced itself now on her sight.

It stood a little in front of her by the bedside. From the breasts downwards its body was unfinished, rudimentary, not quite born. The grey shell was still pregnant with its loathsome shapelessness. But the face—the face was perfect in absolute horror. And it was Louis Carson's face.

Between the black bars of the eyebrows and the black pointed beard she saw it, drawn back, distorted in an obscene agony, corrupt and malignant. The face and the body, flesh and not yet flesh, they were the essence made manifest of untold, unearthly abominations.

It came on to her, bending over her, peering at her, so close that the piled mattresses now hid the lower half of its body. And the frightful thing about it was that it was blind, parted from all controlling and absolving clarity, flesh and yet not flesh. It looked for her without seeing her; and she knew that, unless she could save herself that instant, it would find what it looked for. Even now, behind the barrier of the piled-up mattresses, the unfinished form defined and completed itself; she could feel it shake with the agitation of its birth.

Her heart staggered and stopped in her breast, as if her breast had been clamped down on to her backbone. She struggled against wave after wave of faintness; for the moment that she lost consciousness the appalling presence there would have its way with her. All her will rose up against it. She dragged herself upright in the bed, suddenly, and spoke to it:

"Louis! What are you doing there?"

At her cry it went, without moving; sucked back into the greyness that had borne it.

She thought: "It'll come back. It'll come back. Even if I don't see it, I shall know it's in the room."

She knew what she would do. She would get up and go to the Derings. She longed for the open air, for Rolf and Martha, for the strong earth under her feet.

She lit the candle on the night-table and got up. She still felt that it was there, and that, standing upon the floor, she was more vulnerable, more exposed to it. Her terror was too extreme for her to stay and dress herself. She thrust her bare feet into her shoes, slipped her travelling coat over her night-gown and went downstairs and out through the house door, sliding back the bolts without a sound. She remembered that Rolf had left a lantern for her in the verandah, in case she should want it—as if they had known.

She lit the lantern and made her way down the villa garden, stumbling from terrace to terrace, through the olive wood and the steep lane to the Derings' house. Far down the hill she could see a light in the window of the spare room. The house door was on the latch. She went through and on into the lamp-lit room that waited for her.

She knew again what she would do. She would go away before Louis Carson could come to her. She would go away tomorrow, and never come back again. Rolf and Martha would bring her things down from the villa; he would take her into Italy in his car. She would get away from Louis Carson forever. She would get away up through Italy.

III

Rolf had come back from the villa with her things, and he

had brought her a letter. It had been sent up that morning from Cap Martin.

It was from Louis Carson.

My DARLING MILDRED,

You see I couldn't wait a fortnight without seeing you. I *had* to come. I'm here at the Cap Martin Hotel.

I'll be with you sometime between half-past ten and eleven—

Below, at the bottom of the lane, Rolf's car waited. It was half past ten. If they went now, they would meet Carson coming up the lane. They must wait till he had passed the house and gone up through the olive wood.

Martha had brought hot coffee and rolls. They sat down at the other side of the table and looked at her with kind anxious eyes as she turned sideways, watching the lane.

"Rolf," she said suddenly, "do you know anything about Louis Carson?"

She could see them looking now at each other.

"Nothing. Only the things the people here say."

"What sort of things?"

"Don't tell her, Rolf."

"Yes. He *must* tell me. I've got to know."

She had no feeling left but horror, horror that nothing could intensify.

"There's not much. Except that he was always having women with him up there. Not particularly nice women. He seems," Rolf said, "to have been rather an appalling beast."

"Must have been," said Martha, "to have brought his poor little wife there, after—"

"Rolf, what did Mrs. Carson die of?"

"Don't ask *me*," he said.

But Martha answered: "She died of fright. She saw something. I told you the place was beastly."

Rolf shrugged his shoulders.

"Why, you said you felt it yourself. We both felt it."

"Because we knew about the beastly things he did there."

"*She* didn't know. I tell you; she saw something."

Mildred turned her white face to them.

"I saw it too."

"You?"

"What? What did you see?"

"Him. Louis Carson."

"He must be dead, then, if you saw his ghost."

"The ghosts of poor dead people don't kill you. It was what he *is*. All that beastliness in a face. A face."

She could hear them draw in their breath short and sharp. "Where?"

"There. In that room. Close by the bed. It was looking for me. I saw what *she* saw."

She could see them frown now, incredulous, forcing themselves to disbelieve. She could hear them talking, their voices beating off the horror.

"Oh, but she couldn't. He wasn't there."

"He heard her scream first."

"Yes. He was in the other room, you know."

"*It* wasn't. He can't keep it back."

"Keep it back?"

"No. He was waiting to go to her."

Her voice was dull and heavy with realization. She felt herself struggling, helpless, against their stolidity, their unbelief.

"Look at that," she said. She pushed Carson's letter across to them.

"He was waiting to go to her," she repeated. "And—last night—he was waiting to come to me."

They stared at her, stupefied.

"Oh, can't you *see*?" she cried. "It didn't wait. It got there before him."

CHEMICAL
ALGERNON BLACKWOOD

It is odd how trivial a thing can cause a first, instinctive dislike: the way a man wears his hat, the smirk with which a woman uses her mirror and lipstick in a public place—and the aversion is suddenly aroused. Later knowledge may justify this first dislike, but the actual start has been the merest triviality.

Some think, however, this cause has not been so trivial as it appears; that gesture, being an unconscious expression of the entire personality, may betray far more than speech, which is calculated. Moleson, thinking over the brusqueness of the stranger on the doorstep, the unnecessary way he pushed ahead of him and up the stairs, his whole air, indeed, of general resentment and disapproval, found himself recalling a rather significant answer that a very wise old man had once given in his hearing to a commonplace question. The question was not his own: he was listening to two friends discussing a third.

"Everything indicates," said the first, carelessly enough, "that I ought to like X. I have nothing against him. Quite the reverse, in fact. Yet I do not like him. I simply cannot like him, try as I will. Now—why don't I?"

"Your dislike," was the reply, "is probably chemical. Merely chemical."

This came back to Moleson's mind now, as he unpacked his things and arranged himself in the top-floor bed-sitting room he had engaged that afternoon. It was in Bloomsbury, close to the British Museum. The November twilight was setting in; the gas, electric light stopping at the second floor, was poor; his reading lamp was not yet unpacked. "Chemical...!" he thought. "I wonder...!" as he looked out a moment into the rather dismal street, where the Museum buildings blocked the sky with their sombre and formidable mass. He had, of course, the layman's vague knowledge of the loves and hates of atoms, their intense attraction and repulsion for each other, the dizzy rapidity with which they rushed towards, or away from, those they respectively liked or disliked. Had all the atoms of which he was composed, then, turned their backs instinctively upon those which made up the stranger's body, racing away at a headlong speed that caused him this acute and positive discomfort? Was his instantaneous loathing "chemical merely...?"

As he bustled about arranging his things, his dislike of the fellow remained vivid and persistent. The recent scene again passed through his mind in detail.

He had called in the morning and interviewed Mrs. Smith, with the result: "Not at the moment, sir, I haven't got a room free"; then, after a rather curious hesitation, "But later a little, maybe"; then more hesitation, "This afternoon, per'aps—I—I might be able to manage it—if you could make it convenient—to call in again...." whereupon, seeing that the house was so admirably close to the Reading Room where his daily work would be, Moleson offered to pay in advance, but was then quick enough to see that it was not the question of money alone that troubled the woman. Her hesitation, he perceived, was not mere independence, nor was it due to his unprosperous appearance. She wanted a lodger, clearly enough—if she could "manage it," whatever that might mean—and it was not himself that she objected to. It was, he felt sure, a calculation of sorts she was trying to make in her own mind. He wisely decided to give her time to make it.

"I'll look in again," he said, "about three o'clock, say," and he added, with his pleasant smile, that most of his time would be spent working in the Museum opposite.

It was on his return in the afternoon that the scene occurred.

He had rung the bell and was waiting just inside the narrow hall while the maid hurried downstairs to fetch Mrs. Smith, the street door still ajar behind him, when somebody, another lodger evidently, pushed past brusquely, offensively, almost resentfully, half shoving him, yet without actual contact, from where he stood at the foot of the stairs—slightly in the way, perhaps—and without so much as By your Leave. There might, of course, have been a grunt of apology, for Moleson was a little deaf, but the man's attitude made it unlikely, and the pose of the head and shoulders, the face being turned away and not visible, was far more of resentful disapproval than of apology. Moleson, on the instant, loathed him, not because of the rudeness, but because of some presentment his appearance offered that stirred an intense, instinctive dislike amounting to positive repulsion. A moment later, when Mrs. Smith arrived, panting and labouring, the man was up the stairs and out of sight, but at first the impression left was so vivid that Moleson would not have been altogether displeased if he had heard that no room was, after all, available. The contrary, however, took place. A bargain was struck, money passed hands, and the room was his.

The majority of young men in these circumstances would probably have given their attention to the landlady, to whom money must be paid, and on whose goodwill they must depend for their comfort and the like. Moleson, instead, found himself thinking only of this rude fellow-lodger. Over his dinner in a neighbouring restaurant, he reflected that his sudden dislike was odd; he had never set eyes upon the fellow before, and as yet, had not even seen the face nor heard the voice, yet this loathing had leaped into being. Revulsion, he called it. Its oddness, of course, lay in this want of proportion. He gave a passing thought, too, to his landlady, yet chiefly using her as a means of comparison with the other. Her rather sombre visage, an overwhelming melancholy in it, though certainly not attractive, woke nothing stronger in him than a vague, tolerant sympathy. He felt no dislike, at any rate; she merely didn't matter; a worthy soul, he decided, worn into sadness by life. Whereas the other human being gave him this instinctive, deep revulsion. Chemical? He wondered. For why, if chemical, should one unpleasing soul awake pity, and another, equally unpleasing, stir violent antipathy?

Over his coffee, he dismissed the little puzzle. His room was admirably close to the Museum; Bloomsbury liked him; and it was the number in the street Number eleven—his Manchester friend and employer had mentioned. The price, too, suited him, for money was scarce, otherwise he would not be "devilling" for another man—looking up certain seventeenth-century facts for a writer who would probably clear one thousand pounds over his silly book, yet "must be sure of my dates and facts, you know. Your expenses and five pounds a week, if you'll do it for me...." The street and number, close to the Museum, were added. Young Moleson, ignorant of London, jumped at it.

It was some years before our Great Date this happened. Jim Moleson, engaged to a sweet girl, and now married to her, told me the details recently. The War intervened, of course. He had learnt something. At that time, I should have described him as highly strung, sensitive at any rate, imaginative certainly, poetic probably. I, his senior by a quarter of a century, rather believed he wrote "Celtic" poetry in his bedroom. The War undeceived us about that type, revealed *them* rather: their amazing courage, the splendour of their "imagination," translated into reckless, inspired action. Jim, anyhow, was always headstrong, fierce-tempered, "nasty" once his feelings were stirred, only these feelings were usually for others—for a lame dog, an injured cat, a bird in a cage, an overworked horse. Slights, even insults to himself he could stand, to the point of cowardice, some thought; but this was wrong; he was easygoing to that point; beyond it he saw red and—killed. This savage temper, rarely roused, and then with a curious suddenness, was an item I overlooked. But it was a human, not merely an animal, temper.

His work at the Museum, apparently, absorbed him; no more painstaking and accurate "devil" ever devilled; and he got back to his room, tired mentally and physically. A nice-looking, upstanding lad with his mop of dark hair and blue eyes, he soon made a friend of Mrs. Smith—over his letters first: "Lef' at Number 7," she informed him, the printed name of his employer's Institute on the envelope catching her trained, if mournful, eye perhaps. "The postman arst me, and I thought they was for you," she explained. So his slight deafness had again betrayed him, and his employer had said "Number 7," instead of "Number 11." They talked on a bit. He had the feeling *she* wanted to talk a bit, but wanted to talk about something in particular, and to him. He explained about the letters and his troublesome deafness in one ear; he heard her say "your glass of porter" when she actually said, "hot bath water," and then, after a nice little chat about the weather, prices, and "'ow times was changing," he noticed that she suddenly stuck.

This was after a week in the house, he told me. The appalling melancholy of her face came over him, but rather in a new way; he realized it in some personal sense, I think, as they stood awkwardly staring at one another, each waiting for the other to speak, so that through his sensitive, imaginative mind ran the thought: "That's no ordinary sadness, I'll be bound...!" —and then *he* stuck.

The impulse to say something kind rose in him, only he could think of nothing to say, nothing suitable. It was here he got his first clear, instinctive impression about this common-place woman: that she was interested, namely, to ask some definite question of him, that, liking and trusting him, and, further, having watched carefully and waited anxiously the whole week, she now longed to put this definite query to him, yet was afraid. The same hesitation he had seen first on the doorstep showed itself in her face and sorrowful eyes.

He had been vaguely aware of this for some time evidently, but had not recognized it. It was not, he felt sure, any question about his comfort, for he was old enough to know that landladies rarely took that risk. Something, none the less, she wanted to know, something personal to himself. The suffering in her face made him wonder. A queer sympathy moved through him. He recalled the stationer round the corner in Bury Street, when he bought his paper and materials: "Oh yes, I know, sir; that's Mrs. Warley's," saying he would send the parcel round, and, being corrected:

"No, Mrs. Smith's." He looked blank a moment, troubled a little, but in a kindly sense, before he agreed: "Oh yes, to be sure, sir—Mrs. Smith's—now. So it is. ..." That "now" was suggestive. She had changed her name, married again, no doubt, yet there had been trouble of some sort, Moleson gathered. And, though he had not pursued the matter at the time, this little memory came back now, as he stood chatting with her, trying to think of something pleasant he might say. He wondered...

"I'm very comfortable," he said on impulse, presently. "The room's just what I wanted—" and he was about to add some kind and soothing word when she interrupted in an eager way that startled him:

"Oh, then everything *is* all right, sir? There's nothing, I mean, interfering with your quiet? If anything annoys"—she changed the verb, before it was completed, to "disturbs," then stopped dead.

It was not the words—-commonplace enough: it was her face that startled him. It had been on the tip of her tongue, he felt, to say "anyone" instead of "anything." He knew it in his bones. Also, she could have cut off that tongue for having let it say what it *had* said. That, too, he perceived. This question she longed yet feared to ask had nearly slipped out in spite of herself. Her face, anyhow, betrayed an emotion that for an instant obliterated its usual sadness. It was the emotion of terror.

Moleson, as he caught it, felt shocked. The sharp instinct came suddenly to him that it was wiser not to ask. He cut the talk short, as nicely as he could. "Nothing, nothing," he replied, gave her his pleasant smile, and went up quickly to his room.

Her question was an approach to the real one she wanted so much to ask. That, of course, he realized. Terror lay in it; it was wrapped round with terror as in a cocoon. Once the cocoon burst, was broken, out would come all the hideous wriggling things that lay concealed inside. This was the feeling Moleson carried upstairs with him. It was as though he had just caught a glimpse, behind her suddenly pale skin, of the hideous wriggling things that caused her sadness and her terror. But another certainty lay in him too at this moment: the question she had asked, this preliminary question that was an approach to another, referred—he felt positive of it—to someone he particularly sought to keep out of his thoughts as much as ever he could. She referred, indirectly thus, to the other lodger.

It was his habit at night, after his dinner round the corner, to sort out the Notes of his day's work before an early bed. Tonight, however, this talk stayed by him and prevented. He sat thinking about it ...and eventually, it seems, thought circling and circling but coming to no satisfactory conclusion of course, he dropped asleep, to wake very suddenly much later in a state of uncommon distress—"acute distress," he called it, "funk."

This, I think, is one of the most curious and betraying things about the whole business: that, even when he told it all to me later, he kept off that unpleasant lodger, as he called him —kept him so long in the background. He had begun by emphasizing his unusual repulsion towards the fellow, dwelling upon it, stressing it, just as I have done in this written account. But then, when I was expecting the lodger to appear in some dreadful and dramatic guise a sneak-thief, a forger with coining apparatus, a blackmailer in league with Mrs. Warley-Smith (as I styled her), even a murderer hiding from the police with the woman's help—Moleson merely left him out. He ignored him, made no mention of him. He talked about his work, about Mrs. Smith, his liking the house, yet disliking the room—feeling it disliked him and wanted him out—about anything except the sinister lodger. Having first firmly fixed him in my mind as an ominous character, he just left him there. Thus, when I tried to bring him to the point—this suggestive point of the sinister lodger, and a point he had himself established in opening his tale—he stopped abruptly, and stared into my face, his features working, his eyes gone positively googly. Some fear, I saw, still operated in him, unreleased. His face gave me a touch of goose flesh. There was an ingredient of salutary "confession" in his delayed account, I began to gather. He lowered his voice. "I knew you'd ask that before long," he said. "You see—I shirked him myself."

"Refused to acknowledge him, you mean?" I queried vaguely. "Tried to pretend he wasn't in the house?"

He nodded, looking down at his boots.

"You disliked him," I insisted, "to *that* point?" The expression in his eyes, as he glanced up quickly, answered me better than his words.

"It's unbelievable," he whispered, "how that fellow obsessed me. Obsessed is the term."

I asked if he saw him often.

"After that first encounter on the front-door steps—only twice, all told."

The intensity, a sort of inner secrecy in him still, made me hesitate, but as he said nothing, I presently asked boldly:

"But—in the end—you found out who he was, what he was doing there? In a word—why you loathed him so?" I got no straight answer, but I got the full story, told in his own evasive, curious way.

"I mentioned how I dropped asleep in my chair, and woke up suddenly feeling frightened," he went on. "Well—that's the point, you see."

"What is?" I asked, justifiably dense.

He cast his eyes down as though he were ashamed of it.

"I'd been frightened all along," he muttered. "Damned frightened. Ever since I'd been in that awful house, I'd been frightened."

"Of—him?"

He nodded.

He believed he had discovered why the fellow resented his being there: it was because Moleson occupied his room. Mrs. Smith had hesitated that first morning whether she could turn him out or not—his rent probably overdue, and what not—but eventually had spoken to him—and Moleson, as described, cash in hand, had moved in. It was a sufficiently obvious explanation.

"But that didn't explain my own abhorrence—did it?"

Obviously not.

"He may have felt resentful, furious, because I'd got his room, but that couldn't have made me feel the physical repulsion, to the point of nausea, which I did feel. And dread too. I only saw him twice after that first meeting, but though I saw him so rarely, I knew he was in the house with me. I never forgot it. He was all over the house expresses it better. I was always expecting to meet him, to run across him on the stairs, to find him in the hall. When I came down the street, I imagined him standing on the doorstep, fumbling with his latchkey. When I went to my bath halfway down the stairs, I thought we should pass. At night, if I went out to post a letter; in the morning when I opened my door to take my hot water in. But, no; he made no sign, I did not meet him. What he did all day I have no notion: he never went out, so far as I saw or knew. But then I myself was out from nine to five, then again for my dinner between eight and nine, you see."

At a great rate he rattled this off. He gave me a good deal in a very few words.

A definite question halted his rambling account, though it was my object, otherwise, to hear the tale just as he cared to tell it.

"Describe him?" He repeated my words. "As I first saw him —? Oh yes. Though I didn't see the features, remember, that time." Then he startled me by raising his voice most unexpectedly in his excitement: "Misshapen!" he shouted in my face, so that I jumped. "Well, you asked me; and that's what I felt about him. But mentally, morally, rather than physically. That's the impression he made on me." And then he barked out another word: "A monster!" A little shudder ran over him. "I didn't see the face," he went on, "because he didn't mean me to see it. He moved sideways; the shoulder next to me humped up a trifle so as to hide it. A bit of a beard I saw, or whiskers, straggly hair, anyhow, that left in my mind some faint notion of pretence, of a wig perhaps. But my mind at the moment was on my business with Mrs. Smith, and I wasn't trying to see what a stranger pushing rudely past me was like. I had no particular interest in him then. Clothes? ...Oh, that I couldn't say with accuracy either, but a dark suit, and a bowler hat on his head. *Dark*," he emphasized, "the whole look and feel of the man was dark."

I was still anxiously waiting for that account of his waking up frightened in his chair, for my interest was now deeply held. But I was patient; I had to be. He went on to tell me how he was forever expecting to see the man again, yet did not see him. This repetition, in the tale as he told it, was not redundant, though, when written, it may seem so. It led up with a bang, as it were, to the meeting—the sight, rather—when it came. Every morning on going out to his work he was positive he must pass the fellow on the darkish stairs, but the stairs were empty; on the landing when he opened his door, on the front-door steps when he returned in the evening, but landing and steps were unoccupied. He would have a good look at the door first from a little way up the street, before coming to it, for the dread of meeting was established, horribly established, in his being—"expectant dread," he called it. Then, suddenly, he did see him. This was the second time.

"I was hardly settled at my desk in the Reading Room," he

described the incident, "when I found I'd left my employer's letter on the mantelpiece. It had questions for me to verify, you see. I hurried back for it. It only took five minutes—that's why the house suited me so—but I had a good squint first from a distance to see if the doorstep was free. No one was visible. I ran up. Just as I slipped my latchkey in, I glanced up—something made me—and there he was, staring down at me from the window."

"In your room!"

"I saw the face for the first time, but only for a second, just long enough for our eyes to meet. He withdrew it instantly—awfully quick, I mean. It was dark, unshaven, the beard not a real intended beard. I saw hanging lips. No, it was not what you'd call an evil face, not in that sense, but it was dreadful in the sense of being out of relation with any world I knew. Horrible, appalling, in that way. It was a mad face. Behind its darkness there was white—the white of terror. The face was all I really saw, with just a bit of the neck that had a thin red scarf about it ... The key dropped out of my fingers with a clatter on the steps. I was shaking all over.

"Ferreting about in *my* room! ... was my first thought—the room that used to be his! ... But a second thought came with it simultaneously, and it was this second thought that unsettled me most, I believe. I realized in a flash that the fellow had been actually watching me ever since my arrival, keeping out of my way on purpose, waiting an opportunity, waiting for me to go out—oh, I can't describe it exactly—but he knew my every movement, I mean."

"You rushed up—?" I interrupted. It was a stupid question, but the dread of this mysterious lodger in my mind excited me.

Moleson hesitated. "I've got a vile temper, you know," he said, shyly rather, as though I was not supposed to be aware of this. "*Vile*," he repeated with emphasis and a touch of shame, "curiously sudden too—"

"That brute in your own room," I helped him. For a moment I feared I was to hear of a violent assault.

"I was up those stairs in a second or two," he went on, "and the first thing I noticed on getting to the top was that my door was moving. There was no one on the landing. The room itself was empty." He paused, looking at me significantly. "The fellow," he then added, "had got out—just in time." Again he paused for a moment. "I shouldn't have waited to ask any questions, you know."

I knew he meant it, but I was glad to have been spared details of an ugly assault. This savage temper in Moleson always alarmed me rather. I verily believe he would have done the fellow in. His face, as he told it, betrayed him. By this time, moreover, I already had a shrewd suspicion of what was to prove the explanation of this unpleasant and mysterious lodger: a mad mind certainly, a maniac probably (I had glimpses of a homicidal maniac), he would turn out to be the son of Mrs. Smith. That I was partly right, yet at the same time curiously wrong, is a tribute perhaps to the unconscious skill with which Moleson told his story, concealing its climax admirably, yet disdaining to mislead me by using false clues.

The crime of murder, at any rate, was meanwhile spared him. The room was empty, nothing had apparently been touched, and the corridor was empty too. His suggestion of having been "watched" I disregarded. Later, however, I inclined to accept it.

"Across my landing," Moleson continued, "was one door only—the door of what I felt convinced was his room. It was closed. My first instinct was to bang at it and ask him what the devil ... Well"—he laughed a little—"I didn't do it, that's all. My anger had cooled down somehow. I just snatched up the letter I'd come to fetch and went back to the Museum Reading Room."

I looked at him, impressed by his admirable brevity, thinking of the MC gained in Flanders, of that runaway he once stopped, of the two hefty ruffians he fought, half killing one of them, in a Surrey lane when they objected to his interfering on behalf of their overloaded horses. He had various things to his credit of this sort, and he was delicate, of slight build, no muscles or brawn at all. Moleson, with his fierce, perhaps great, spirit, was not negligible. Any story he told, I mean, had value ... "Now," I thought to myself, "at last we'll get to this business about waking up frightened!" Not a bit of it. He must tell me something about Mrs. Smith first. And though it delayed the thing *I* wanted to hear; it was worth listening to.

Poor lodging houses have secrets, secret lodgers, as well, no doubt. His room was cheap, too cheap. But it was not his business, after all. "Better leave it at that!" he decided. Only one thing troubled me about Mrs. Smith—her interest, namely, in ascertaining if he was "not interfered with"—as though she had rather expected that he *would* be disturbed. Her phrase had anchored itself in his mind; he was always recalling it; he couldn't forget it apparently. Why should he be "interfered with?" What—who should interfere with him? Who, indeed, he reflected, but this man? This man who had been turned out for him? This man whose room he now undoubtedly occupied? And so it was that, since Mrs. Smith came to no closer terms with the real question she longed to ask, he now, for his part, decided to come to closer terms with the question he wanted to ask: "Who is your other lodger?" For the floor below being empty, he knew, there was none but himself and this other lodger in the house.

After various hints, suggestions and the rest, chances he provided but she did not take, the expression in her face invariably making him pause—after numerous futile leads, he came abruptly one day to the direct question. Tired of fencing, a touch of his queer anger stirred in him. He made up his mind to know whether her feelings were upset or not. He put the brutal question, though he did it delicately enough:

"By the by," he said, as they were in the narrow hall, money having just passed, "I meant to ask you sooner, Mrs. Smith—my typewriter at night—does it disturb anyone? The gentleman opposite, I mean?"

If he was prepared for evasion of some kind, he was certainly not prepared for the answer he received.

"She denied there being any gentleman opposite at all?" I asked, as Moleson hesitated, wondering, I fancied, how best to make her answer sound credible to a Philistine like myself.

"She *didn't* answer," he said briefly. "Her face turned white as a sheet. She fell back against the hat rack. She screamed. It was a curious scream, rather low, not noisy a bit. And it was pain, not fear. She was hurt, terribly hurt. She began to cry...."

Further explanation of the amazing collapse, beyond that her "'eart caught me sudden—it's always been weak,"—there was none. It was in this brief fashion that Moleson related the incident, then left it there without another word—as I, too, must therefore leave it.

For some days after that nothing happened. He did not see the lodger. He avoided the landlady. He began to look forward to the end of his stay, hurrying his work at the Museum purposely. But his mind was forever going back, he says, to that odd question about being "interfered with," and one night in particular, as he sat over his notes after dinner, memory carried him away rather forcibly, rather persistently, to that phrase which had inserted his original uneasiness. He sat in his chair, lolling back, and thinking about it, wondering afresh about this mysterious lodger, about what he did, why he hid so carefully, why he watched him. The old notions slipped through his mind, for no new ones occurred to him: was he a coiner of counterfeit money, a blackmailer, a lunatic, a man wanted by the police, a man who ought by rights to be shut up, a suicidal maniac ... and so, eventually, he dropped asleep in his chair ... to wake up suddenly "frightened, and in acute distress."

So, at last, we had got to it.

It was late. The night was very still, all noises in the street had stopped. No footsteps even were audible on the pavement through the open window.

"I woke up cold," he said, "cold to the bone. The room, in spite of the warm summer air, was icy. I was shivering."

And at first, rather bewildered after his sleep, he sat there listening, waiting, wondering why he felt cold, wondering for some minutes what the matter was. That something was the matter, he felt sure. Something had been happening, had just happened, while he was asleep. But what? He collected his senses, remembering exactly where he was. Details, of course, came back quickly then. He says the first thing he noticed was that a change had come over the room.

The room was somehow different. It had curiously altered. When he dropped off to sleep it had been one thing, now it was another. He glanced about him, searching uncomfortably for evidence of this change, but finding no single detail altered, nothing out of place, the furniture exactly as it always was— until his eye rested on the door. The door, he phrased it, "drew" his attention, although a closed door—and it was closed now—must always, it seemed to me, look much the same.

"Well," he said, "it didn't." He used the tone of challenge, anticipating disbelief. "That door," he declared, "had been opened and shut while I was asleep." He waited a moment. "It had only just been shut."

The imaginative statement struck me as singularly dramatic. Proof, of course, was not possible, yet a door, I reflected, is easily the most significant feature of a house, opened, closed, tapped on, locked; it is a frontier, a threshold, and when passed, either in exit or entrance, leads necessarily to other conditions of living, to other states of mind, since it leads to other people and other atmosphere. I could understand in a fashion that Moleson used those words. He rather convinced me, I mean, that he was possibly right.

"That's what made you wake," I offered, filling the pause he left.

"Yes," he returned flatly. "While I slept, that door had been opened, someone had looked in, come in, moved about the room, done something, then gone out again—gone out just that instant."

Aware of this change in the room, or in the atmosphere about him, he sat for some time staring at that door. He listened intently. A glance at his wristwatch showed that it was two in the morning, so that he had slept several hours. The deep silence of the house came over him unpleasantly, and his distress, instead of passing, increased. He found himself still shivering. But a moment later his cold skin turned hot and broke out in a profuse perspiration—at a sound. It was a sound he recognized, having heard it before: the dragging of furniture or luggage across the landing, of heavy and awkward articles, difficult to move. He had heard it already several times, late at night, early in the morning, through his dreams as well, and he had always ascribed it to the lodger, busy arranging things in his room opposite, and using the landing sometimes in so doing. He had paid no particular attention to it, beyond a passing annoyance at the choice of hours, and the sounds had usually ceased after a few minutes at the most. Now, however, he was conscious of a difference, for in the first place it was two in the morning, when ordinary people were asleep; secondly, he realized distinctly, it was not furniture or luggage being moved—it was *a* piece of luggage, a heavy piece, for the sound was unmistakable. He thought of a trunk or portmanteau. Moreover—it was going on immediately outside his own door.

"The fellow was dragging this luggage of his across the landing just beyond my door," Moleson underlined the fact. "At two o'clock in the morning, if you please!"

The first effect upon him was one of a queer paralysis, mental and physical. He could neither think nor move.

"I just sat listening to the fellow dragging his great bag, or whatever it was, across the landing—dragging it, I supposed, towards his own room opposite. Then, very gradually, my mental numbness lifted, and I found myself wondering *why*. At two in the morning! Dragging luggage about! What was he doing with luggage on the landing of a Bloomsbury lodging house at that unearthly hour? So close to my own door too? The bumping and scraping were audible enough; there was no pretence of doing it quietly. Where was he taking his luggage from? Where to? My mind worked quickly, once it started. A score of questions rushed over me. What could it be, this bag, this portmanteau, this heavy bundle so difficult to move? What could it contain? What had he put inside it? Taken?"

"Taken?" I repeated, not quite following him.

"Some of the questions, racing through my mind," he explained, "brought a kind of answer with them. That's the only way I can put it," he added apologetically, a sop to me, the sceptical recipient of his confession.

"*What* had he taken?" he repeated, looking at me rather hard.

I had no notion.

"But I had," said Moleson with decision, interpreting my blank expression. "I guessed at once—half guessed, at least."

He had me at a loss there, I admit; but I made no comment, merely nodding my head affirmatively. His next words took me completely by surprise:

"His great bag or bundle, whatever it was," whispered Moleson, "contained something he had just taken out of my room. While I slept, the fellow had sneaked in, crept about, found what he wanted, taken it, and sneaked out again with it —in his bag."

Again, I made no comment, the explanation being too preposterous to argue about. Moleson, besides, was now too earnest and convinced—he knew, remember, the climax, whereas I was still in ignorance—too eager to make his full confession for me to interfere and cavil with commonplace criticism. It might have stopped him, for one thing.

"You missed anything?" I asked, no disbelief in my face or voice. I had to repeat it before he replied, and his reply, when it came, again took me by surprise. Also, it sent a shiver through me, as though the hair were moving on my scalp:

"What he had taken," he told me in a lowered voice, and speaking very slowly, "was not in my room at that time when I fell asleep, I mean. But it *had* been there—some time before."

The statement, naturally, left me without a rejoinder. I lit a cigarette and waited in silence.

"At that moment," he said impressively, still in his whisper, and loathing coming into his face with a leap, as it were, "I knew—he was a—horror. Oh, in every meaning of the word. And a queer, sudden revulsion rushed over me—the intense desire to see him close, to look at him face to face, to speak to

34

him—I never once heard his voice, you know—to—yes, even to touch the brute; and in so doing—somehow—God knows how to get rid of him. So far, he had avoided me deliberately. All this time he had evaded, escaped me. He meant to avoid and escape me, but now at last I had him close—a few feet away—busy, occupied, within reach, unable to get away—if I just opened that door. I need only open that door, and I should see him—catch him in the act."

Longing to ask, "In what act?" I ventured instead: "You felt angry all of a sudden?" and hit the mark better than I knew.

He admitted it, ashamed a little, with a nod. "I felt cold all over, mind you," he went on, always in that low voice, "scared as well, really scared, but at the same time, as you say, I felt"—he chose a queer word—"vicious. Exasperated, too, a bit. I wanted to be done with it. I wanted to get at the fellow. Why the devil should he make this infernal row at two in the morning? How dared he? How dared he come into another man's room, even if it had once been his own? Why should he watch me, bother me, haunt me, get into my mind—and all the rest of it? Yes,"—with a touch of fierceness—"you're right—I did feel angry all of a sudden. I decided abruptly I'd go out—"

"Open that door?"—I simply couldn't keep it back. Personally, I should *not* have opened that door at two in the morning under the circumstances.

"Yes, open the door, go out, and tell the brute to go to hell. I decided to do that—and more—"

I knew what that "more" meant.

"—but when I tried to get up from my chair, I found I couldn't move. I just sat there, furious angry, struggling—like a mechanical doll whose machinery had run down. I was dying to get at the fellow. I was perspiring all over. I felt that if he answered back, showed any insolence, I'd strangle him—just go for him and be done with it. Throttle the devil! I felt my fingers at his throat, the prickle of his filthy beard, saw his hanging lips drop wider as he fought for breath, his beastly eyes bulge out, his face turn black—oh, I was in this odd, sudden fury, I admit—and yet—I couldn't move an inch.

"Perhaps—probably—I made a noise of some kind, cursed aloud most likely, but anyhow the sound of the dragging luggage suddenly stopped. A deep, rather an extraordinary, silence followed. I could hear the blood beating in my head. I sat fixed in my chair like a dummy, staring at the door. Only that door separated us. He existed there—breathing, vivid, intense—a few feet from where I sat rigid in my chair, unable to get at him, unable to move a muscle. He seemed to exert some tremendous pressure on me, paralysing my will, holding me helpless where I was."

Moleson mopped his forehead a moment.

"I was so angry," he went on, rather breathless now in his excitement, as though he lived over again his fury and exasperation, "that I felt murder in me. Positively, I felt myself a murderer."

Curiously, he stopped dead suddenly. A look of shyness came over him. He stared at me; I stared back at him. Such language, of course, in anybody else, would have been merely extravagant, hysterical. In his case it was real. I knew his sudden, ungovernable temper; I knew, too, he was ashamed of it. In a less civilized country he must always have been in trouble with his gun. He was the type that saw red and killed. And a quick flash of understanding somehow came into me, so that I guessed in that instant the explanation both of his abrupt pause and of his queer shyness. Having this dangerous thing in himself, he recognized it in others too. That sympathy existed.

"That's how I knew," he muttered, looking down, having guessed my thought.

"What *he* was?" I asked, fumbling with my cigarette.

"A murderer," he said quietly.

I waited in silence, wondering what he was going to tell me. His face was rather white, his excitement only kept under by his doubt of being believed. It was best now, I felt, to ask no questions. In his own way he would presently go on. But curiosity, I confess, devoured me. Did he open that door? Did he see the other fellow, speak to him, touch him, perhaps go for him?

His own mind, however, was an odd psychological revelation—of himself.

"And the instant I realized *that*," he went on, "the power to move came back to me. My muscles acted. The pressure the fellow exerted was lifted, because we understood one another. There was that ghastly sympathy between us. I got out of my chair and crossed the floor. I reached the door. Then I stopped a moment and listened. He, too, I knew, was listening a few inches away from my face, nothing but half an inch of thin boards between us, listening to my movements, bending to the keyhole probably, crouching, his luggage neglected for a moment while he waited to see what I was going to do. A second later I caught the handle, turned it, and flung the door wide open with a rush.

"There he was before me. Quite close. He was bending down, exactly as I had imagined, crouching, his head lowered; and at his feet, less than a yard beyond me, I saw on the floor the dark blotch that was his luggage.

"What happened then happened so quickly that it seemed less than a second. From the stooping position he did not rise, nor make any attempt to rise. One hand, still stretched out upon the bag, began to work. He pulled at it. He had been pulling at it when I opened the door, and he went on pulling at it—dragging it, dragging it away from me, away from the door, and across the landing floor. I, for my part, had one hand raised to strike, to clutch, to kill, if necessary, but my hand did not fall, I did nothing violent, because I made in that very instant a horrible discovery. I suddenly realized that he did not see me. He had not noticed me. He was not aware of my being there close beside him. He did not react to my presence in any way, because he was simply not conscious of it. He continued doing what he had been doing just before—dragging his luggage across the landing floor. I saw the dark mass of it go hitching along in jerks as he pulled. It was very heavy.

"And this—this not being aware of me, I mean—came as a tremendous shock. The surprise of it, perhaps. It was the last thing in the world I'd expected. I had rather looked for something sudden, violent. I was prepared for it. This way he just ignored me turned me cold. It struck me as unnatural. I stood and stared, for I didn't know what else to do, and my body was trembling, and I felt queerly uncertain of my legs. I watched him go on dragging at that heavy thing, which I now saw was not luggage after all, not ordinary luggage, at least. It was neither bag nor portmanteau, nor anything like that. It was a sack of awkward shape and outline. It was unpleasant, I thought, the way it bulged. But more than that, more than unusual, it gave me a turn—I felt it somewhere awful. And realizing this, I made an unconscious movement evidently, for I felt my breath catch, and I must have staggered a little. I caught at the edge of the door to steady myself, and the door, naturally, yielded with my weight; I lurched with it, sideways at first, then a little outwards as the door came with me, and then—forwards. Before I could recover balance, I was against him. I was right into him.

"But I didn't fall. I didn't, thank God, collide with the monstrous creature and his awful sack, but I was so close against him that the shock of finding nothing solid—there was no substance there at all—stopped my heart for a second. It seemed to rush up into my throat. Then my breath came back, and I let out a yell into the night that must have been heard in the street. At which moment, still dragging at his bundle, he made a sudden, rather violent, movement. He turned in a new way. I saw his face clearly.

"By 'clearly' I mean close—dreadfully close. It was turned up, but I saw it obliquely rather, a kind of sideways glimpse, and even then, he wasn't looking *at* me. The light from the open door behind fell on it, and I saw the eyes, blazing eyes, the hanging lips, the white skin smudged with unshaven hair of the growing black beard, and—to my utter amazement—tears upon the cheeks. It was a maniac's face, if ever I saw one. The other thing that I saw clearly was that the thin red scarf about the neck was not a scarf at all. It was a thin red line of contused blood in the flesh of the neck itself, a line that only a rope, drawn very tightly, could have made." Moleson stopped then and sank back in his chair, looking away from me, and glad, I think, that he had got so far without interruption. His words and manner, his facial expression above all, conveyed his horror far better than his jerked-out sentences. I smoked a moment in silence, handing him a cigarette too, which he refused. But he said nothing for some little time, while I also kept back a dozen questions that rushed up in me."

"What happened then?" I ventured at length. "What did you do?"

"Nothing," he replied briefly, looking up at me again, his manner now quiet and collected. "I did nothing. It seemed, somehow, there was nothing I wanted to do. A feeling I must shout, strike out, do something violent passed. What was done next, *he* did. I merely looked on and watched. There was no emotion in me of any sort. I was just numb. My whole consciousness, I think, was in my eyes. I stared ... as he went on dragging that heavy mass across the landing, always a little farther from me, hitching and shoving it along with great effort—towards the door of his room. Then he opened the door, but the light from my room did not reach to it, and as it was not lit inside, I saw nothing but a black space. I watched. I saw everything he did, every movement he made. He stepped to one side, across the bundle, so that he was then pushing instead of dragging. His whole body was bent double with the effort to get the thing through the door and inside the room. Apparently, it was difficult to do. He accomplished it after several minutes. He closed the door, putting his weight against it heavily from outside, and then—after that—well—he wasn't there anymore."

"He'd gone into the room?"

Moleson shrugged his shoulders. "Can't say," he answered rather curtly. "I tell you he simply wasn't there. I couldn't see him anymore. I'd lost sight of him." He added sheepishly: "Something happened to my eyes, I suppose. I didn't see him go—but he *was* gone."

Fully five minutes passed, Moleson then told me slowly, before he could think, much less move. He was struck dumb with terror and amazement. He felt stupid, empty of life, unable to act at all.

"It may have been five minutes," he said, "but it may just as well have been twenty—for all I know. The only thing I remember clearly is that my awful yell—that wild shriek I let out into the night some time before—still seemed to me echoing through the house and down the stairs. I had a feeling it must have been heard in the street and the police would be in. But nothing happened. The fellow's disappearance bewildered me to a point I can't describe properly. I *knew* I hadn't been dreaming, but I knew damned little else, it seems to me.

"I moved at last, after a bit. I moved backwards. I threw my own door as wide as it would go, so as to get all the light there was, and the light streamed across the landing and fell on the door—his door. I knew I was going to open that door. I had to."

His pluck hardly surprised me, for I already knew it. I admired it. Nothing in this world or the next could have induced me to go near that door, much less open it. Moleson, however, did more: he went over and knocked loudly against its boards.

"The sound echoed," he told me, "but not inside. It echoed down the stairs, I mean. The boards sounded dull. That dullness explained itself," he added, with a quick glance up at me as though, of course, I understood what he meant. But I did not understand, and my eyebrows went up in query and response, "It wasn't an ordinary door," he said.

"You—opened it?" I had no inkling what he meant.

"I guessed it wasn't a proper door," he replied, changing his adjective, but leaving me more ignorant than before. "I'd felt that some time before."

"Sham?"

"Not an ordinary door into an ordinary room," he explained, with a hint of impatience at my stupidity. "When I knocked," he went on, "and got no answer, I knew I was right. The dead sound proved it."

"Oh!"

"Yes," he went on quietly, "the dead muffled sound it made. I waited a moment. Then I opened it. It was the door of a cupboard—a rather shallow cupboard." He paused, then said something that made my blood curdle: "That's why the creature had to shove it in so hard—*stuff* it in—to make it stay—"

"Upright?" I gasped, catching the ghastly meaning at last.

"Upright," was all he replied.

~

The dusk was now fallen into our room between us, and I saw the glow of my cigarette-end in the mirror, behind his chair. It had been a dreadful story. I longed for light and a glass of whisky. Moleson had so convinced me of the truth, the reality, of his confession, yet I got the feeling that he hoped I would tear it to pieces and demolish it utterly, proving to his satisfaction how absurd it all was, and using nice words like hallucination, overwrought nerves, and the like.

Instead, I remained rather quiet and non-committal, and certainly dumb; I could not honestly comfort him in the way he wished.

"I told you," he resumed, his voice much lower now, "that I imagined that shriek of mine still echoing in the house and down the stairs? Well, a few moments later, while I still stood glaring at that ghastly cupboard, all black and empty ... I heard a sound on the stairs. It was below me, coming nearer. I couldn't move—not an inch, one way or the other. I was just stuck to the floor. But I felt sure of one thing it wasn't—" but he couldn't say the word he meant, the word in his mind—"it wasn't—" He stuck again.

"*Who* was it?" I asked quickly, eager to help him, but to help myself at the same time.

"I saw the light first," he said, "the light of a candle, evidently, flickering on the wall, then on the ceiling. Next came the shadow, enormously magnified and grotesque. Then came a large white face of melancholy and terror mixed, looming at me over the banisters. There was a thin voice:

"'...interfered with....'... I heard from what seemed an immense distance... 'He showed hisself, then, did he? ... May

God forgive me....' and something about a 'broken promise' and a 'room I didn't oughter 'ave let to anyone....' And then, as, to my shame, I felt myself being helped up from the floor—for I had no idea I had let my legs give way like that—something— oh, horrible and dreadful—about '... they 'anged him for it; oh, they 'anged him at the Scrubs ... it was 'is own father, you see ... and now over twenty years ago....'"

There were gulping sounds, he remembers, and these odd, broken words.

Moleson, curiously enough, had never gone to the trouble to verify anything, and it was my vile curiosity that had to find its own satisfaction. The British Museum, where he had worked so hard, gave me certain facts in the newspapers of long before the war. The "Warley Parricide," I discovered, and the unpleasant details about how the body was found stuffed into a cupboard, and how the public signed a petition and the lawyers urged homicidal mania, but without the intended result. The Home Secretary, one paper dared to mention, had married again and had stepsons of his own....

THE DUENNA
MRS. BELLOC LOWNDES

"Que vous me coutez cher, O mon cœur, pour vos plaisirs."

I

Laura Delacourt, after a long and gallant defence of what those who formed the old-fashioned world to which she belonged would have called her virtue, had capitulated to the entreaties of Julian Treville. They had been friends—from tomorrow they would be lovers.

As she lay enfolded in his arms, her head resting on his breast, while now and again their lips met in a trembling clinging kiss, the strangest and, in some ways, the most incongruous thoughts flitted shadow-wise through her mind, mingled with terror at the possible, though not the probable, consequences of her surrender.

Her husband, Roger Delacourt, was thirty years older than herself. Though still a vigorous man, he had come to a time of life when even a vigorous man longs instinctively for warmth; so he had left London the day after Christmas Day to join a friend's yacht for a month's cruise in the Mediterranean. And now, just a week later, the wife whom he considered a negligible quantity in his self-indulgent, still agreeable existence, had consented to embark on what she knew must be a perilous adventure in a one-storied stone house, well named The Folly, built by Julian Treville's great-grandfather.

Long, low, fantastic—it stood at the narrow end of a wide lake on the confines of his property; and a French dancer, known in the Paris of her day as *La Belle Julie*, had spent there a lifetime in exile.

Though Laura in her lover's arms felt strangely at peace, her homing joy was threaded with terror. Constantly her thoughts reverted to her child, David, who, till the man who now held her so closely to him had come into her life, had been the only thing that made that then mournful life worth living.

The boy was spending the New Year with his mother's one close woman friend and her houseful of happy children, so Laura hoped her little son did not miss her. At any other time the thought that this might be so would have stabbed her with unreasonable pain, but what now filled her heart with shrinking fear was the dread thought of David's father, and of the punishment he would exact if he found her out.

Like so many men of his type and generation Roger Delacourt had a poor opinion of women. He believed that the woman tempted always falls. But, again true to type, he made, in this one matter, an exception as to his own wife. That Laura might be tempted was a possibility which never entered his shrewd and cynical mind; and had he been compelled to admit the temptation, he would have felt confident as to her power of resistance. So it was that she faced the awful certainty that were she ever "found out," immediate separation from her son, followed by a divorce, would be her punishment.

She had been a child of seventeen when her mother had

elected to sell her into the slavery of marriage with the voluptuary to whom she had now been married ten years. For three years she had been her husband's plaything, and then, suddenly, when their boy was about two years old, he had tired of her. Even so, they lived, both in London and in the country, under the same roof, and many of the people about them thought the Delacourts got on better than do most modern couples. They were, however, often apart for weeks at a time, for Roger Delacourt still hunted, still shot, still fished, with unabated zest, and his wife did none of these things.

As time went on, Laura's joyless life was at once illumined and shadowed by her passionate love for her child, for all great love brings with it fear. A year ago, by his father's decree, David had been sent to a noted preparatory school, leaving his young mother forlornly lonely. It was then that she had met Julian Treville.

By one of those odd accidents of which human life is full, he and she had been the only two guests of an aged brother and sister, distant connections of Laura's own, in a Yorkshire country house. Cousin John and Cousin Mary had watched the sudden friendship with approval. "Dear Laura Delacourt is just the friend for Julian Treville," said old Mary to old John. She had added, pensively, "It is so very nice for a nice young man to have a nice married woman as a nice friend."

That had been eight months ago, and since then Treville had altered the whole of his life for Laura's sake, she, till today, taking everything and giving nothing, as is so often the way with a woman who believes herself to be good....

During their long drive the lovers scarcely spoke; to be alone together, as they were now, was sufficient bliss.

Treville had met her at a distant railway junction where a motor had been hired in the name of "Mrs. Darcy." This was part of the plan which was to make the few who must perforce know of her presence at The Folly believe her there as the guest of Treville's stepmother, who was now abroad.

Darcy had been Laura's maiden name, and it was the only name she felt she had the right to call herself. She and her lover were both amateurs in the most dangerous and most exciting drama for which a man and woman can be cast.

The hireling motor had brought them across wide stretches of solitary downland, but now they were speeding through one of the long avenues of Treville Place, their journey nearly at an end.

His neighbours would have told you that Julian Treville was a reserved, queer kind of chap. Laura Delacourt was the first woman he had ever loved; and even now, in this hour of unexpected, craved-for joy, he was asking himself if even his great love gave him the right to make her run what seemed an exceedingly slight risk of detection and consequent disgrace.

Each felt a sense of foreboding, though Laura's reason told her that her terrors were vain, and that it was conscience alone that made her feel afraid. Every possible danger had been countered by her companion. Her pride, her delicacy, her sense of shame—was it false shame?—had been studied by him with a selfless devotion which had deeply moved her. Thus, he was leaving her to spend a lonely evening, tended by the old Frenchwoman, who, together with her husband, waited on The Folly's infrequent occupants.

The now aged couple in their hot youth had been on the losing side in the Paris Commune of 1871. They had been saved from imprisonment, possibly worse, by Julian Treville's grandmother, a lawless, high-minded Scotchwoman who called herself a Liberal. She had brought them to England, and for fifty odd years they had lived in a cottage a quarter of a mile from The Folly. There was small reason, as Treville could have argued with perfect truth, to be afraid of this old pair. But Laura did feel afraid, and so it had been arranged between the lovers that only tomorrow, after she had spent at The Folly a solitary night and day, would he, at the close of a day's hunting, share "Mrs. Darcy's" simple dinner....

The motor stopped, and the man and woman, who had been clasped in each other's arms, drew quickly apart.

"We have to get out here," muttered Treville, "for there is no carriageway down to The Folly. I'll carry your bag."

Keeping up the sorry comedy she paid off and dismissed the chauffeur.

In the now fading daylight Laura saw that to her left the ground sloped steeply down to the shores of a lake whose now grey waters narrowed to a point beyond which there stood a low, pillared building. It was more like an eighteenth-century orangery than a house meant for human habitation. Eerily beautiful, and yet exceedingly desolate, to Laura The Folly appeared unreal—a fairy dwelling in that Kingdom of Romance whither her feet had never strayed, rather than a place where men and women had joyed and sorrowed, lived and died.

"If only I could feel that you will never regret that you came here," Treville whispered.

She answered quickly, "I shall always be glad, not sorry, Julian."

He took her hand and raised it to his lips. Then he said: "Old Célestine will have it that The Folly is haunted by *La Belle Julie*. You're not afraid of ghosts, my dearest?"

Laura smiled a little wanly in the twilight. "Far more afraid of flesh and blood than ghosts," she murmured.

"Where do Célestine and her husband live, Julian?"

"We can't see their cottage from here; but it's quite close by." His voice sank: "I've told them that you're not afraid of being in the house alone at night."

They went down a winding footpath, she clinging to him for very joy in his nearness, till they reached the stone-paved space which lay between the shore of the lake and the low grey building. And then, suddenly, while they were walking towards the high front door, Laura gave a stifled cry, for a gnome-like figure had sprung, as if from nowhere, across their path.

"Here's old Jacques," exclaimed Treville vexedly. "He always shows an excess of zeal!"

The little Frenchman was gesticulating and talking eagerly, explaining that fires had been burning all day in the three rooms which were to be occupied by the visitor. He further told, at unnerving length, that Célestine would be at The Folly herself very shortly to install "Madame."

When the old chap had shuffled off, Julian Treville put a key in the lock of the heavy old door; taking Laura's slight figure up into his strong arms, he lifted her over the threshold straight into an enchanting living room where nothing had been altered for over a hundred years. She gave a cry of delight. "What a delicious place, Julian! I never thought it would be like this—"

A log fire threw up high flames in the deep fireplace, and a lighted lamp stood on a round, gilt-rimmed, marble table close to a low and roomy, if rather stiff, square armchair. The few pieces of fine Empire furniture were covered with faded yellow satin which had been brought from Paris when Napoleon was ironing out the frontiers of Europe, for the Treville of that day had furnished The Folly to please the Frenchwoman he loved. The walls of the room were hung with turquoise silk. There was a carved-wood gilt mirror over the mantelpiece, and on the right-hand wall there hung an oval pastel of *La Belle Julie*.

Hand in hand they stood, looking up at the lovely smiling face.

"According to tradition," said Treville, "that picture was the only thing the poor soul brought with her when she left France. The powdered hair proves it must have been done when Julie was in her teens, before the Revolution. My great-great-grandfather fell in love with her when she must have been well over thirty—"

Then, dropping the mask he had worn since they had left the motor, "Laura!" he exclaimed; "Beloved! At last—at last!"

For him, and for her, too, the world sank away, though, even so, that which is now called her subconscious self was listening, full of shrinking fear, for the sound of a key in the lock.....

He said at last in a low, shaken voice, "And now I suppose that I must leave you?"

Her lips formed the words telling him that he had been over-scrupulous in his care for her, that they might as well brave the curious eyes of old Célestine tonight as tomorrow. And then, before she could utter them, there came the sound of steps on the stone path outside.

"It's Célestine, come before her time," muttered Treville. The front door opened and Laura, turning round quickly, saw a tall, thin, old woman, clad in a black stuff dress; a white muslin cap lay on her white hair, and over her shoulders a fur cape.

Standing just within the door, which she had shut behind her, she cast a long, measuring glance at her master, and at the lady who had come to spend a week at The Folly at this untoward time of the year.

It was a kindly, even an indulgent, glance, but it made Laura feel suddenly afraid.

"I come to ask," exclaimed Célestine in very fair English, "if Madame is comfortable? Is there anything I can do for Madame besides laying the table and cooking Madame's dinner?"

"I don't think so—everything is delightful," murmured Laura.

The old woman, taking a few steps forward, vanished into what the newcomer was soon to learn was the dining room. Treville said wistfully, "And now I must leave you—"

Laura whispered faintly, "I am a coward, Julian."

He answered eagerly, "I would not have you other than you are."

She took his hand in hers, and laid it against her cheek.

"It's because of David—only because of David—that I feel afraid."

And as she said the word "afraid," the old Frenchwoman came back into the room. "Would Madame like me to come in to sleep each night?" she asked.

Treville answered for Laura. "Mrs. Darcy prefers being here alone. She will live as does my stepmother, when she is staying at The Folly."

He turned to Laura. "I will say good night now, but after I come in from hunting tomorrow, I'll come down, as you have kindly asked me to do, to dinner."

She answered in a low voice, "I shall be so glad to see you tomorrow evening."

"By the way—" he waited a moment.

Why did Célestine stand there, looking at them? Why didn't she go away, as she would have hastened to do if his companion had been his stepmother?

But at last, he ended his sentence with "—there's a private telephone from The Folly to my study, if you have occasion to speak to me."

After her lover had left her with a quiet clasp of the hand, and after old Célestiné had gone off, at last, to her own quarters, Laura sat down and covered her face with her hands; she felt both happy and miserable, exultant and afraid.

At last, she threw a tender thought to *La Belle Julie*, who had given up everything that to her should have seemed worth living for, in a material sense, to follow the man she loved into what must have been a piteous exile. And yet Laura felt tonight that she, too, would have had that cruel courage, had she not been the mother of a child.

She got up at last, and walked across the room, wondering how lovely Julie had fared during the long, weary hours she must have waited here for her lover.

Would the Treville of that day have done for his Julie what Julian had done for his Laura tonight? Would he have respected her cowardly fears? She felt sure not. Julie's Treville might have gone away, but Julie's Treville would have come back. Well, she knew that Laura's Treville would not return tonight.

And then she turned round quickly, for across the still air of the room had fallen the sound of a deep sigh.

Swiftly Laura went across to the door, masked by a stiff curtain of tapestry, which led into the corridor linking the various rooms of The Folly.

She lifted the curtain, and slipped out into the dimly lit corridor, but there was no one there.

Coming back into the sitting room she sat down again by the fire, convinced that her nerves had played her a trick, and once more she found herself thinking of *La Belle Julie*. She felt as if there was a bond between herself and the long dead dancer; the bond which links all poor women who embark on the danger-fraught adventure of secret, illicit love.

II

That evening Célestine proved that her hand had not lost its French cunning. But Laura was too excited, as well as too tired, to eat. The old woman made no comment as to that, but when at last she found with delight that "Mrs. Darcy" spoke excellent French, she did tell her that if she heard strange signs, or may be a stifled sob, she was not to feel afraid, as it would only be the wraith of *La Belle Julie* expatiating her sin where that sin had not only been committed but exulted in.

But it was not the ghost of Julie of whom Laura was afraid —it was Célestine, with her gleaming brown eyes and shrewd face, whom she feared. She breathed more easily when the old Frenchwoman was gone....

The bedchamber where she was to sleep had also been left unaltered for a hundred years and more. It was hung with faded lavender silk, and on the floor lay an Aubusson carpet, while at the farther end of the room was the wide, low, *Directoire* bed which had been brought from the Paris of the young Napoleon.

The telephone of which Treville had told her stood on a table close to her pillow. How amazed would Julie have been to hear that a day would come when a woman lying in what had been her bed would be able to speak from there to her lover— the man who, like Julie's own lover, was master of the great house which stood over a mile away from The Folly.

Célestine had forgotten to draw the heavy embroidered yellow silk curtains, and Laura walked to the nearest window and looked out on to the gleaming waters of the lake.

Across to the right rose dense clumps of dark ilexes; to the left tall trees, now stripped of leaves, stood black and drear against the winter sky.

The telephone bell tinkled. She turned and ran across the room, and then she heard Julian Treville's voice as strong, as clear, as love-laden, as if he were with her here, tonight.

The next day's sun illumined a beautiful soft winter morning, and Laura felt not only tremblingly happy, but also what she had not thought to feel—at peace. She went for a walk round the lake, then enjoyed the luncheon Célestine had prepared for her. Célestine, so much was clear, was set on waiting on her far more assiduously than she did on her own mistress, old Mrs. Treville.

About three o'clock Laura went again out of doors, to come in, an hour later, to find the lamp in the drawing-room lit, though it was not yet dark.

She went through into her bedroom, and then she heard the telephone ring—not loudly, insistently, as it had rung last night, but with a thin, tenuous sound.

Eagerly she went over to the side of the bed and took off the receiver, and then, as if coming from infinitely far away, she heard Julian Treville's voice.

"Are you there, my darling? I am in darkness, but our love is my beacon, and my heart is full of you," and his voice, his dear voice, sank away.

Then he was home from hunting far sooner than he had thought to be? This surely meant that very soon he would be here.

She took off her hat and coat, put on a frock Julian had once said he loved to see her wear, and then went back to wait for his coming in the sitting-room. But the moments became minutes, and the minutes quarters of an hour, and the time went by very slowly.

At last, a key turned in the lock of the front door, and she stood up—then felt a pang of bitter disappointment, for it was only the old Frenchwoman who passed through into the room.

Célestine shut the door behind her, and then she came close up to where Laura had sat down again, wearily, by the fire.

"Madame!" she exclaimed. And then she stopped short, a tragic look on her pale withered face.

Laura's thoughts flew to her child. She leapt up from her chair. "What is it, Célestine? A message for me?"

Very solemnly Celestine said the fearful words: "Prepare for ill news."

"Ill news?" Oh! how could she have left her child? "What do you mean?" cried Laura violently.

"There is no message come for you. But—but—our good kind master, Mr. Treville, is dead. He was killed out hunting today. I was in the village when the news was brought." She went on, speaking in quick gasps: "His horse—how say you? —" she waited, and then, finding the word she sought, "stumbled," she sobbed.

Laura for a moment stood still, as if she had not heard, or did not understand the purport of, the other's words, and then she gave a strangled cry, as Célestine, gathering her to her gaunt breast, said quickly in French, "My poor, poor lady! Well did I see that my master loved you—and that you loved him. You must leave The Folly tonight, at once. They have already telegraphed for old Mrs. Treville."

III

An hour later Laura was dressed, ready for departure. In a

few minutes from now Célestine would be here to carry her bag to the car which the old Frenchwoman had procured to take her to the distant station where Julian Treville had met her yesterday. Yesterday? It seemed aeons of time ago.

Suddenly there came a loud knock on the heavy door, and at once she walked across the room and opened it wide. Nothing mattered to her now; and when Roger Delacourt strode into the room she felt scarce any surprise, and that though she had believed him a thousand miles away.

"Are you alone, Laura?" he asked harshly. There was a look of savage anger in his face. His vanity—the vanity of a man no longer young who has had a strong allure for women—felt bruised in its tenderest part.

As she said nothing, only looked at him with an air of tragic pain and defiance, he went on, jeeringly, "No doubt you are asking yourself how I found out where you were, and on what pretty business you were engaged? I will give you a clue, and you can guess the rest for yourself. I had to come back unexpectedly to England, and the one person to whom you gave this address—I presume so you might have news of the boy—unwittingly gave you away!"

She still said nothing, and he went on bitterly: "I thought you—fool that I was—a good woman. But from what I hear I now know that your lover, Julian Treville, is no new friend. But I do not care, I do not enquire, how often you have been here—"

"This is the first time," she said dully, "that I have been here."

And then it was as if something outside herself impelled her to add the untrue words, "I am not, as you seem to think, Roger, alone—" for with a sharp thrill of intense fear she had remembered her child.

"Not alone?" he repeated incredulously. And then he saw

the tapestried curtain which hung over the door, opposite to where he stood, move, and he realized that someone was behind it, listening.

He took a few steps forward and pulled the curtain roughly back. But the dimly illumined corridor was empty; whoever had been there eavesdropping had scurried away into shelter. He came back to the spot where he had been standing before. Baffled, angry, still full of doubt, and yet, deep in his heart, unutterably relieved. Already a half-suspicion that Laura was sheltering some woman friend engaged in an intrigue had flashed into his mind, and the suspicion crystallized into certainty as he looked loweringly into her pale, set face. She did not look as more than once, in the days of his good fortunes, he had seen a guilty wife look.

Yes, that must be the solution of this queer, secret escapade! Laura, poor fool! had been the screen behind which hid a pair of guilty lovers. Thirty years ago, a woman had played the same thankless part in an intrigue of his own.

"Who is your friend?" he asked roughly.

Her lips did not move, and he told himself, with a certain satisfaction, that she was paralysed with fear.

"How long have you and your friend been here? That, at least, you can tell me."

At last, she whispered what sounded like the absurd answer: "Just a hundred years."

Then, turning quickly, she went through the door which gave into the dining room, and shut it behind her.

Roger Delacourt began pacing about the room; he felt what he had very seldom come to feel in his long, hard, if till now fortunate, life, just a little foolish, but relieved—unutterably relieved—and glad.

The Folly? Well named indeed! The very setting for a secret

love affair. Beautiful, too, in its strange and romantic aloofness from everyday life.

He went and gazed up at the pastel, which was the only picture in the room. What an exquisite, flower-like face! It reminded him of a French girl he had known when he was a very young man. Her name had been Zélie Mignard, and she had been reader-companion to an old marquise with whose son he had spent a long summer and autumn on the Loire. From the first moment he had seen Zélie she had attracted him violently, and though little more than a boy, he had made up his mind to seduce her. But she had resisted him, and then, in spite of himself, he had come to love her with that ardent first love which returns no more.

Suddenly there fell on the air of the still room the sound of a long, deep sigh. He wheeled sharply round to see that between himself and the still uncurtained window there stood a slender young woman—Laura's peccant friend, without a doubt!

He could not see her very clearly, yet of that he was not sorry, for he was not and he had never been—he told himself with an inward chuckle—the man to spoil sport.

Secretly he could afford to smile at the thought of his cold, passionless wife acting as duenna. Hard man as he was, his old heart warmed to the erring stranger, the more so that her sudden apparition had removed a last lingering doubt from his mind.

She threw out her slender hands with a gesture that again seemed to fill his mind with memories of his vanished youth, and there floated across the dark room the whispered words,

"Be not unkind." And then—did she say "Remember Zélie?" No, no—it was his heart, less atrophied than he had thought it to be, which had evoked, quickened into life, the name of his first love, the French girl who, if alive, must be—hateful, disturbing thought—an old woman today.

Then, as he gazed at her, the shadowy figure swiftly walked across the room, and so through the tapestry curtain. He waited a moment, then slowly passed through the dining room, and so into the firelit bedroom beyond.

His wife was standing by the window, looking as wraith-like as had done, just now, her friend. She was staring out into the darkness, her arms hanging by her side. She had not turned round when she had heard the door of the room open.

"Laura!" said her husband gruffly. And then she turned and cast on him a suffering alien glance.

"I accept your explanation of your presence here. And, well, I apologize for my foolish suspicions. Still, you're not a child! The part you're playing is not one any man would wish his wife to play. How long do you—and your friend—intend to stay here?"

"We meant to stay ten days," she said listlessly, "but as you're home, Roger, I'll leave now, if you like."

"And your friend, Laura, what of her?"

"I think she has already left The Folly."

She waited a moment, then forced herself to add, "Julian Treville was killed today out hunting—as I suppose you know."

"Good God! How awful! Believe me, I did not know—" Roger Delacourt was sincerely affected, as well he might be, for already he had arranged, in his own mind, to go to Leicestershire next week.

And, strange to say, as the two travelled up to town together, he was more considerate in his manner to his wife than he had been for many years. For one thing, he felt that this curious episode proved Laura to have more heart than he had given her credit for. But, being the manner of man and of husband he happened to be, he naturally did not approve of her having risked her spotless reputation in playing the part of duenna to a friend who had loved not wisely but too well. He trusted that what had just happened would prove a lesson to his wife and, for the matter of that, to himself.

A VISITOR FROM DOWN UNDER

L. P. HARTLEY

And who will you send to fetch him away?

After a promising start, the March day had ended in a wet evening. It was hard to tell whether rain or fog predominated. The loquacious bus-conductor said "A foggy evening" to those who rode inside, and "A wet evening" to such as were obliged to ride outside. But in or on the buses, cheerfulness held the field, for their patrons, inured to discomfort, made light of climatic inclemency. All the same, the weather was worth remarking on: the most scrupulous conversationalist could refer to it without feeling self-convicted of banality. How much more the conductor, who, in common with most of his kind, had a considerable conversational gift.

The bus was making its last journey through the heart of London before turning in for the night. Inside it was only half full. Outside, as the conductor was aware by virtue of his sixth sense, there still remained a passenger too hardy or too lazy to seek shelter. And now, as the bus rattled rapidly down the

Strand, the footsteps of this person could be heard shuffling and creaking upon the metal-shod stairs.

"Anyone on top?" asked the conductor, addressing an errant umbrella-point and the hem of a mackintosh.

"I didn't notice anyone," the man replied.

"It's not that I don't trust you," remarked the conductor, pleasantly giving a hand to his alighting fare; "but I think I'll go up and make sure."

Moments like these, moments of mistrust in the infallibility of his observation, occasionally visited the conductor.

They came at the end of a tiring day, and if he could he withstood them. They were signs of weakness, he thought; and to give way to them matter for self-reproach. "Going barmy, that's what you are," he told himself, and he casually took a fare inside to prevent his mind dwelling on the unvisited outside. But his unreasoning disquietude survived this distraction and murmuring against himself he started to climb the stairs.

To his surprise, almost stupefaction, he found that his misgivings were justified. Breasting the ascent, he saw a passenger sitting on the right-hand front seat; and the passenger, in spite of his hat turned down, his collar turned up and the creased white muffler that showed between the two, must have heard him coming; for though the man was looking straight ahead, in his outstretched left hand, wedged between the first and second fingers, he held a coin.

"Jolly evening, don't you think?" asked the conductor, who wanted to say something. The passenger made no reply, but the penny, for such it was, slipped the fraction of an inch lower in the groove between the pale freckled fingers.

"I said it was a damn wet night," the conductor persisted irritably, annoyed by the man's reserve. Still no reply.

"Where you for?" asked the conductor, in a tone suggesting that, wherever it was, it must be a discreditable destination.

"Carrick Street."

"Where?" the conductor demanded. He had heard all right, but a slight peculiarity in the passenger's pronunciation made it appear reasonable to him, and possibly humiliating to the passenger, that he should not have heard.

"Carrick Street."

"Then why don't you say Carrick Street?" the conductor grumbled as he punched the ticket.

There was a moment's pause, then "Carrick Street," the passenger repeated.

"Yes, I know, I know; you needn't go on telling me," fumed the conductor, fumbling with the passenger's penny. He couldn't get hold of it from above, it had slipped too far, so he passed his hand underneath the other's and drew the coin from between his fingers.

It was cold, even where it had been held.

"Know?" said the stranger suddenly. "What do you know?"

The conductor was trying to draw his fare's attention to the ticket, but could not make him look round. "I suppose I know you are a clever chap," he remarked. "Look here now. Where do you want this ticket? In your buttonhole?"

"Put it here," said the passenger.

"Where?" asked the conductor. "You aren't a blooming letter rack."

"Where the penny was," replied the passenger. "Between my fingers."

The conductor felt reluctant, he did not know why, to oblige the passenger in this. The rigidity of the hand disconcerted him: it was stiff, he supposed, or perhaps paralysed. And since he had been standing on the top his own hands were none too warm. The ticket doubled up and grew limp under his repeated efforts to push it in. He bent lower, for he was a good-hearted fellow, and using both hands, one above and one below, he slid the ticket into its bony slot.

"Tight you are, Kaiser Bill."

Perhaps the passenger resented this jocular allusion to his physical infirmity; perhaps he merely wanted to be quiet. All he said was:

"Don't speak to me again."

"Speak to you!" shouted the conductor, losing all self-control. "Catch me speaking to a stuffed dummy!"

Muttering to himself, he withdrew into the bowels of the bus.

At the corner of Carrick Street quite a number of people got on board. All wanted to be first, but pride of place was shared by three women, who all tried to enter simultaneously.

The conductor's voice made itself audible above the din: "Now then, now then, look where you're shoving! This isn't a bargain sale. Gently *please*, lady; he's only a poor old man." In a moment or two the confusion abated, and the conductor, his hand on the cord of the bell, bethought himself of the passenger on top whose destination Carrick Street was. He had forgotten to get down. Yielding to his good nature, for the conductor was averse to further conversation with his uncommunicative fare, he mounted the stairs, put his head over the top and shouted, "Carrick Street! Carrick Street!" That was the utmost he could bring himself to do. But his admonition was without effect; his summons remained unanswered; nobody came. "Well, if he wants to stay up there, he can," muttered the conductor, still aggrieved. "I won't fetch him down, cripple or no cripple." The bus moved on. He slipped by me, thought the conductor, while all that Cup-tie crowd was getting in.

The same evening, some five hours earlier, a taxi turned into Carrick Street and pulled up at the door of a small hotel.

The street was empty. It looked like a cul-de-sac, but in reality, it was pierced at the far end by an alley, like a thin sleeve, which wound its way into Soho.

"That the last, sir?" enquired the driver, after several transits between the cab and the hotel.

"How many does that make?"

"Nine packages in all, sir."

"Could you get all your worldly goods into nine packages, driver?"

"That I could; into two."

"Well, have a look inside and see if I have left anything." The cabman felt about among the cushions. "Can't find nothing, sir."

"What do you do with anything you find?" asked the stranger.

"Take it to New Scotland Yard, sir," the driver promptly replied.

"Scotland Yard?" said the stranger. "Strike a match, will you, and let me have a look."

But he, too, found nothing, and reassured, followed his luggage into the hotel.

A chorus of welcome and congratulation greeted him. The manager, the manager's wife, the ministers without portfolio of which all hotels are full, the porters, the liftman, all clustered around him.

"Well, Mr. Rumbold, after all these years! We thought you'd forgotten us! And wasn't it odd, the very night your telegram came from Australia we'd been talking about you! And my husband said, 'Don't you worry about Mr. Rumbold. He'll fall on his feet all right. Some fine day he'll walk in here a rich man.' Not that you weren't always well-off, but my husband meant a millionaire."

"He was quite right," said Mr. Rumbold slowly, savouring his words; "I am."

"There, what did I tell you?" the manager exclaimed, as though one recital of his prophecy was not enough. "But I wonder you're not too grand to come to Rossall's Hotel."

"I've nowhere else to go," said the millionaire shortly. "And if I had, I wouldn't. This place is like home to me."

His eyes softened as they scanned the familiar surroundings. They were light-grey eyes, very pale, and seeming paler from their setting in his tanned face. His cheeks were slightly sunken and very deeply lined; his blunt-ended nose was straight. He had a thin straggling moustache, straw-coloured, which made his age difficult to guess. Perhaps he was nearly fifty, so wasted was the skin on his neck, but his movements, unexpectedly agile and decided, were those of a younger man.

"I won't go up to my room now," he said, in response to the manageress's question. "Ask Clutsam—he's still with you?—to unpack my things. He'll find all I want for the night in the green suitcase. I'll take my despatch-box with me. And tell them to bring me a sherry-and-bitters in the lounge."

As the crow flies, it was not far to the lounge. But by way of the tortuous, ill-lit passages, doubling on themselves, yawning with dark entries, plunging into kitchen stairs—the catacombs so dear to *habitués* of Rossall's Hotel—it was a considerable distance. Anyone posted in the shadow of these alcoves, or arriving at the head of the basement staircase, could not have failed to notice the air of utter content which marked Mr. Rumbold's leisurely progress: the droop of his shoulders, acquiescing in weariness; the hands turned inwards and swaying slightly, but quite forgotten by their owner; the chin, always prominent, now pushed forward so far that it looked relaxed and helpless, not at all defiant. The unseen witness would have envied Mr. Rumbold, perhaps even grudged him his holiday airs, his untroubled acceptance of the present and the future.

A waiter whose face he did not remember brought him the *apéritif*, which he drank slowly, his feet propped unconventionally upon a ledge of the chimneypiece; a pardonable relaxation, for the room was empty. Judge therefore his surprise when, out of a fire-engendered drowsiness, he heard a voice which seemed to come from the wall above his head. A cultivated voice, perhaps too cultivated, slightly husky, yet careful and precise in its enunciation. Even while his eyes searched the room to make sure that no one had come in, he could not help hearing everything the voice said. It seemed to be talking to him, and yet the rather oracular utterance implied a less restricted audience. The utterance of a man who was aware that, though it was a duty for him to speak, for Mr. Rumbold to listen would be both a pleasure and a profit.

"—A Children's Party," the voice announced in an even, neutral tone, nicely balanced between approval and distaste, between enthusiasm and boredom; "six little girls and six little" (a faint lift in the voice, expressive of tolerant surprise) "boys. The Broadcasting Company has invited them to tea, and they are anxious that you should share some of their fun." (At the last word the voice became almost positively colourless.) "I must tell you that they have had tea, and enjoyed it, didn't you, children?" (A cry of "Yes," muffled and timid, greeted this leading question.) "We should have liked you to hear our table talk, but there wasn't much of it, we were so busy eating." For a moment the voice identified itself with the children. "But we can tell you what we ate. Now, Percy, tell us what you had."

A piping little voice recited a long list of comestibles; like the children in the treacle-well, thought Rumbold, Percy must have been, or soon would be, very ill. A few others volunteered the items of their repast. "So you see," said the voice, "we have not done so badly. And now we are going to have crackers, and afterwards" (the voice hesitated and seemed to dissociate itself from the words) "children's games." There was an impressive pause, broken by the muttered exhortation of a little girl: "Don't cry, Philip, it won't hurt you." Fugitive sparks and snaps of sounds followed; more like a fire being mended, thought Rumbold, than crackers. A murmur of voices pierced the fusillade.

"What have you got, Alec, what have you *got*?"

"I've got a cannon."

"Give it to me."

"No."

"Well, lend it to me."

"What do you want it for?"

"I want to shoot Jimmy."

Mr. Rumbold started. Something had disturbed him. Was it imagination, or did he hear, above the confused medley of sound, a tiny click? The voice was speaking again. "And now we're going to begin the games." As though to make amends for past lukewarmness a faint flush of anticipation gave colour to the decorous voice. "We will commence with that old favourite, Ring-a-ring-of-Roses."

The children were clearly shy, and left each other to do the singing. Their courage lasted for a line or two, and then gave out. But fortified by the speaker's baritone, powerful though subdued, they took heart, and soon were singing without assistance or direction. Their light wavering voices had a charming effect. Tears stood in Mr. Rumbold's eyes.

"Oranges and Lemons" came next. A more difficult game, it yielded several unrehearsed effects before it finally got under way. One could almost see the children being marshalled into their places, as though for a figure in the Lancers. Some of them no doubt had wanted to play another game; children are contrary, and the dramatic side of "Oranges and Lemons," though it appeals to many, always affrights a few. The disinclination of these last would account for the pauses and hesitations which irritated Mr. Rumbold, who, as a child, had always had a strong fancy for this particular game. When, to the tramping and stamping of many small feet, the droning chant began, he leaned back and closed his eyes in ecstasy. He listened intently for the final accelerando which leads up to the catastrophe. Still the prologue meandered on, as though the children were anxious to extend the period of security, the joyous care-free promenade which the great Bell of Bow, by his inconsiderate profession of ignorance, was so rudely to curtail. The Bells of Old Bailey pressed their usurers' question; the Bells of Shoreditch answered with becoming flippancy; the Bells of Stepney posed their ironical query, when suddenly before the great Bell of Bow had time to get his word in, Mr. Rumbold's feelings underwent a strange revolution. Why couldn't the game continue, all sweetness and sunshine? Why drag in the fatal issue? Let payment be deferred; let the bells go on chiming, and never strike the hour. But heedless of Mr. Rumbold's Squeamishness, the game went its way. After the eating comes the reckoning.

> *"Here is a candle to light you to bed,*
> *And here comes a chopper to chop off your head!*
> *Chop, chop, chop ..."*

A child screamed, and there was silence.

Mr. Rumbold felt quite upset, and great was his relief when, after a few more half-hearted rounds of "Oranges and Lemons," the voice announced, "Here we come gathering Nuts and May." At least there was nothing sinister in that. Delicious sylvan scene, comprising in one splendid botanical inexacti-

tude all the charms of winter, spring, and autumn. What supe-
riority to circumstance was implied in the conjunction of nuts
and may! What defiance of cause and effect! What a testimony
to coincidence! For cause and effect are against us, as witness
the fate of Old Bailey's Debtor; but coincidence is always on
our side, always teaching us how to eat our cake and have it!
The long arm of coincidence; Mr. Rumbold would have liked to
clasp it by the hand.

Meanwhile his own hand conducted the music of the
revels and his foot kept time. Their pulses quickened by enjoyment, the children put more heart into the singing; the game
went with a swing; the ardour and rhythm of it invaded the
little room where Mr. Rumbold sat. Like heavy fumes the
waves of sound poured in, so penetrating, they ravished the
sense, so sweet they intoxicated it, so light they fanned it to a
flame. Mr. Rumbold was transported. His hearing, sharpened
by the subjugation and quiescence of his other faculties, began
to take in new sounds; the names, for instance, of the players
who were "wanted" to make up each side and of the champions who were to pull them over. For the listeners-in, the
issues of the struggles remained in doubt. Did Nancy Price
succeed in detracting Percy Kingham from his allegiance?
Probably. Did Alec Wharton prevail against Maisie Drew? It
was certainly an easy win for someone: the contest lasted only
a second, and a ripple of laughter greeted it. Did Violet
Kingham make good against Horace Gold? This was a dire
encounter, punctuated by deep irregular panting. Mr. Rumbold
could see, in his mind's eye, the two champions straining backwards and forwards across the white motionless handkerchief,
their faces red and puckered with exertion. Violet or Horace,
one of them had to go: Violet might be bigger than Horace, but
then Horace was a boy: they were evenly matched: they had
their pride to maintain. The moment when the will was

broken, and the body went limp in surrender. would be like a moment of dissolution. Yes, even this game had its stark, uncomfortable side. Violet or Horace, one of them was smarting now; crying perhaps under the humiliation of being fetched away. The game began afresh. This time there was an eager ring in the children's voices: two tried antagonists were going to meet: it would be a battle of giants. The chant throbbed into a war cry.

> *"Who will you have for your Nuts and May,*
> *Nuts and May, Nuts and May?*
> *Who will you have for your Nuts and May*
> *On a cold and frosty morning?"*

They would have Victor Rumbold for Nuts and May, Victor Rumbold, Victor Rumbold; and from the vindictiveness in their voices they might have meant to have his blood too.

> *"And who will you send to fetch him away*
> *Fetch him away, fetch him away?*
> *Who will you send to fetch him away*
> *On a cold and frosty morning?"*

Like a clarion call, a shout of defiance, came the reply:

> *"We'll send Jimmy Hagberd to fetch him away,*
> *Fetch him away, fetch him away;*
> *We'll send Jimmy Hagberd to fetch him away,*
> *On a wet and foggy evening."*

This variation, it might be supposed, was intended to promote the contest from the realms of pretence into the world of reality. But Mr. Rumbold probably did not hear that his abduction had been antedated. He had turned quite green, and his head was lolling against the back of the chair.

~

"Any wine, sir?"

"Yes, Clutsam, a bottle of champagne."

"Very good, sir."

Mr. Rumbold drained the first glass at one go.

"Anyone coming into dinner besides me, Clutsam?" he presently enquired.

"Not now, sir, it's nine o'clock," replied the waiter, his voice edged with reproach.

"Sorry, Clutsam, I didn't feel up to the mark before dinner, so I went and lay down."

The waiter was mollified.

"Thought you weren't looking quite yourself, sir. No bad news, I hope?"

"No, nothing. Just a bit tired after the journey."

"And how did you leave Australia, sir?" enquired the waiter, to accommodate Mr. Rumbold, who seemed anxious to talk.

"In better weather than you have here," Mr. Rumbold replied, finishing his second glass, and measuring with his eye the depleted contents of the bottle.

The rain kept up a steady patter on the glass roof of the coffee room.

"Still, a good climate isn't everything; it isn't like home, for instance," the waiter remarked.

"No, indeed."

"There's many parts of the world as would be glad of a good day's rain," affirmed the waiter.

"There certainly are," said Mr. Rumbold, who found the conversation sedative.

"Did you do much fishing when you were abroad, sir?" the waiter pursued.

"A little."

"Well, you want rain for that," declared the waiter, as one who scores a point. "The fishing isn't preserved in Australia, like what it is here?"

"No."

"Then there ain't no poaching," concluded the waiter philosophically. "It's every man for himself."

"Yes, that's the rule in Australia."

"Not much of a rule, is it?" the waiter took him up. "Not much like law, I mean."

"It depends what you mean by law.'"

"Oh, Mr. Rumbold, sir, you know very well what I mean. I mean the police. Now, if you was to have done a man in out in Australia—murdered him, I mean—they'd hang you for it if they caught you, wouldn't they?"

Mr. Rumbold teased the champagne with the butt end of his fork and drank again.

"Probably they would, unless there were special circumstances."

"In which case you might get off?"

"I might."

"That's what I mean by law," pronounced the waiter. "You know what the law is: you go against it, and you're punished. Of course, I don't mean you, sir; I only say 'you' as—as an illustration to make my meaning clear."

"Quite, quite."

"Whereas if there was only what you call a rule," the waiter pursued, deftly removing the remains of Mr. Rumbold's chicken, "it might fall to the lot of any man to round you up. Might be anybody; might be me."

"Why should you or they," asked Mr. Rumbold, "want to round me up? I haven't done you any harm, or them."

"Oh, but we should have to, sir."

"Why?"

"We couldn't rest in our beds, sir, knowing you was at large. You might do it again. Somebody'd have to see to it."

"But supposing there was nobody?"

"Sir?"

"Supposing the murdered man hadn't any relatives or friends; supposing he just disappeared, and no one ever knew that he was dead?"

"Well, sir," said the waiter, winking portentously, "in that case he'd have to get on your track himself. He wouldn't rest in his grave, sir, no, not he, and knowing what he did."

"Clutsam," said Mr. Rumbold suddenly, "bring me another bottle of wine and don't trouble to ice it."

The waiter took the bottle from the table and held it up to the light. "Yes, it's dead, sir."

"Dead?"

"Yes, sir, finished—empty—dead."

"You're right," Mr. Rumbold agreed. "It's quite dead."

It was nearly eleven o'clock. Mr. Rumbold again had the lounge to himself. Clutsam would be bringing his coffee presently. Too bad of Fate to have him haunted by these casual reminders; too bad, his first day at home. "Too bad, too bad," he muttered, while the fire warmed the soles of his slippers. But it was excellent champagne, he would take no harm from it: the brandy Clutsam was bringing him would do the rest. Clutsam was a good sort, nice, old-fashioned servant ... nice, old-fashioned house ... Warmed by the wine, his thoughts began to pass out of his control.

"Your coffee, sir," said a voice at his elbow.

"Thank you, Clutsam, I'm very much obliged to you," said Mr. Rumbold, with the exaggerated civility of slight intoxication. "You're an excellent fellow. I wish there were more like you."

"I hope so, too, I'm sure," said Clutsam, trying in his muddle-hearted way to deal with both observations at once.

"Don't seem many people about," Mr. Rumbold remarked. "Hotel pretty full?"

"Oh yes, sir, all the suites are let, and the other rooms too. We're turning people away every day. Why, only tonight a gentleman rang up. Said he would come round late, on the off chance. But, bless me, he'll find the birds have flown."

"Birds?" echoed Mr. Rumbold.

"I mean, there ain't any more rooms, not for love nor money."

"Well, I'm sorry for him," said Mr. Rumbold, with ponderous sincerity. "I'm sorry for any man, friend or foe, who has to go tramping about London on a night like this. If I had an extra bed in my room, I'd put it at his disposal."

"You have, sir," the waiter said.

"Why, of course I have. How stupid! Well, well. I'm sorry for the poor chap. I'm sorry for all homeless ones, Clutsam, wandering on the face of the earth."

"Amen to that," said the waiter devoutly.

"And doctors and such, pulled out of their beds at midnight. It's a hard life. Ever thought about a doctor's life, Clutsam?"

"Can't say I have, sir."

"Well, well, but it's hard; you can take that from me."

"What time shall I call you in the morning, sir?" the waiter asked, seeing no reason why the conversation should ever stop.

"You needn't call me Clutsam," replied Mr. Rumbold in a sing-song voice, and running the words together as though he were excusing the waiter from addressing him by the waiter's own name. "I'll get up when I'm ready. And that may be pretty late, pretty late." He smacked his lips over the words. "Nothing like a good lie, eh, Clutsam?"

"That's right, sir. You have your sleep out," the waiter encouraged him. "You won't be disturbed."

"Goodnight, Clutsam, you're an excellent fellow, and I don't care who hears me say so."

"Goodnight, sir."

Mr. Rumbold returned to his chair. It lapped him round, it ministered to his comfort; he felt at one with it. At one with the fire, the clock, the tables, all the furniture. Their usefulness, their goodness, went out to meet his usefulness, his goodness, met and were friends. Who could bind their sweet influences or restrain them in the exercise of their kind offices? No one. No one; certainly not a shadow from the past. The room was perfectly quiet. Street sounds reached it only as a low continuous hum, infinitely reassuring. Mr. Rumbold fell asleep.

He dreamed that he was a boy again, living in his old home in the country. He was possessed, in the dream, by a master passion; he must collect firewood whenever and wherever he saw it. He found himself one autumn afternoon in the woodhouse; that was how the dream began. The door was partly open, admitting a little light, but he could not recall how he got in. The floor of the shed was littered with bits of bark and thin twigs; but, with the exception of the chopping block which he knew could not be used, there was nowhere a log of sufficient size to make a fire. Though he did not like being in the woodhouse alone he stayed long enough to make a thorough search. But he could find nothing. The compulsion he knew so well descended on him, and he left the woodhouse and went into the garden. His steps took him to the foot of a high tree, standing by itself in a tangle of long grass at some distance from the house. The tree had been lopped; for half its height it had no branches, only leafy tufts, sticking out at irregular intervals. He knew what he would see when he looked up into the dark foliage. And there, sure enough it was; a long dead bough, bare in patches where the bark had peeled off, and crooked in the middle like an elbow.

He began to climb the tree. The ascent proved easier than he expected, his body seemed no weight at all. But he was visited by a terrible oppression, which increased as he mounted. The bough did not want him; it was projecting its hostility down the trunk of the tree. And every second brought him nearer to an object which he had always dreaded: a growth, people called it. It stuck out from the trunk of the tree, a huge circular swelling thickly matted with twigs. Victor would have rather died than hit his head against it.

By the time he reached the bough twilight had deepened into night. He knew what he had to do: sit astride the bough, since there was none near by from which he could reach it, and press with his hands until it broke. Using his legs to get what purchase he could, he set his back against the tree, and pushed with all his might downwards. To do this he was obliged to look beneath him, and he saw, far below him on the ground, a white sheet spread out as though to catch him; and he knew at once that it was a shroud.

Frantically he pulled and pushed at the stiff brittle bough; a lust to break it took hold of him; leaning forward his whole length, he seized the bough at the elbow joint and strained it away from him. As it cracked, he toppled over, and the shroud came rushing upwards....

Mr. Rumbold waked in a cold sweat to find himself clutching the curved arm of the chair on which the waiter had set his brandy. The glass had fallen over, and the spirit lay in a little pool on the leather seat.

I can't let it go like that, he thought, *I must get some more.*

A man he did not know answered the bell.

"Waiter," he said, "bring me a brandy and soda in my room in a quarter of an hour's time. Rumbold, the name is." He followed the waiter out of the room. The passage was completely dark except for a small blue gas jet, beneath which was huddled a cluster of candlesticks. The hotel, he remembered, maintained an old-time habit of deference towards darkness. As he held the wick to the gas jet, he heard himself mutter, "Here is a candle to light you to bed." But he recollected the ominous conclusion of the distich, and, fuddled as he was, he left it unspoken.

Shortly after Mr. Rumbold's retirement the doorbell of the hotel rang. Three sharp peals, and no pause between them.

"Someone in a hurry to get in," the night porter grumbled to Clutsam, who was on duty till midnight. "Expect he's forgotten his key."

He made no haste to answer the summons, it would do the forgetful fellow good to wait: teach him a lesson. So dilatory was he that by the time he reached the hall door the bell was tinkling again. Irritated by such importunity, he deliberately went back to set straight a pile of newspapers before letting this impatient devil in. To mark his indifference, he even kept behind the door while he opened it; so that his first sight of the visitor only took in his back. But this limited inspection sufficed to show that the man was a stranger and not a guest at the hotel.

In the long black cape, which fell almost sheer one side and on the other stuck out as though he had a basket under his arm, he looked like a crow with a broken wing. A bald-headed crow, thought the porter, for there's a patch of bare skin between that white linen thing and his hat.

"Good evening, sir," he said, "what can I do for you?"

The stranger made no answer but glided to a side table and began turning over some letters with his right hand.

"Are you expecting a message?" asked the porter.

"No," the stranger replied. "I want a room for the night."

"Was you the gentleman who telephoned for a room this evening?"

"Yes."

"In that case I was to tell you we're afraid you can't have one, the hotel's booked right up."

"Are you quite sure?" asked the stranger. "Think again."

"Them's my orders, sir. It don't do me no good to think." At this moment the porter had a curious sensation as though some important part of him, his life maybe, had gone adrift inside him and was spinning round and round. The sensation ceased when he began to speak.

"I'll call the waiter, sir," he said.

But before he called, the waiter appeared, intent on an errand of his own.

"I say, Bill," he began, "what's the number of Mr. Rumbold's room? He wants a drink taken up, and I forgot to ask him."

"It's thirty-three," said the porter unsteadily. "The double room."

"Why, Bill, what's up?" the waiter exclaimed. "You look as if you'd seen a ghost."

Both men stared round the hall, and then back at each other. The room was empty.

"God," said the porter. "I must have had the horrors. But he was here a moment ago. Look at this."

On the stone flags lay an icicle, an inch or two long, around which a little pool was fast collecting.

"Why, Bill," cried the waiter, "how did that get here? It's not freezing."

"*He* must have brought it," the porter said.

They looked at each other in consternation, which changed into terror as the sound of a bell made itself heard, coming from the depths of the hotel.

"Clutsam's there," whispered the porter. "He'll have to answer that, whoever it is."

Clutsam had taken off his tie, and was getting ready for bed. What on earth could anyone want in the lounge at this hour? He pulled on his coat and went upstairs.

Standing by the fire he saw the same figure whose appearance and disappearance had so disturbed the porter.

"Yes, sir," he said.

"I want you to go to Mr. Rumbold," said the stranger, "and ask him if he is prepared to put the other bed in his room at the disposal of a friend."

In a few moments Clutsam returned.

"Mr. Rumbold's compliments, sir, and he wants to know who it is." The stranger went to the table in the centre of the room. An Australian newspaper was lying on it, which Clutsam had not noticed before. The aspirant to Mr. Rumbold's hospitality turned over the pages. Then with his finger, which appeared, even to Clutsam standing by the door, unusually pointed, he cut out a rectangular slip, about the size of a visiting card, and, moving away, motioned the waiter to take it.

By the light of the gas jet in the passage Clutsam read the excerpt. It seemed to be a kind of obituary notice; but of what possible interest could it be to Mr. Rumbold, to know that the body of Mr. James Hagberd had been discovered in circumstances which suggested that he had met his death by violence?

After a long interval Clutsam returned, looking puzzled and a little frightened.

"Mr. Rumbold's compliments, sir, but he knows no one of that name."

"Then take this message to Mr. Rumbold," said the stranger.

"Say 'would he rather that I went up to him, or that he came down to me?'"

For the third time Clutsam went to do the stranger's bidding. He did not, however, upon his return open the door of the smoking room, but shouted through it:

"Mr. Rumbold wishes you to Hell, sir, where you belong, and says 'Come up if you dare.'"

Then he bolted.

A minute later, from his retreat in an underground coal cellar, he heard a shot fired. Some old instinct, danger-loving or danger-disregarding, stirred in him, and he ran up the stairs quicker than he had ever run up them in his life. In the passage he stumbled over Mr. Rumbold's boots. The bedroom door was ajar. Putting his head down he rushed in. The brightly lit room was empty. But almost all the movables in it were overturned, and the bed was in a frightful mess. The pillow with its fivefold perforation was the first object on which Clutsam noticed bloodstains. Thenceforward he seemed to see them everywhere. But what sickened him and kept him so long from going down to rouse the others was the sight of an icicle on the windowsill, a thin claw of ice curved like a Chinaman's nail, with a bit of flesh sticking to it.

That was the last he saw of Mr. Rumbold. But a policeman patrolling Carrick Street noticed a man in a long black cape who seemed, from the position of his arm, to be carrying something heavy. He called out to the man and ran after him; but though he did not seem to be moving very fast the policeman could not overtake him.

THE LOST TRAGEDY
DENIS MACKAIL

Mr. Bunstable's bookshop represents a type of establishment which has pretty well disappeared from our modern cities. Indeed, but for the fear of becoming involved in correspondence with strangers, I should be prepared to go considerably further, and to say that it is the only shop of its kind still in existence. In any case, it is most distinctly and unmistakably a survival from the past.

As all who have considered the subject must agree, the principal object of any bookseller is to obstruct, as far as possible, the sale of books. The method generally adopted today is to fill the premises with intelligent young men with knobby foreheads who chase intending customers from shelf to shelf, thrusting novels at antiquarians, theological works at novel readers, and two-volume biographies at those who obviously cannot afford them, until finally they have chased their victims right out into the street. This is called scientific salesmanship, and is largely responsible for the profits shown by the circulating libraries.

The old-fashioned method was directed at the same end,

but by a totally different route. The intending customer was left utterly and entirely to himself. If he knew what he wanted to read, he read it without let or hindrance and equally without payment. If he were just vaguely in search of an unidentified book—let us suppose for a wedding present—then he would wait for a period which varied according to his patience and temperament, and ultimately would take his departure and buy a silver sauceboat elsewhere.

Mr. Bunstable was, and still is, a skilled exponent of this second and earlier form of bookselling. He does not go in for window-dressing, and the wares which are visible from the street seem to have been chosen principally for their power to exclude the daylight from the interior of his shop, and secondarily for a lack of interest which shall ensure their remaining undisturbed. If you persist in disregarding the warning of this window, your next difficulty is with the door. Owing to a slight settlement in the fabric of Mr. Bunstable's premises it is impossible to open this door without the exercise of both strength and skill, but if you do succeed in opening it, then beware of the step which lurks just inside. Inexperienced customers usually arrive in the shop with a crash and a cry of alarm, and perhaps it is because of this that Mr. Bunstable has never troubled to repair the bell which hangs over his lintel, and was originally intended to give notice of his clients' approach.

As your eyes become accustomed to the darkness within, you now detect one or more figures, standing more or less erect with their legs more or less twisted round each other, and profoundly absorbed in the books which they are reading. Here again, and before they have discovered that these figures are wearing hats, inexperienced customers have mistaken them for members of Mr. Bunstable's staff. But no contretemps has ever arisen from this misapprehension. The figures are so intent on their studies that they are deaf to any words which may be addressed to them, and the customer can retrieve his error without any spoken explanation. One imagines that towards closing time Mr. Bunstable must go round his shop removing the volumes from these students' hands, and gently pushing them back into the outer world. But it is almost as easy to suppose that some of them remain there all night, for so far as my own observation goes Mr. Bunstable regards them as part of the fittings and fixtures. One day I must really go there at closing time and see what happens.

Meanwhile your eyes are becoming more and more acclimatized. You see vistas and vistas of books. Books heaped up on the dusty floor; books rising in tiers to the mottled ceiling; books on tables; books piled precariously on a stepladder; books bursting out of brown-paper parcels; books balanced on the seats of chairs. You long to sneeze—for the violence of your entrance has sent a quantity of dust flying up your nose—but you control yourself heroically.

The atmosphere of the place would make such an action an outrage. It would be worse than sneezing in church.

It was at this stage, in my own case, and just as I was wondering how on earth one ever bought anything in this extraordinary shop, that another of my senses was unexpectedly assailed. Somewhere—for the moment I couldn't tell where—a tune was being whistled. A short, monotonous air which suggested, "Here we go round the mulberry bush," and other works of that nature, and yet refused to be identified as anything that I had heard before. I looked at the two drugged readers who were the only other visible occupants of the shop, but the sound wasn't coming from them. Nor, on the other hand, did they give any sign of interest or annoyance at the constant repetition.

You will sympathize, I hope, when of that little tune I say

that it had now become my most pressing requirement to track the whistler to his lair; and with this object in view, I penetrated still farther into the darkness of the shop, stepping over the heaps of books and the brown-paper parcels, and soon losing all sense of direction in a labyrinth of shelves. All this while the tune continued, but as I felt my way forward, I noticed another peculiarity about it. The whistler seemed to have some rooted objection to giving us the last note of his melody. Each time that he reached this point, and each time that I was convinced the keynote must be coming, he suddenly broke off, paused for a moment, and began again at the beginning. It was all that I could do not to supply the missing note myself. And yet if, as I was now coming to believe, the music was proceeding from the proprietor of the shop, this was hardly the conventional way of introducing myself to his notice.

Again, I controlled myself, and then suddenly—as I turned yet another corner—I beheld the explanation of my puzzle. I was at the door of an inner sanctum or den, bursting with books also, yet differing from the dusty profusion through which I had come in that they were all neatly and carefully arranged; and between me and the window, which opened on to a prospect of unrelieved brickwork, there hung a small bird cage.

"Oh," I exclaimed aloud. "A bullfinch." At the same moment a second, and human, silhouette appeared before the window. Afterwards I saw that it had risen from a large desk, but at the time it had the startling effect of emerging as from a trapdoor, and what with this and my embarrassment at having been overheard, I took a hasty step backward.

"Don't go, sir," said the silhouette. "Was there anything I could find for you?"

It was in this way that I first met Mr. Edward Bunstable,

the sole proprietor of the shop which I have attempted to describe, and the individual to whom I owe the story that I am trying to relate. He was, and still is, a shortish gentleman of a genial but moderate rotundity, the possessor of a beard and a pair of steel-rimmed spectacles. He knows more about out-of-the-way books than anyone I have ever met, and how in the world he keeps his trade going and pays rent, rates, and taxes out of it, it is impossible to guess. I have enjoyed the privilege of his acquaintanceship for a number of years now, but though he has frequently shown me volumes which he has bought, I have never yet been able to discover any volume which he has sold. Sometimes I think that he must be an eccentric millionaire—so utterly unbusinesslike are his ways of business; at other times I am fain to believe that he is some kind of fairy, or ghost, or magician, or that he has escaped from the pages of one of his mustiest volumes—but I think this is because secretly he rather enjoys mystifying me. There has been a hint of a twinkle from behind those steel-rimmed spectacles during some of our talks which seems to me to support this view.

I have no idea where he sleeps, when he eats, or what—within about forty years—his age may be. On the other hand, I know all these particulars about his bullfinch, for within three minutes of our first meeting—and while I was still trying to give him the name of the book that I wanted he had told me that the bullfinch never left his room, that it subsisted on millet seed, and that it was fifteen years old.

"I bought him cheap," he said, "because he never could learn the last note of his song. I spent ten years trying to teach it him, but it was no use. That bird's got *character*, he has."

"Oh yes," I said. "But about this book, I was wondering if—"

"That bird," interrupted Mr. Bunstable, "is a regular Londoner. He's as sharp as they're made, that bird is."

He told me a great deal more about his bullfinch's alleged characteristics before I could succeed in giving him the particulars of the book that I was after. Then he nodded his head with an air of infinite wisdom.

"I've got it," he said. "I can't just lay my hands on it at the moment, but if you were to come back say in two- or three-days' time...."

Knowing no better, I did as I was asked. Mr. Bunstable said that he was still searching for the book. He was more convinced than ever that it was somewhere on the premises, but his general attitude towards the affair was that it was no use hurrying things. The suggestion conveyed to me at the time was that if once the book became aware that he was looking for it, it might take fright and disappear for good. After telling me a number of anecdotes of a literary flavour and showing me several of his most recent purchases—which he was careful to explain were not to be included in his stock—he proposed that I should pay him another visit, say in about a week or ten days.

"I'll be certain to have it for you by then," he added. "I *know* I've got it put away somewhere."

To cut a long story short, the object of my original enquiry has eluded Mr. Bunstable's search to this day. He is still hopeful about it, though I have long since abandoned any expectation of its ever coming to light just as I have long since outgrown the whim which made me ask for it. If he should ever find it, of course I would offer to buy it. This would at least be due to a man who, at a very moderate reckoning, has spent about a fortnight of working days in trying to oblige a customer. I shall not be surprised, however, if—in the event of its turning up—Mr. Bunstable refuses to part with it. For, in the meantime, there have been one or two near shaves when I have tried to purchase other volumes from his collection, and each time he has managed to prevent the sale taking place.

"Don't take it now, sir," he has said. "I'll find a better copy if you'll wait." Or, "I wouldn't have it, if I were you, sir. There'll be a new edition out in the spring." If I am still persistent, he enmeshes me in one of his long and hypnotic anecdotes, edging me quietly towards the door as he tells it. By this means I am caused to forget the quest which had drawn me to his shop, and his honour as an old-fashioned bookseller is preserved.

An inexplicable old gentleman. Even now, as I set this description on paper, I find myself wondering whether he and his shop can really exist. And perhaps this uncertainty is one of the reasons why I keep on going back there. I want to convince myself that I haven't made it all up.

So we arrive at the story which Mr. Bunstable told me one evening last autumn—beginning it in the recesses of his inner sanctum, with the bullfinch contributing its familiar *obbligato*, and finishing it at the front door of his shop, as he bowed me out into the foggy street. A good title for it might be "The Lost Tragedy."

Personally (said Mr. Bunstable) I'm a great one for reading, and perhaps you'll say that's natural enough. But there've been some big men in my trade—men who are up to all the tricks of the auction-room—who'd buy and sell books by the thousand, and yet never read anything but a catalogue or a newspaper, or maybe a railway timetable. Not that they weren't fond of books. But it was the bindings they cared for, or the leaves being uncut, or the first edition with all the misprints and the suppressed preface—*you* know, sir; the things that run up the value of a book without any reference to what that book's about. Of course, we've all got to watch out for these details, but to my mind—when all's said and done—a book's a thing to read. You can't get away from *that*, sir.

But the man I learnt the business from—old Mr. Trumpett —I was twenty years in his shop in Panton Street before I set up on my own—*he* wouldn't have agreed with me. Not he, sir. He'd got an eye for rarities which was worth a fortune; he'd got a collection of old editions which was worth another fortune; and he could run rings round anyone in the saleroom. But he didn't worry about what was inside a book. Not he. Many a time he's hauled me over the coals for sitting reading in his shop.

"You stick to the title pages, my boy," he said. "That's all a bookseller needs to know about."

And I'll say this for Mr. Trumpett, he certainly practised what he preached.

He used to travel about a good deal, attending sales outside London or helping in valuations for probate where there was a big library; and sometimes—though not as often as I'd have liked—he'd take me along with him. It was a wonder to me the way he'd go into a room full of books in an old country house —all arranged anyhow and with no catalogue or anything to help him—and yet he'd pick out all the plums within five or ten minutes of getting there. It was almost as if he could *smell* 'em out, sir. Uncanny, you'd have called it, if you'd seen him on the job. Partly for practice and partly to amuse myself I'd try sometimes if I couldn't find something valuable that he'd missed; but I can't say that I ever succeeded. The nearest I ever came to it was with this book that I'm telling you about.

We'd gone down to a big country house where the owner had died, to see if we could pick anything up. The young fellow who'd come into the property was all for selling everything that he could, but when it came to the library the whole place was in such a mess that no one could trouble to make a proper inventory. The auctioneer's instructions were to sell the old books off in bundles as they stood on the shelves; and seeing the quantity of litter there was, I can't say it was a bad idea. The bindings had been pretty good in their day, though that had been some time ago, but as for the stuff inside—well, it was just the typical sermons and county histories and so forth that you could buy up anywhere. A regular lot of rubbish.

We got down there the morning of the day when that part of the sale was coming on, and old Mr. Trumpett didn't take long to size it all up. He marked down a few bundles which might about cover our railway fares, if he got them at a proper price, and then he was just thinking about getting some lunch when I pointed out to him that there was a shelf over one of the doors that we hadn't looked at.

"Nonsense," he said, for he didn't like admitting he could have missed anything. "I saw them when I first came in."

Of course, we both knew quite well that he'd done nothing of the sort, but it wasn't going to pay me to get into an argument with him, so I just made up my mind that I'd come back after he'd gone and have a glance at those books myself.

Perhaps I'll get a chance, I thought, *to show him I'm not so ignorant as he thinks.*

So just as we were going out of the front door, I pretended I'd left my pencil-case in the library, and I went back there alone. To my surprise—for I hadn't been gone more than a minute and we certainly hadn't met anyone on the way—there was a gentleman standing on a chair with his back to me, reaching up at that particular shelf over the inner door. He'd got a cloak on—rather like people used to wear in Scotland—and as I could see a pair of rough stockings underneath it, I made up my mind he was a golfer. He was running through the books very quick and anxious-like, but he must have heard my step, for he stopped suddenly and turned round on his chair. He was rather a short gentleman, and a bit pale; rather thin on the top, if you know what I mean, and with a little pointed beard. It struck me that I'd seen him somewhere before, or else his photograph, but I couldn't put a name to him at the time, and of course—well, I'll come to that later.

He was looking at me so curiously that I felt I had to say something, so I thought I'd better explain what I'd come back for.

"When you've finished, sir," I said, "I wanted to have a look through that shelf for myself." And as he didn't answer, though I was certain he'd heard me quite clearly, added: "I've come down from London for the sale."

He nodded very gravely and politely, and turned back to the bookshelf. He kept on taking out one volume after another and shoving them back again as soon as he'd looked inside. Then all of a sudden, he gave a little gasp, and I saw him staring at an old quarto, bound in calf, that he'd just opened. The next moment he'd popped it under his cloak and jumped off the chair.

Well, I'd seen some pretty cool customers in the book trade before now, but this seemed to me to be a bit too cool.

"Here," I called out, backing between him and the door-way. "What are you doing with that book? You can't take it away like that."

"Can't I?" he said—and it seemed to me that he spoke like some kind of West-countryman. "It's mine."

"But you're not Mr. Hatteras, are you?" I asked—naming the heir to the property. For, you see, this gentleman was about fifty, I should judge.

"No," he said. "But the book is mine. If I choose to take it with me, what is that to you? It should never have been printed."

Well, sir, at that last remark of his, I'll admit that I thought he was a little bit—well, *you* know what I mean. (Here Mr. Bunstable tapped his forehead expressively.) But that didn't seem to me any reason why he should make off with something that wasn't his.

"Look here, sir," I said, "I don't want to make any trouble, but I saw you putting a book from that shelf under your cloak, and unless you put it back where it came from, I shall have to tell the auctioneer."

"The auctioneer?" he repeated, looking a bit puzzled.

"Yes," I said. "If you want any book out of this room, you can bid for it at the sale this afternoon." And as he still looked kind of silly, I pointed to the card that had been pinned over the shelf. "Lot 56," I said. "If you want that book, the proper way to get it is to bid for Lot 56."

For a moment I thought he was going to make a dash past me, but I wasn't surprised when he changed his mind, for he was a very nervous-looking gentleman, and he wouldn't have stood much chance if I'd wanted to stop him.

"So be it," he said, and he climbed on to the chair again and put the book back where he'd found it. Then with a funny sort of look at me, he went straight out of the room. "I wonder where I've seen that face before," I kept on thinking—but still I couldn't put a name to it.

Well, sir, by this time I saw that if I was going to get any lunch, I should have to run for it, and as I was a young man in those days, I decided to leave that last bookshelf and try to slip in again before the sale started. As I was going out through the hall, I ran into the auctioneer's clerk, and I thought it mightn't be a bad thing if I told him what I'd seen.

"All right," he said, when I'd finished. "I'll lock the library door, if there's anything of that sort going on. But did you say the gentleman had come out just now?"

"Yes," I said. "Just about a minute before I did."

"That's funny," he answered. "I was in the hall here the whole time, and I could have sworn nobody came by."

Well, it *was* funny, if you see what I mean, sir; and we both laughed a good deal at the time.

"Though apart from the principle of the thing," I said, "there's precious few books in there that are worth more than sixpence."

"That's as it may be," said the clerk cautiously. And I left him, and hurried off to the inn.

When I told Mr. Trumpett, he said, "H'm. That sounds like Badger of Liverpool. He'll get shut up one of these days if he's not careful." And he pulled out his copy of the sale catalogue and made a pencil mark against Lot 56. "He's a cunning old bird," he added. "If there's anything I've missed, we'll give him a run for his money."

And we did. I had no opportunity of seeing that shelf again, for the library was still locked when I got back, and the sale was to take place in the dining room. But there was Mr. Badger of Liverpool, in his cloak and his golf-stockings, watching each lot as it came up and was knocked down, and when we got to Lot 56, he started bidding like a good 'un.

Mr. Trumpett sat there nodding his head to the auctioneer —for everyone but these two had soon dropped out—but when the price for the odd dozen books had run up to a hundred and twenty-five pounds, I suppose he felt he'd gone far enough for a pig in a poke. He closed his eyes and shook his head, in the way he had when he'd finished bidding, and the auctioneer brought his hammer down with a thump.

Of course, I thought we'd heard the last of Lot 56, but just as I was crossing it off my list, I heard the auctioneer having some kind of an argument with the successful bidder.

"These are no good to me," he was saying, holding out a handful of coins. "I can't take foreign money for my deposit."

Mr. Badger was a very nervous-looking gentleman, as I think I've told you, and he didn't seem to know what to make of this. He kept on snapping his fingers and starting sentences that he couldn't finish, but it was no use. The auctioneer simply dropped the money on his desk for Mr. Badger to take or leave as he chose, and announced that he was putting the lot up again. The little mystery and excitement that there'd been sent it up to seven-pound-ten, but at that figure the competition stopped, and Mr. Trumpett got what he'd wanted. I could see the auctioneer looking pretty sick, but he was quite right, of course. Whatever those coins were, they'd have been no good to his employers. Why, some of them were scarcely even round!

Well, sir, we stopped on and picked up one or two more lots, and when we'd arranged for having them sent up to London, we took a fly back to the station and caught our train. In the carriage I suddenly remembered rather a curious thing, and I mentioned it to Mr. Trumpett.

"Did you see where Mr. Badger went to?" I asked. "I never saw him leaving the room, but he wasn't there when we came away; that I'll swear."

Mr. Trumpett looked at me quite queer-like.

"Badger?" he repeated. "What do you mean?"

"Why," I said, "the gentleman who bid against you, sir, for Lot 56."

"That wasn't Badger," he says.

"Then who was it?" says I.

But Mr. Trumpett had no idea. "I feel as if I'd seen his face

95

somewhere," he said presently; "or else he's very like someone I've met. But I'm bothered if I can place him."

"If you ask me," he said, a little later on, "he'd broken loose from somewhere. Did you see the way his eyes were rolling?"

"Yes," I said. "Quite a fine frenzy, wasn't it?"

But of course, my little literary allusion was wasted on Mr. Trumpett. He only grunted, and we dropped the subject for good.

Well (resumed Mr. Bunstable, who had now got me out of his labyrinth into the main part of the shop), a few days after that the packing case came along from the sale, and though Mr. Trumpett would likely enough have let it lie in his cellar for weeks—for he took his time over most things—I thought I'd go down and look through the stuff myself.

You see, I'd still got it in the back of my head that our golfing friend might have known a bit more than we'd given him credit for; that there really might be some sort of "find" in Lot 56. And if there was, then I meant to get to the bottom of it.

So late that afternoon I took a candle down to the cellar—we'd no gas except in the shop itself in those days—and I got a tack-lifter and a hammer, and started opening the case. Out it all came—most of it just about fit for a barrow in the street, though every now and then I'd find one of the books that Mr. Trumpett had spotted—and presently I'd got right down to the straw. And there—the last book to come out—was the calf-bound quarto that the gentleman in the cloak had tried to make away with. The label had come off the back and the leaves were still uncut, but when I turned to the title page— well, I tell you, sir, I thought for a moment I must be dreaming.

What would *you* say, sir, I wonder, if you picked up an old book and found it was a play by Shakespeare that no one had ever imagined as existing? Would you believe your eyes? I tell you, I could hardly believe mine. Yet there it was—paper, type and binding all above suspicion, as I knew well enough—and on the title page *The Tragedie of Alexander the Great by Mr. William Shakespeare.* I felt like Christopher Columbus and Marconi rolled into one. The biggest discovery of the century, and I—down there by myself in Mr. Trumpett's cellar—had made it. I sat down on the edge of that packing-case and fairly gasped for breath. It was the most tremendous moment in my life.

Of course, I knew it was my real duty to rush up the ladder into the shop and tell Mr. Trumpett what I'd found, and, of course, I meant to do this as soon as I'd collected my wits. But while I sat there staring at the title page, I realized more and more clearly what Mr. Trumpett would do. The book would go straight into his safe—uncut as it was, so as to keep up the value; when it left the safe it would be to go direct to the sale-room, and from there—unless an Act of Parliament stopped it —-to an American collector. If I carried out my duty without a thought of the consequences, my first opportunity of reading *The Tragedie of Alexander the Great* would be in a facsimile or reprint, just as if the original had never been in my hands at all. And I wanted to read it *now*. I was enough of a bookseller to recognize its enormous value, but—unlike Mr. Trumpett—I was too much of a book lover to let that American collector read it first.

I wasn't going to cut the leaves, of course. I knew better than to do that. But there were pretty wide margins, and by twisting the pages carefully I could manage well enough; and so—sitting down on the packing-case and by the light of my candle—I began right away. "*Act I, Scene 1. A Room in King*

Philip's Palace." Yes, sir; I remember that. But I'm thankful that I can't remember any more.

Did I say "thankful?" Well, sir, I'm afraid I mean it. I don't pretend to be a poet myself and in the ordinary way I'll admit there may be better critics. But when it comes to a real piece of downright incompetent, careless writing, of bad scansion and worse grammar, of loud-sounding, pretentious and meaningless clap-trap—then I'll take leave to say that I'm as good a judge as most men. It was awful, sir; it was terrible. It was like a parody of the worst kind of Elizabethan poetry, and yet, if you see what I mean, it was Elizabethan poetry. Not a word, not a phrase to give the show away—as there are in Chatterton's forgeries. It was like Shakespeare read through some kind of distorting lens, with all the faults and weaknesses—for he had faults and weaknesses, sir—magnified ten thousand times, and all the beauty cancelled right out.

"No wonder they kept this out of the First Folio," I kept on telling myself. And yet I couldn't put it down. However bad it might be, it *was*—unless some contemporary had played an expensive practical joke—the discovery that I had taken it for. And I was the first of my own contemporaries to read it. In spite of myself, though, my excitement had given way to an almost overwhelming sense of depression. If you're really fond of books, sir, that's always the way a piece of thoroughly bad workmanship takes you.

I don't know how long I'd been down in that cellar (resumed Mr. Bunstable, after a short and mournful pause), when all of a sudden, I heard a kind of thud overhead; and looking up I saw that someone had closed the trap at the top of the ladder.

Good heavens, I thought, *there's Mr. Trumpett going off for the night, and if I don't hurry after him, I shall be locked in.*

I jumped up, picked up my candle and was just moving to

the foot of the ladder, when to my astonishment I saw that two men were standing in my way. It seemed to me that they were in some kind of fancy dress, and what with this and my bewilderment at the way they'd managed to get in, I very nearly dropped the candle. Then, as I recovered it, I recognized the shorter of them. It was the old gentleman that I'd seen last week at that sale down in the country; the gentleman that I'd taken for Mr. Badger of Liverpool.

"What's the matter?" I asked in a shaking kind of voice. "What do you want, sir?"

He didn't answer me, but turned to his companion—a big, burly sort of fellow, who struck me as knowing pretty well what the bottom of a pint-pot looked like.

"Did you bolt the trap, Ben?" he asked. "Are you sure the old man's gone?"

"What do you take me for?" said the big fellow, speaking with a kind of rough, Cockney accent. "Of course he's gone. Now, then," he added, looking at me, "we've come for that book. Where have you put it?"

I had it under my arm, but before I could answer him, he'd spotted it.

"Aha!" he called out. "There you are, Will. What did I tell you? Didn't I say we'd find it here?"

They both seemed tremendously excited, and I was convinced that they'd been drinking; but I wasn't going to stand any nonsense.

"I don't know what you're doing here," I said, retreating behind the packing case, "or how you've forced your way in. But this book has been bought and paid for by my employer, Mr. Trumpett, and let me remind you that you've no right in the private part of the shop."

The big man only laughed at this, but the other started talking sixteen to the dozen.

"And let me tell *you*," he said, "that that book was published without any authority, that the script was stolen from the theatre and that anyone who keeps it is a receiver of stolen goods. Do you know what I spent in buying up that edition from the blackguard who printed it? Two hundred angels. And do you know how long I've been hunting for the copy he kept back? Nearly three hundred years! But I've found it at last, and I'm going to see that it's destroyed. I've got my reputation to protect the same as anyone else, and if I did a bit of pot-boiling because I'd got into debt that's no reason why it should be brought up against me now. I've had enough trouble over *Pericles* and *Titus Andronicus*, without being saddled with a bit of balderdash like *Alexander the Great*. You got the better of me down in Gloucestershire last week, but it's my turn now. I've got good friends, I have, who'll see that justice is done. If I'm a bit scant of breath myself, here's my old colleague Jonson, who's killed his man more than once and will do it again for the honour of the profession. Now, then, young sir, are you going to hand that play over, or do you want a taste of Ben's dagger in your gullet?"

That's the way he ran on, sir, though I may not have got all his words quite right, and all the time the other man was rocking and shaking with laughter. I was so scared I could hardly think, for it was no joke being shut up down there with two fellows like that. Mad, they might be, or drunk, or both together; but whatever they were, I could see they would stick at nothing. And yet ....

Well, sir, it's no use reproaching myself now. And, besides, after all these years I'm not at all sure that the actual upshot wasn't the best for everybody. The big fellow had jumped right over the packing-case and twisted my arms together behind my back, while the little one snatched the book from where it had fallen, tore out the sheets and burnt them one by one in the flame of my candle. Then he threw the empty binding down on the cellar floor.

"All's well that ends well," he said. "He's had his lesson, Ben. You can let him go."

And then he stooped down and blew out the candle.

As he reached this stage in his remarkable narrative, Mr. Bunstable stretched past me with one hand and opened the door of his shop. A cold draught accompanied by wisps of London fog blew in through the aperture, causing me to shiver and Mr. Bunstable to utter his little, dry, grating cough. Far away I heard the indomitable bullfinch once more embarking on his incomplete melody. The rest was silence.

"You mean," I said presently, "that it was a dream?"

"Eh?" said Mr. Bunstable, starting from his thoughts. "Well, sir, as to that I should hardly like to say. I certainly spent the night in that cellar, as Mr. Trumpett could tell you if he were alive. And I'll have to admit that there were no traces of that book on the floor—no ashes, even—when I looked for them in the morning. And yet that doesn't seem to me to explain everything. Because, sir, there was no calf-bound quarto there either. You've only got my word for it, of course, but...."

And here, gently but firmly, Mr. Bunstable shut me out into the fog.

SPINSTERS' REST
(VARIATIONS OF AN OLD TUNE)
CLEMENCE DANE

"*Every day the poor girl had to sit and spin till her fingers bled ... and in the sorrow of her heart she jumped into the well ... When she came to herself, she was in a lovely meadow where many thousands of flowers grew. Along she went till she came to an oven, and the bread cried: 'Take me out! I shall burn' ... and to a tree covered with apples which called to her: 'Shake me! Shake me!' ... and at last, to a little house out of which an old woman peeped and called out: 'Dear child, stay with me! If you will do the work of the house properly you shall be the better for it. I am Mother Holle.'*

"*So the girl took courage and agreed to enter her service. She stayed some time, and then she became sad. At first, she did not know what was the matter with her, but at last she said to Mother Holle: 'I have a longing for home.' ... Thereupon Mother Holle led her to a great door and, opening it, said: 'This is the reward of your service.'*"—Grimm's Fairy Tales

"*Holda (Hulda, Holle, Frau Holl) ... A being of the sky... a motherly deity. She assumes the shape of an old woman and has the*

*oversight of spinners. When it snows, she is said to be making her
bed. She carries off unchristened infants."*—Grimm's Mythology

I

The old woman had looked so kind. She had been such a
friendly sight after London, beastly London, crazy London,
after the struggle at the railway station and the sordid rhythm
of the train, after the solitary walk through the rainy village
and the soaked January lanes. She had been such a cheerful
heart, she and her firelit room, to the huge stone house with its
unlighted endless casement rows and its prison front. The
chance of such an employer, such a place of employment,
seemed too good to be true! She was all a-strain to fit herself
into the picture, as she sat on the edge of the chair, hands in
lap, answering questions. Her body was still, her manner was
still, her eyes were fixed respectfully upon the old woman's
face. Yet the effect she produced, even to herself, was not a
peaceful one. She felt like a wire stretched to snapping point,
like her own mantelpiece statue of the praying boy, beseeching
hands eternally arrested in midair. Her voice as she answered
was flat:

"Mary—Mary Pawle. No, quite alone. Both dead. I have a
little money of my own. Oh no, I don't mind telling you ninety
pounds a year. At the office I got three pounds a week."

"I can't offer a companion more than board and lodging."

"I don't care. I want a change. I was ten years at the office."

"Ten years in an office! A girl shouldn't be at any one piece
of work for more than a year, my dear. We need change, we
women. That's why we're given children."

Children! That was the word that had driven like a wedge

between the dry preliminaries of the interview and its fantastic heart of dreams. Children! What devil's dice had tossed up that number? What senile whim induced the old woman to strike just that forbidden note? These rich old ladies, she thought, were like pampered house cats; too full fed to claw, but they must pat you for their amusement. Well, she was yet her own mistress—where were her gloves? Yet she had hoped to be approved: she had hoped to be taken on: it would have been a change. But such dissertations were more than even her sullen patience proposed to endure. You do not talk to an employer of the secret flowers withering in your heart like pansies in a London window box—not in the first five minutes—no, nor for bed and board. She repeated stonily, her sallow cheeks flushing:

"I want a change, that's all!" and reached for her handbag.

"Ah?" The knitting needles were flashing in the knotted ivory hands. Such bright pointed lights flickered from them: she could not take her eyes away.

"I hate London," she added, and flushed anew. She had not meant to say it.

"Quarrelled with him?" said the old lady, for the first time fixing her with eyes sharper and brighter than the needles.

Then had come panic. She had risen hurriedly, giddily, so that her chair tilted backwards and fell clattering. She picked it up with fumbling hands, crying:

"I can't talk. I can't!" in a high, terrified voice.

"To me? Oh, my girl, if we're to be companions—"

There were the velvet paws again! And yet the voice was sweet, like a dream she had had once of sighing trees. All her happy times had been in dreams. She was enchanted by that kind voice, even while she said, trembling:

"I'd better go. I don't think I should do." And saying it, gazing into the bright eyes of the old lady, she sat down again, slowly, obediently, like an animal quieted. She even answered the unspeakable question, saying, "It wasn't a quarrel." And then, "I haven't even that."

The bright steels that had stopped for a moment began to click again.

"Not even that, eh? Well—go on!"

And she went on. She felt the terrors and pangs of a prisoner tortured into speech as she cried out in spite of herself, twisting her fingers:

"He never looked at me. He only cared to spoil things."

"Spoilt things, did he?"

"Oh," she said piteously, "it was only a dream—like playing with dolls to some girls—but—but I'd lived for it somehow. I'd trained myself—fairy tales and sewing and things. I wasn't silly. I wasn't horrid. It wasn't to get married. It was the children, to have children one day. But he—he spoilt it all. Did I ask to fall in love?"

So she spoke, her eyes fixed on those two bright eyes as if they were the crystals in which she read aloud her own fate. She listened, as if they were a stranger's, to her own shameless avowals.

"I always thought I'd get married, you see. One does. Home —husband—children—one knows it'll come. One's brought up to it. Can I help that? And I'm good with children. I looked so to have my own. One does. I know their names. I know how they look. I can feel their hands some-times, touching me. I can—oh, I wish you'd let me stop! I wish—"

Again, the movement of the needles had been passes in the air quelling and compelling her.

"You wish—? Go on!" said the old woman.

Go on? Of course she must go on. She could no more stop— she would like to see anyone stop her! All the agonies of her dying youth rose under the compulsion of those strange eyes to the surface of her mind at last, like some heaven or hell's brew on the bubble, on the boil, ready to brim over, to scald anew, to complete the ruin of the seared and suffering spirit; and yet, when she tried to speak, she could express herself only in the pitifully inadequate phrases of her untrained and illiterate consciousness:

"Husbands—love—troublesome, I used to think: rather hateful; but to be put up with, you know, because of children, Children get on with me, I'd have been such a good mother. But now—"

"Now—?"

"I can't have any, ever." And then, twisting herself like a prisoner straining in bonds, "I won't talk any more. I don't want to. I'm tired."

"Now—?" The bright eyes were becoming two lamps into which she must stare. She yielded.

"He stopped it, for good and all."

"Did you—?"

"Love him? He was at my boarding house. He sat opposite me at meals. He talked to me. He used to smile when I came in. I thought for a little while—oh, I was so happy. I was a fool. He didn't even guess. He was killed, you know, in the War. He married a girl I know. They asked me to the wedding." And then fiercely: "Did I ask for it to happen to me? I could have married before, just nicely. But now—other men—how can I? It would be adultery. Besides, oh, besides, it's a blow, a thing like that, a blow to your mind. It's like a tree falling on you in a storm, crushing. Oh, it's nothing: I don't feel much anymore. I'm only tired. I wish you'd let me shut my eyes."

"Shut them!" said the old woman's voice, a blessed, decisive voice, a voice that knew your business for you, that told you what to do. She obeyed.

"Once upon a time—" began the old woman softly, and the

clickings of the needles were like the tripping heels of a tune—
"Once upon a time there was a poor girl—"

How familiar was the voice, the voice of her nurse telling her fairy-tales dreams, nightmares; for the interview, of course, was a dream, the latest stage of the dull nightmare of her life. Well, if it lightened to mere dream again, at least it was a change. How familiar was the voice! It was her own voice, surely her own voice, dreaming over Grimm's on the hearthrug, spelling out by firelight her favourite fairy tale—

"And at last, she came to a house out of which an old woman was looking, and the girl was so frightened that she wanted to run away—"

Familiar words, familiar as a forgotten dream!

"What are you afraid of, dear child? Stay with me for a year, and you shall be the better for it; but you must take care to shake my bed till the feathers fly, for then it snows in the world. I am—"

She broke in triumphantly:

"Mother Holle! You're Mother Holle—Grimm's fairy tales —the blue-and-gold cover! I know you! You're Mother Holle!" And she would have risen from her chair as people rise in dreams from a strange bed; but the needle lights flashed round her head like swords, like lightnings, and the soft voice forced her back into the dream's velvet deeps like a strong hand ramming home a sword into its protectant scabbard. She lost even the desire to struggle. With closed eyes and rested heart, she let herself wander, as she had not done for twenty years, into the half-light, the half-consciousness of that accessible Middle Land that a child enters so easily, and that some children grow never too old to enter. She was such a child, though she had forgotten it, and it was as easy as waking to drift over the cobwebbed border on the wings of that controlling voice, a voice, a windy voice that spoke to her from the apple tree:

"Shake me! Shake me!"—a comfortable croaking voice from the oven door: "Burning! Burning! Take me out!"—as she shook down the apples and pulled out the scorched cakes, and so wandered on through its flowery grass and sunny weather, happy, happy, happy, in the happy land.

A timeless land—all its hours and minutes, its days and seasons melted into one, as a thousand scents puff by in every breath of summer. She did her year's service, wandering dreamily to and fro, from the cows with their aching udders to the dropping autumn apple trees, and back to the little house with its spring garden quick with furtive life: newborn butterflies clinging weakly to the grey cabbage leaves: young thrushes busy with snails: till (how eagerly she stooped!) under a gooseberry bush one evening, one frosted, moon-lit evening, she found—

"That shall be the reward of your service!" said Mother Holle. "In the meantime, board and lodging."

She heard her own voice:

"I don't care. I want a change" and so jerked herself back into consciousness, consciousness and relaxed on the sofa like a kitten on forbidden coverlets, facing the bright windows that leaped towards her like an eager dog, and near the fire, brighter than the fire, the bright eyes of her employer. "Employer" was the right term; for the bargain had been struck, and her hand of herself, guiltily warm once more and the bright fire she found, given and held a moment in a firm hand clasp, in a clasp stirring words to life in her mind:

"Good-bye! Good luck! Come back safe! Good-bye!"

She tried to disengage her hand and herself, she tried to say, "I won't come to you! You're bad for me. You're making me cry." But the words turned themselves on her lips to: "Thank you! Yes!—yes! Very well!"

She was to live at the inn in the village and come to Spinsters' Rest daily, "to be with me, to read aloud, and sew and be silent, and look after my guests."

"Guests?"

"Not arrived yet," said her employer, and with a gleaming smile had closed the extraordinary interview.

II

She settled down, as far as unpacking a thin suitcase went, and learning her duties, and going, on her free afternoons, for aimless walks. It was the easiest place in the world for a poor girl—gratefully she admitted it. She might not have existed for all the ripple she made in the pond-like life of the village. She felt sometimes as if she and her employer were the only waking creatures in a tapestry world: that the sunlight outside the window was glimmering on mere stitchwork walls: that it was only her own shadow falling on them as she passed to and fro from her lodging that stirred her neighbours to unreal and momentary life. Yet she liked the faded quiet, just as she liked the grey street with its pebbled pavements and slate roofs streaked with velvet. The village was like herself, she thought, in a rare moment of self-analysis, stagnant, neither alive nor dead. She was in touch with it, and liked it better than the surrounding emerald wheatlands set off with startling hedgerows of white and yellow; for the winter was more than over. She could not but stare in daily wonder at the washed perfection of the spring; but it had not lost, she found, its old power to hurt her. It roused her, made her think and remember and long for her own past with a sick violence of regret that thinned her cheeks till the skin grew taut and polished over the bones, and her eyelids were swelled and darkened with the weight of tears restrained.

Before the spring was a month old, she was as restless and hopeless as ever she had been in London.

She might be restless; but she was not the only one. That discovery she made, and in a moment of expansion imparted it to her employer.

"How queer the village people are! They whisper and point. They follow me, d'you know—truly it's not my fancy. One woman came right up to the door."

"A beggar?"

"Yes—no. Begging, but not a beggar. A dog with a hurt paw, that's the look. And if I turn suddenly, they back away."

Said her employer thoughtfully, compassionately "I can't do anything. It's too early in the year. They know that." And then "Aren't the primroses out yet in the hedges?"

She answered, "I haven't looked."

And was then amused and in the end, half frightened by the look she got—such blue eyes were the old woman's, with such flashes in them when she chose. But the answer was merely whimsical. How else should she take it?

"Not looked for primroses? My dear, how wicked!"

She shrugged her shoulders.

"I hate the spring. It makes me restless."

"You'll stay on through the summer all the same," said her employer placidly. "There'll be plenty to do." She clicked thoughtfully a moment, murmuring to herself in the fashion with which the girl had become familiar:

> "Some to kill cankers in the musk-rose buds:
> Some war with rear mice for their leathern wings."

And then, flicking the words at her not so much from mouth or eye as from those sharp needle-points, flicking them forth at the end of invisible threads like a fisherman flicking a fly delicately forth upon the too clear water: "I've some children coming down next week," and for an instant paused in her eternal knitting, the girl felt, watchfully.

But this once-caught fish, sullen beneath her root, would not rise: though she knew all about the slum children and their yearly pilgrimage to shriek and scatter orange peel and wreck the byways of the garden.

Her landlady had told her their story, among others: "Oh yes, miss, the children come regularly. Squalling brats! I don't hold—but children always have come, somehow, to Spinsters' Rest. My grandmother, she said her mother said it was the same in her time."

"But that must be—oh, a hundred years ago! She couldn't—I mean, who lived there then?"

"I don't know, miss, now you ask. But I'd say there'd always been a friendly person, as it were, at Spinsters' Rest. And children and beasts, they know it—oh yes! I tell you, miss, I seen a sick fox once walk in at the gate like a Christian. And swallows—! Miss, where *do* the swallows go in winter—our swallows? Miss, there's an old man here, and his father's mother told him what she saw once. She'd gone up to Spinsters' Rest, wanting a herb or such—for the oldest trouble in the country, she told him—and as she went up the lane (in the autumn it was) she saw the swallows swinging round and round the house like flies round a paper ball, she said; and up went the sash of a window, and there was a hand that beckoned, and in they swept very quick and quiet, every last one of them, like a flight of fish in clear water, the woman said, and the window shut down. She said the sky seemed so big and empty all at once, with the swallows gone, and the house stood up so black against it, that she just took and ran. And never a swallow seen again till April. Never see birds here in winter, you know, nor squirrels and such. They say the house takes them. They say it takes folks, too. There was a time, miss, they say, when the house took too many: poor creatures, you know, that nobody missed: tramps and trollops and now and then a come-by-chance. Not people to be missed. Then one day a young lady! That startled them, and they searched and searched, but they never found anyone. So they took the woman of the house to be a witch and swam her and stretched her and burnt her at last on her own doorstep. They say the brickwork's blackened still over the front door."

The modern girl shuddered.

"Yes, miss, and not her fault, as it turned out. For the beggars were back when the New Year came, trailing into the village again by twos and threes, and the young lady with them. They had nothing to say for themselves, just went about mooning, smiling, a bit too friendly. So it was put about that it was kidnapping, and they hanged the lot, all but the young lady. That was before they built the high wall round it."

"Who built it?"

"I don't know, miss—one of the ladies. There's always been a lady living there, at least since the Queen's time."

"Which queen?"

"The one on the sign. The story got about, you know, and she came to see for herself. Stayed in this very room. It's her bed you're setting on."

"But to see *what* for herself?" For the assumption that she must understand irritated her.

"Well, miss, she never had chick nor child, did she? Yes, she spent a day at Spinsters' Rest, they say, and she left a paper behind her that the house should never be troubled. The rector has it."

"Is that history?" demanded the girl.

"Not board school, miss, but—well, they say so, hereabouts. The Rector'd tell you."

But the Rector was not interested in anything so modern as Good Queen Bess; though, a mild amateur of antiquities, he was only too glad to chat with anyone employed in a house where a Roman pavement had been unearthed. He had not, alas! been privileged to examine it himself. The occupant of Spinsters' Rest took little interest in matters parochial, was not, in fact (he lowered his voice), a communicant; but he understood that it was a singularly interesting specimen. According to his theory—mere theory, my dear young lady!— the local legends all pointed to a grove or temple in Roman times, of—Minerva, possibly?—the patroness of spinners, eh? —doubtless, re-sanctified later as a Christian fane. But in the sixth century, of course, all records were obliterated—Teuton hordes—"fierce Pagans," as Roger hath it—"setting up strange gods"; but it was certainly a nunnery in later years. Hilda, Abbess Hilda (the convert, you remember?) is said to have been the founder. The good nuns were famous for their linen in—er —1250 I fancy, and privileged in consequence. Hence the name —Spinsters' Rest! Dispossessed under Henry VIII, of course. An iniquitous business! From him passed to his daughter—the spinster queen! Explains your landlady's—er—surmise. Oh, mere surmise—I know nothing of any paper; except, of course, the deed of gift to a waiting-maid—dependent—who was, curiously enough, burnt under James I. The road to Endor, eh? Strait is the gate—yes, indeed! And now, alas! in private hands: oh, no doubt very respectable hands; but, as I say,—*not* being a communicant...." He sighed himself away.

She would lie at night listening to the curiously musical creak of the Queen's Head board as it swung and started beneath her window in the spring wind, and ponder these things, and others: and not least among others, the fact that she was sleeping where she was, and not, as would have been so natural, in her employer's house.

"The rooms are wanted," her employer had stated in her brief, unarguing fashion that inclined Mary Pawle, at least, to accept any statement without question, without even an inward stir of surprise. But in the stillness of the shortening nights surprise would lift a head nevertheless, belatedly, like a memory of wrongdoing long past, long forgotten, but once roused never again to be quieted. Who and what was her employer? And what did the charwoman *do* on Sundays?

"And get me my meals on Sundays, my dear! I like my good woman to get her Sundays off!" That had been the actual phrase of her instructions, the wording of her bond: and yet once—twice—for three Sundays running she had come upon the clod-hopping familiar figure, in unfamiliar Sunday clothes, lurking in the bushes in the early morning as she let herself in, scurrying into the darkness of the drive as she left the house behind her in the evening. And once, as she swept away the breakfast crumbs, she had seen her through the half-open door, passing across the patterned floorwork of the vestibule, and heard her too, heard the labouring feet creaking the stairs as she climbed them.

She had spoken then in her surprise:

"I thought she had her Sundays off!"

"So she does," said her employer. "Shake the crumbs to the birds, my dear!"

She had laughed a little as she obeyed that regular command. No need to scatter the crumbs: she was accustomed to pushing the robins out of the way with her crumb-brush, to have the mixed crew on the threshold of the window rise but a bare half-yard into the air at her scattering gesture, and settle again a little nearer, always a little nearer. She said:

"But I see her here almost every Sunday."

Said the old lady, "What do *you* do with your afternoons off?"

She considered the question as she went to her next duty, standing on the chair to snip the dead leaves from the great trail of old-man's-beard that had grown into the room through a crack in the cornice and now swung its powdery length over a blackened portrait (the original, she guessed, of the inn signboard).

At last, she said slowly, flushing, "You know what I do."

"Sit and think?"

"Sit and think." And then: "What else can I do?"

"What my good woman does."

"Come back here?"

"Why not? Prowl about the house, my dear! Amuse you. Fine pictures. Beds to rest on. Beautiful views—upstairs."

She got up irresolutely and opened the door as she spoke over her shoulder:

"I've never been upstairs."

The wide staircase was lighted by a skylight so large that you guessed the hall had once been open to the sky and the staircase ended in a landing, long, low-ceilinged, with doors to right and left. It turned sharply at its farther end like a rabbit's bolt hole.

"However many doors!"

"Many, many," chuckled the old woman, and startled the girl, for she had thought, not spoken.

"You wouldn't say it was such a long passage," she commented, "from the outside."

"It could be bounded in a nutshell," said her employer complacently.

She frowned, puzzled, because the incomprehensible phrase was somehow familiar. Then she turned back to the staircase. The problem of the charwoman had roused her curiosity.

"What does she do up there?"

"Rests, I dare say. She's welcome. She's had a sad life. She's a spinner," said the old lady. "That's why her back's bent double."

"A weaver, you mean? I thought that handlooms—"

"Factory work, I mean," said the old woman. "Isn't it factories now? It was looms once. But always the spinning wheel, my dear, behind it. Call it what you like, it works out the same. Swaddle clothes are always wanted, and bride veils and shrouds—and who thanks the spinners? Fourpence an hour—sweating, don't you call it, in your London? Sweat of the spinners, it waters the earth. Bend 'em and break 'em, the women who spin, plenty more where they come from. One man to one woman, and the women over—let 'em spin!"

The girl stood staring, her duties dropping from her hands:

"Me—they're in me, those bitter thoughts. That's what I'm thinking day and night. How do you know what I think?"

Said her employer "You don't rest properly. You talk in your sleep."

It was her duty to laugh at the joke, and she laughed, shakily, as she stooped for the dusters and scissors.

"'Spinster—an unmarried woman—so called because she was supposed to occupy herself with spinning.' I found that in the dictionary." And then, "Do you hear my dreams across the village?"

Said the old woman seriously. "I hear the noise they make."

She had got herself in hand.

"I don't dream about noises."

"Oh, my dear," said her employer, "children are bound to be noisy." And then, as the girl sat shivering, for she was never sufficiently on guard against the crazy accidents of their intercourse that ever and again, like a nail in an old panel, ripped up her garment in passing and bared the naked skin. "By the way, they're coming next week."

Almost she said, "My children?" so utterly had the baring of her thoughts shaken her. But somehow, she held to her sanity as she had done before in the crazy place. She could do it by sheer fierce repetition of the epithet: "Crazy—it's a crazy place! And she—she's crazy! A crazy old woman! That's all! She's crazy!" She said it inwardly now, as she said it twenty times a day, while her tongue said in best companion's manner:

"The London children?"

"Fifty of 'em. You'll see to things, my dear. Tea on the lawn."

"But if it rains?"

"It won't rain," said her employer. And then: "Better give 'em strawberries and cream."

"But"—she was tentative after the snub—"there aren't many. It's been so wet."

"There'll be enough," said her employer.

And when, a few days later, the children were at last ranged in a great circle between the oak tree and the house, and she overlooked the quick-passing pottles that she had been filling all the morning, she saw that there was indeed enough. And the sky was as blue as a forget-me-not.

She was kept busy. The old lady's chair was pushed to the very threshold of the French window, though she did not leave it, did not put down her knitting even to greet the London curate and the London ladies that topped and tailed the excited column that filed past. ("My dear, I daren't! The sun would go in.") She had said it with that swift glance and smile that always dazzled her companion, physically dazzled her, as if her eyes were too weak to support it unblinking. And indeed, at that moment it had seemed to her as if the long thin needles were indeed busy, not with threads of wool but, fantastic notion, threads of sunlight.

However, it was not her business, and the children and their games were. She went down to play with them.

It was while they were playing Nuts and May that she first noticed the child. It stood by itself, watching: a forlorn manling, ridiculous in a woman's coat with gigot sleeves. As they passed and repassed, she made with her hand a little gesture of invitation to join the end of the line. It backed from her hastily, unsmiling, and she heard a laugh from the girl whose hand she held.

"He won't come, miss: he's dumb. We don't play wiv 'im."

"Oh, poor—But why shouldn't he play?"

"He won't, miss. He'll hit out at yer."

"Will he?" She detached herself from the sticky clasp, and went quickly after the small figure that was so pitifully easy to overtake, for it limped in its hurry, and she could see the stocking-shaped support of iron it wore on a pipestem leg. She caught up with it and held out once more the inviting hand, though some delicate instinct restrained her from any premature touch.

"I say—look here—don't you want to play?" She was panting a little from her run.

The child, overtaken, had stopped; and its eyelids were lifted in that cold little look of inquiry with which all children await advances. It had the dark eyes, the pure, lustrous black circles, that so inexplicably shrink and lighten in later life to the common brown "like mine," she thought ruefully, and smiled. And at that suddenly behind the eyes' blank surface something stirred, something looked out at her, signalled— she could swear it, for she felt her own eyes signalling in answer, in yearning answer—and was still again. It was as if a blind had been drawn up and down, as if two strangers had snapshotted each other's souls. But she was a woman grown out of girlhood and this starved child was—what? Four? Five?

She bent forward in her eagerness, and as quickly knew her error. For, as she caught at the small hand it was snatched from her, and the child backed away again and at two yards' distance turned and fled, fled towards the open window at which her employer sat. She did not follow: she was well trained in putting her duties before her wishes; but as she took her place once more, and added her sweet shrill note to the song of the children, she was saying within herself over and over again: "It looked at me! It looked at me! What a fool I am! —but it looked at me!"

Later, she saw it again, momentarily, out of the corner of her eye, as she hurried along the terrace at teatime. It had got itself over the threshold much, she fancied, as the birds did at breakfast, and was now as close as it could push to the big chair in the bewildering green-and-gold-barred shadows of the venetian blinds. Its hands, planted each on one of the old woman's knees, supported the whole weight of the eager, forward-thrust body. She had an odd fancy that the fingers were spread like the rootlets of some small tenacious tree, digging its home into a crag of the hill. The old woman, too, was bent forward till the two faces almost touched; and she heard a delicious whisper in the room, that faint, familiar hush of sighing trees. But the phrase that caught her ears as she passed them was only the banal phrase of old age not used to coping with the youngest generation.

"Run away and play now, there's a good boy! Upstairs anywhere you like!"

She had passed by then, but at the chink of iron she turned her head and stopped in time to see the dumb child push itself upright again and limp out of the room. The sunlight of the big hall showed it in silhouette for a moment, with the dark doorway of the sitting-room for frame. Then, as the creature began to climb the stairs, the lintel cut off the sharp, pallid little face. Once more the tenacious small fingers caught her eye, clutching and lifting, clutching and lifting, on the brown balustrade, and then the hall was empty again save for the shaft of sunshine from the roof and the glittering motes that danced against the darkness. She shot a glance sideways over the threshold. Her employer was knitting, knitting. And yet, as the girl shifted her pile of dishes to the other arm and went on again, she thought she heard a laugh.

When the telegram arrived three days later, she heard it again. Somehow, somewhere, on the route, one of the children had been mislaid. Could Spinsters' Rest help them? Spinsters' Rest could not. For—"Think back, my dear!"—the wagonettes had brimmed over with waving handkerchiefs and flushed faces, and trails of dog-roses whose petals fluttered from their golden holds, as the school-treat drove away, after farewells and false starts, and she had come to rest at the feet of her employer with a "Pouf! And that's that!"—had sat cooling as the garden cooled, till the little sounds of evening fell into the silence like pebbles flung into a lake; but their peace had not been broken by any sight of any child.

An odd business, her employer agreed, as she soothed superintendents and interviewed inspectors. But what was to be done, when the children had not been counted, coming or going? Tickets issued, eh? Tickets, not names! Blank tickets get exchanged, lost, picked up. Could they even be sure that the child was missing? Had it ever started? What did the parents? —Ah, no parents! A stepsister. Not too heart-broken, eh? And its absence had really gone unnoticed three days? Three days astray in London—poor child! Poor children! God pity poor children! They must report progress—let her know. No, nothing seen of any child here, eh, Miss Pawle? No limping child wandering in our garden, with an iron round its leg. No child's voice ah, dumb was it? Dumb, too! Well, Miss Pawle?

But Miss Pawle, fascinated, had seen nothing. And it was odd, as her employer said to her in the later days of brown August, it was odd how soon inquiries died down.

Odd—the phrase stuck in her mind though the incident faded from it—odd how inquiry died down, how soon, how dully one accustomed oneself to change and novelty and a new address. She had hoped to detach, to reattach herself, to fling new tendrils, to strike new roots; and here, after the strangest summer she had ever spent, after six months, only six months in a new world, in a very factory of oddness (what stories might she not have woven, what mysteries unravelled, what ghosts not laid in this forgotten coign of England, were the spirit of adventure yet alive in her!), she could do no more than turn back wearily upon herself, sated and indifferent. London counting house or Spinsters' Rest, it was all the same to her! What more did Spinsters' Rest give her than London gave? Flowers for the picking and summer days: moonlit nights, the song of birds, children that came and went: and queer tales such as she used to love. But if the salt has lost its savour?

"I want to leave!" she blurted out.

Her employer shook her head. "Soon, not yet."

She said:

"I want a change."

"You haven't earned your bonus. You must stay out your year."

Again, she said, as she had said nearly a year ago. "I don't care. I want a change."

"Restless, eh?"

"Desperate." And indeed, with her miserable eyes and twisting hands, she looked it. "Could I—talk to you?"

"I waited for that," said the sweet voice.

"I—I'm ill, I think. Oh, you know what it is! I've nothing to care for." Suddenly she flung herself down at the old woman's feet, caught at the knees as if they were the knees of a god. "Can't you help me? Can't you? You're older than I."

Her eyes were a daze of tears. She saw no face. Yet she heard the voice swell out in answer like a stir of many winds, like the thrash of saving rain:

"Yes, yes, older than you, my daughter, older than you." And then, as she lay there, her face buried in the folds of the dress, crying as she had not cried for many days, came the voice again, the chirpy, commonplace voice of everyday life:

"You want rest, my dear! You go upstairs and lie down."

She did as she was told, as children do, worn out with passion and tears.

III

As she reached the head of the stairs the door of the first room opened and out came the charwoman, breathless and staring.

"I beg your pardon, miss—but do *you* come upstairs?"

"She said I might," she said shyly, apologetically, forgetting her caste.

Said the woman harshly:

"You're young enough. What's *your* trouble?" And then, softening: "But you're welcome. Quiet, ain't it? I've been coming these twenty years. What I'd 'ave done without it—" Then, as the girl, making way for her, laid a hand on the door-knob behind them, she cried: "What are you doing? That's my door, my young madam! You leave touching other folks' doors!" and, pushing by her, re-entered in haste, loosing a January draught on that hot August day against the girl's thin frock. She shivered. What a cold room to choose! Was it only its north aspect that made it so bleak, or were there actually snowflakes afloat on the cold air? Snowflakes? How silly she was! It was only the charwoman shaking up the bed. That must be her employer's room. "When they shake up my pillows, it snows in the world." Where did the phrase come from? Shaking her head over that puzzle, she tried a second door, and a third. They were locked. She opened a fourth and went in.

She found herself in a nursery.

The nursery was her own. She was sure of that; but whether the nursery of her yesterday or tomorrow she could not tell. The high guard round the fire was ancient history: so was the cork carpet and the spread tea-table, and golden-syrup in the jam-pot hand-painted with pink chrysanthemums; but the frieze on the wall, that was the frieze she had always meant to paint round the walls of her children's nursery: and the floor games to teach a child geography, the history soldiers, the bricks for building the cities of the world, these existed nowhere, she could have sworn, but in her own mind. Nor were the windows the small stiff casements of her childhood, but generous glass doors reaching to the ground, even as she had planned, as she had planned. As she threw them open hurriedly because of what she saw without, she tripped and all but fell over some object that clanked as she touched it.

It was a child's iron stocking.

The sight of it, she was aware, should have brought a memory to her mind, a memory factual not fantastic, a memory—but no! Though she picked up the ugly little instrument, fingering it critically, she could not at the moment crystallize the memory it evoked. For the windows were open and the wide champaign that spread itself without was calling to her with the voice of apple trees sighing in the wind—"Shake me! Shake me!" "I burn! I burn!" rose the scent of cakes from the oven: and Mother Holle, it seemed, had once more taken her in; yet not to service, but to wander where she would, swinging from her fingers, as it were a divining rod pointing to hidden treasure, a child's discarded stocking.

"Rested?" said her employer, not so much as looking up at her when, a thousand years later, she returned demurely to spread the evening meal.

She stretched out her hands, tiptoeing in a delicious yawn that sent the good blood to her cheeks with a rush.

"Rested," she said, and her smile was honest and her eyes at peace. Then, shyly, not knowing how to word it: "Did you call? I came back when I heard you call."

"In your sleep?"

"*Was* I asleep?"

In answer she got only:

"I should get your rest while you can. You've only another three months."

She started; all her new-found wellbeing poised for flight.

"I don't want to go, not now," she submitted humbly.

"Didn't I engage you for the year?"

"I thought, if I give satisfaction—"

"Board and lodging for the year, and a present when you go, wasn't it?"

She pleaded, clutching wildly at the first excuse. "The char —the old woman she's been with you years and years."

Said her employer: "Yes, she stays on. She's too old to get the good of her wages. But yours are due by Twelfth Night, my dear, so take your pleasure while you can!"

She took it, desperately she took it, as a man who has once starved hoards crusts against tomorrow. She came with the dawn: she stayed till moonlight blanched the dying fields. It was "Can you spare me for half an hour?" till her employer laughed as she spared her. Indeed, had she been less absorbed in her own dreaming, she might have wondered that she was spared so easily, have been startled at the restless little phrases that escaped her employer as she told stories in the early winter twilight—tales of swan girls from Norway tucking men's hearts under their wings—of a ship out of Egypt that sailed on dry land, scattering corn and blessing through all the Middle Kingdoms, through all the middle years—of the spider in the cornice who was once a spinster too—of a limping queen whose son still drowses under the roots of the mountains with Arthur and Red Beard and Ogier the Dane, awaiting the call to arms. "And his beard has grown through the stone table, and still, he sleeps—or did, a year ago!" And the shorter the days grew, the longer the tales, of journeys "in my car," and of adventures with obstructive village folk merrymaking on Twelfth Night. "Ah, yes, they're sorry when I go! But there: I come again, my dear! They know I come again!" It was not till, years later, as she searched her memory for half-heard tales to please a listener, that she realized what she had lost, what she had wasted, yes, like the carpenter in one of the stories who had mended the car's broken wheel. "When I threw him the chips for his pains, the fool left them lying! And they were gold, my dear, they were gold!"

But why listen to fairy tales when fairyland itself lay across the Roman pavement and up a flight of stairs; when "Can you spare me for half an hour" was open sesame to her own country and her own kind? For the land was peopled. None spoke to her, none crossed her path; yet she was aware of shapes that lay under the poplars and stirred among the apple trees, and looked down at her from the rails of laden ships that sailed to and fro upon the purple rim of the sea which edged that country as ghost moths sail across the blue of the dusk.

Some of the faces were familiar. She thought that she recognized a village crone who had followed her on one of her rambles, and there was a younger woman who might have been her landlady but for her full skirts and mob-cap. Once she saw a pretty girl with a plait of fair hair and a spindle in her hand, singing to herself as she sat on the edge of a well; but the words were in a strange language and the girl did not seem to see her: and once she came face to face with a pinched, white countenance, high-nosed like a parrot, in a parrot's flare of finery, that outfaced her a searching instant before a turn of the stiff shoulders swung the immense ruff between them for a screen, and that shadow swept away into the shadows with a screech of laughter that brought to her mind the creaking signboard of the Queen's Head Inn. "Neither chick nor child, miss, had she?" The words returned to her. Was it indeed the same need that had brought them both to Spinsters' Rest? Was she still searching, the grand, starved ghost, for a heart's love to take back with her into history? "And are you jealous of me, poor queen, because the child has looked at me, not you?"

For it was the dumb child who filled her hours. Ever since, on the threshold of enchantment, she had stumbled on that discarded instrument of pain, she had known what face would turn to her, what eyes would speak to her eyes in good time, unbeckoned. For would it not be lonely, the one male creature in the Spinsters' Rest? Summer is sweet, and draws a child with daisy-chains, but summer is a poor playfellow: she can grow you a cowslip ball, but—can she throw it? Furtively she observed it, flitting from tree to tree, from flower to flower, always wary, yet always circling her, always at play in the human safety of her shadow, and bided her time: and the while tried not to reckon, yet daily reckoned, up her shortening days. She had come to Spinsters' Rest on—Twelfth Night, was it not? And out in the winter world Twelfth Night was once more drawing near, was a month, a fortnight, was a week away. And now it had dwindled into a matter of days, into the last Sunday of all, and she had not won the child!

Lying in the sweet grasses by the river's edge, she watched

it, not a yard away, as it hung over the clover-tufted bank, engrossed in the image that wondered up at it from the clear deep water. And as she watched she began very softly to sing the old rhyme:

"Monday's child is full of grace—"

It did not so much as start.

It's grown accustomed to me, she thought. She sang on:

"Tuesday's child is fair of face—"

Was it? Its grave eyes travelled doubtfully over its own reflection.

"Wednesday's child is loving and giving—"

She stretched out a hand and slipped a finger into the small fist that made room and closed again fast and friendly.

"Thursday's child—"

She shook her head ruefully at their two intent faces,

"—must work for its living—
Friday's child is full of woe—"

And it was clambering into her lap, kneeling upright to stare into her face with piteous intelligence.

"Saturday's child has far to go—"

It was so light a burden to hold. She thought she could carry it to the ends of the earth and back, and never tire.

"But the child that is born on the Sabbath day—"

Its arms were at her neck, it was laughing and loving her as a child should. She finished with a little squeeze that made it chuckle:

"Is blithe and bonny and good and gay!"

And, cheek grazing cheek, waited.

But before that for which she waited could be bestowed, the silence of the land was riven by a cry, a cry half-triumph, half-call, as it were the voice of a wild swan circling for the south, as it were a horn blowing for the departure of hosts. And at that sound the whole painted landscape, the meandering river with its white scarves of ranunculus, the gilded meadows and trees heavy with heat, the vaporous hills, the clouds, the purple yard of ocean, all, all quivered as the air quivers over a gipsy fire, and, rising like a painted gauze curtain, melted and passed utterly away.

She put her hand to her dazed eyes. She was in the garden, the common back garden of Spinsters' Rest, with its orange gravel so carefully swept, with its oak tree and evergreens, and its snow-covered, untouched lawn. And then fear took her, coldly, as the winter air was taking her by the throat and shaking hands; for she was standing, empty-armed, in the centre of that pure surface, and there was not, neither before nor behind her, neither to right nor to left, any track of human feet. Only, as she stared terrified, she could everywhere discern the innumerable tracks of birds.

She remembered the landlady's words—"Never see birds in winter time!" But now the birds had come back.

Thereupon she ran panicking into the house, half knowing what she should find, and found it—a garment discarded, a shrine abandoned, the body of an old, old woman, serenely laid down and left. The wind of winter sleeted in through the garden window and stirred the withered trails of clematis till seeded gossamers floated downwards to mingle with the stray and wind-borne flakes of snow. A brown shadow flurried for a moment at the wainscot and was gone. From the floor a robin rose into the air, hung fluttering, and dropped again to its crumb....

It was a full week later that she turned for the last time into Spinsters' Rest. The weary business of a burying lay behind her and the agent's bored inquisition. Not that he had asked her what her plans were. Why should he? It was of the fate of the house, "a fine property—neglected, of course!"—that he had talked. And on that she had asked, with an effort, who had inherited? He did not know. A distant cousin, he imagined.

A—a woman? She hung, breathless, on his answer, not daring to define what she expected.

A lady, yes. A spinster lady, he believed. A great traveller. As a matter of fact, the firm was uncertain at the moment of her exact whereabouts.

Was Mary Pawle needed? Should she wait?

He raised his eyebrows. He had already told her that they had appointed a former charwoman as a caretaker. Why, then, should she wait?

Why, indeed? The train, the night train for London goes at seven. The luggage has gone already. Say goodbye to Spinsters' Rest, and go!

For the last time she mounted the stairs, carpetless now, and opened the door of her room. Her room? She did not know it anymore. The livid evening pressed its cheek against a curtainless high window: through a broken pane a little wind whistled as it bellied out the dirtied cobweb long since spun from latch to sill. Empty stood the room, empty as her future, empty as her life. Her feet made marks on the grey velvet dust, as she crossed to the casement and looked out.

What had she expected? She did not know; but whatever she looked for, she saw only below, below, not level with her feet, the orange paths, the dull garden, the dreary laurels. Well —there it was! another year frittered away, and—nothing to show! She was sorry that her employer was gone; but it was not for her that she was crying, weakly, miserably, in spite of herself. One dreamed dreams and paid for them. She supposed that it was something to be able even to dream. Some poor women had not even dreams. It had been at least a heaven's own vision. If it had lasted only a moment longer, only a little moment, the child would have kissed her of its own accord. It was something to win a child to you, if only in a dream.

Well—no use waiting: no use wishing. It was getting dark. She would barely grope her way to the station through the unlighted war-time lanes. So goodbye, room! Goodbye, dreams! Goodbye, Mother Holle!

What was that?

She nearly fell with the violence of her own start. What, in God's name, was that shapeless sound? A damned soul clanking its chain? The wail of a lost child? Send us light in our darkness, O Lord, O Lord of the spirits and little children!

As if in answer, over the edge of the sill, broad and benignant rose the winter moon, and the shadows fled before it to the far corners of the room, fled, settled, thickened to a stirring blackness on the silvered floor, to a crouched bundle with white face and wide eyes. She dropped to her knees beside it, and for an instant the two forlorn creatures stared at each other. Then the dark eyes knew her, the pinched lips smiled, the small unmothered arms reached up to her, caught, closed and clung, tightening about her neck till she could hardly breathe. Wild with wonder and delight, she rose to her feet and flinging loose her cloak, wrapped it anew about herself and the child, so that the little creature might lodge on her breast, in the crook of her arm, hidden and safe and warm. Then, stealing down the stairway, tiptoeing over the pavement, she fled from that house of rest, unheard, unseen.

But ever as she hurried down the evening lanes the smiling moon observed her: and the trees sighed after her—"This is the reward of your service."

MRS. LUNT
HUGH WALPOLE

I

"Do you believe in ghosts?" I asked Runciman. I had to ask him
this very platitudinous question more because he was so difficult a man to spend an hour with rather than for any other
reason. You know his books, perhaps, or more probably you
don't know them—*The Running Man, The Elm Tree*, and *Crystal
and Candlelight*. He is one of those little men who are constant
enough in this age of immense overproduction of books, men
who publish every autumn their novel, who arouse by that
publication in certain critics eager appreciation and praise,
who have a small and faithful public, whose circulation is very
small indeed, who, when you meet them, have little to say, are
often shy and nervous, pessimistic and remote from daily life.
Such men do fine work, are made but little of in their own day,
and perhaps fifty years after their death are rediscovered by
some digging critic and become a sort of cult with a new
generation.

I asked Runciman that question because, for some

unknown reason, I had invited him to dinner at my flat, and was now faced with a long evening filled with that most tiresome of all conversations, talk that dies every two minutes and has to be revived with terrific exertions. Being myself a critic, and having on many occasions praised Runciman's work, he was the more nervous and shy with me; had I abused it, he would perhaps have had plenty to say—he was that kind of man. But my question was a lucky one: it roused him instantly, his long, bony body became full of a new energy, his eyes stared into a rich and exciting reminiscence, he spoke without pause, and I took care not to interrupt him. He certainly told me one of the most astounding stories I have ever heard. Whether it was true or not I cannot, of course, say: these ghost stories are nearly always at second or third hand. I had, at any rate, the good fortune to secure mine from the source. Moreover, Runciman was not a liar: he was too serious for that. He himself admitted that he was not sure, at this distance of time, as to whether the thing had gained as the years passed. However, here it is as he told it.

"It was some fifteen years ago," he said. "I went down to Cornwall to stay with Robert Lunt. Do you remember his name? No, I suppose you do not. He wrote several novels; some of those half-and-half things that are not quite novels, not quite poems, rather mystical and picturesque, and are the very devil to do well. De la Mare's *Return* is a good example of the kind of thing. I had reviewed somewhere his last book, and reviewed it favourably, and received from him a really touching letter showing that the man was thirsting for praise, and also, I fancied, for company. He lived in Cornwall somewhere on the seacoast, and his wife had died some two years before; he said he was quite alone there, and would I come and spend Christmas with him; he hoped I would not think this impertinent; he expected that I would be engaged already, but he could not resist the chance. Well, I wasn't engaged; far from it. If Lunt was lonely, so was I; if Lunt was a failure, so was I; I was touched, as I have said, by his letter, and I accepted his invitation. As I went down in the train to Penzance I wondered what kind of a man he would be. I had never seen any photographs of him; he was not the sort of author whose picture the newspapers publish. He must be, I fancied, about my own age— perhaps rather older. I know when we're lonely how some of us are forever imagining that a friend will somewhere turn up, that ideal friend who will understand all one's feelings, who will give one affection without being sentimental, who will take an interest in one's affairs without being impertinent— yes, the sort of friend one never finds.

"I fancy that I became quite romantic about Lunt before I reached Penzance. We would talk, he and I, about all those literary questions that seemed to me at that time so absorbing; we would, perhaps, often stay together and even travel abroad on those little journeys that are so swiftly melancholy when one is alone, so delightful when one has a perfect companion. I imagined him as sparse and delicate and refined, with a sort of wistfulness and rather childish play of fancy. We had both, so far, failed in our careers, but perhaps together we would do great things.

"When I arrived at Penzance it was almost dark, and the snow, threatened all day by an overhanging sky, had begun gently and timorously to fall. He had told me in his letter that a fly would be at the station to take me to his house; and there I found it—a funny old, weather-beaten carriage with a funny, old weather-beaten driver. At this distance of time my imagination may have created many things, but I fancy that from the moment I was shut into that carriage some dim suggestion of fear and apprehension attacked me. I fancy that I had some absurd impulse to get out of the thing and take the night train back to London again, an action that would have been very unlike me, as I had always a sort of obstinate determination to carry through anything that I had begun. In any case, I was uncomfortable in that carriage; it had, I remember, a nasty, musty smell of damp straw and stale eggs, and it seemed to confine me so closely as though it were determined that, once I was in, I should never get out again. Then, it was bitterly cold; I was colder during that drive than I have ever been before or since. It was that penetrating cold that seems to pierce your very brain, so that I could not think with any clearness, but only wish again and again that I hadn't come. Of course, I could see nothing—only feel the jolt over the uneven road— and once and again we seemed to fight our way through dark paths, because I could feel the overhanging branches of the trees knock against the cab with mysterious taps, as though they were trying to give me some urgent message.

"Well, I mustn't make more of it than the facts allow, and I mustn't see into it all the significance of the events that followed. I only know that as the drive proceeded, I became more and more miserable: miserable with the cold of my body, the misgivings of my imagination, the general loneliness of my case.

"At last, we stopped. The old scarecrow got slowly off his box, with many heavings and sighings, came to the cab door, and, with great difficulty and irritating slowness, opened it. I got out of it, and found that the snow was now falling very heavily indeed, and that the path was lightened with its soft, mysterious glow. Before me was a humped and ungainly shadow: the house that was to receive me. I could make nothing of it in that darkness, but only stood there shivering while the old man pulled at the doorbell with a sort of frantic energy as though he were anxious to be rid of the whole job as quickly as possible and return to his own place. At last, after what seemed an endless time, the door opened, and an old man, who might have been own brother to the driver, poked out his head. The two old men talked together, and at last my bag was shouldered and I was permitted to come in out of the piercing cold.

"Now this, I know, is not imagination. I have never at any period of my life hated at first sight so vigorously any dwelling place into which I have entered as I did that house. There was nothing especially disagreeable about my first vision of the hall. It was a large, dark place, lit by two dim lamps, cold and cheerless; but I got no particular impression of it because at once I was conducted out of it, led along a passage, and then introduced into a room which was, I saw at once, as warm and comfortable as the hall had been dark and dismal. I was, in fact, so eagerly pleased at the large and leaping fire that I moved towards it at once, not noting, at the first moment, the presence of my host; and when I did see him, I could not believe that it was he. I have told you the kind of man that I had expected; but, instead of the sparse, sensitive artist, I found facing me a large, burly man, over six foot, I should fancy, as broad-shouldered as he was tall, giving evidence of great muscular strength, the lower part of his face hidden by a black, pointed beard.

"But if I was astonished at the sight of him, I was doubly amazed when he spoke. His voice was thin and piping, like that of some old woman; and the little nervous gestures that he made with his hands were even more feminine than his voice. But I had to allow, perhaps, for excitement, for excited he was; he came up to me, took my hand in both of his, and held it as though he would never let it go. In the evening, when we sat over our port, he apologized for this. 'I was so glad to see you,' he said; 'I couldn't believe that really you would come; you are the first visitor of my own kind that I have had here forever so long. I was ashamed indeed of asking you, but I had to snatch at the chance—it means so much to me."

"His eagerness, in fact, had something disturbing about it; something pathetic, too. He simply couldn't do too much for me: he led me through funny crumbling old passages, the boards creaking under us at every step, up some dark Stairs, the walls hung, so far as I could see in the dim light, with faded yellow photographs of places, and showed me into my room with a deprecating agitated gesture as though he expected me at the first sight of it to turn and run. I didn't like it any more than I liked the rest of the house; but that was not my host's fault. He had done everything he possibly could for me: there was a large fire flaming in the open fireplace, there was a hot bottle, as he explained to me, in the big four-poster bed, and the old man who had opened the door to me was already taking my clothes out of my bag and putting them away. Lunt's nervousness was almost sentimental. He put both his hands on my shoulders and said, looking at me pleadingly: 'If only you knew what it is for me to have you here, the talks we'll have. Well, well, I must leave you. You'll come down and join me, won't you, as soon as you can?"

"It was then, when I was left alone in my room, that I had my second impulse to flee. Four candles in tall old silver candlesticks were burning brightly, and these, with the blazing fire, gave plenty of light; and yet the room was in some way dim, as though a faint smoke pervaded it, and I remember that I went to one of the old lattice windows and threw it open for a moment as though I felt stifled. Two things quickly made me close it. One was the intense cold which, with a fluttering scamper of snow, blew into the room; the other was the quite deafening roar of the sea, which seemed to fling itself at my very face as though it wanted to knock me down. I quickly shut the window, turned round, and saw an old woman standing just inside the door. Now every story of this kind depends for its interest on its verisimilitude. Of course, to make my tale convincing I should be able to prove to you that I saw that old woman; but I can't. I can only urge upon you my rather dreary reputation of probity. You know that I'm a teetotaller, and always have been, and, most important evidence of all, I was not expecting to see an old woman; and yet I hadn't the least doubt in the world but that it was an old woman I saw. You may talk about shadows, clothes hanging on the back of the door, and the rest of it. I don't know. I've no theories about this story, I'm not a spiritualist, I don't know that I believe in anything especially, except the beauty of beautiful things. We'll put it, if you like, that I fancied that I saw an old woman, and my fancy was so strong that I can give you to this day a pretty detailed account of her appearance. She wore a black silk dress and on her breast was a large, ugly, gold brooch; she had black hair, brushed back from her forehead and parted down the middle; she wore a collar of some white stuff round her throat; her face was one of the wickedest, most malignant, and furtive that I have ever seen—very white in colour. She was shrivelled enough now, but might once have been rather beautiful. She stood there quietly, her hands at her side. I thought that she was some kind of housekeeper. 'I have everything I want, thank you,' I said. 'What a splendid fire!' I turned for a moment towards it, and when I looked back, she was gone. I thought nothing of this, of course, but drew up an old chair covered with green faded tapestry, and thought that I would read a little from some book that I had brought down with me before I went to join my host. The fact was that I was not very intent upon joining him before I must. I didn't like him. I had already made up my mind that I would find some excuse to return to London as soon as possible. I can't tell you why I didn't like him, except that I was myself very reserved and had, like many Englishmen, a great distrust of demonstrations, especially from another man. I hadn't cared for the way in which he had put his hands on my shoulders, and I felt perhaps that I wouldn't be able to live up to all his eager excitement about me.

"I sat in my chair and took up my book, but I had not been reading for more than two minutes before I was conscious of a most unpleasant smell. Now, there are all sorts of smells—healthy and otherwise—but I think the nastiest is that chilly kind of odour that comes from bad sanitation and stuffy rooms combined; you meet it sometimes at little country inns and decrepit town lodgings. This smell was so definite that I could almost locate it; it came from near the door. I got up, approached the door, and at once it was as though I were drawing near to somebody who, if you'll forgive the impoliteness, was not accustomed to taking too many baths. I drew back just as I might had an actual person been there. Then, quite suddenly, the smell was gone, the room was fresh, and I saw, to my surprise, that one of the windows had opened and that snow was again blowing in. I closed it and went downstairs.

"The evening that followed was odd enough. My host was not in himself an unlikeable man; he did his very utmost to please me. He had a fine culture and a wide knowledge of books and things. He became quite cheerful as the evening went on; gave me a good dinner in a funny little old dining room hung with some admirable mezzotints. The old serving man looked after us—a funny old man, with a long white beard like a goat—and, oddly enough, it was from him that I first recaught my earlier apprehension. He had just put the dessert on the table, had arranged my plate in front of me, when I saw him give a start and look towards the door. My attention was attracted to this because his hand, as it touched the plate, suddenly trembled. My eyes followed, but I could see nothing. That he was frightened of something was perfectly clear, and then (it may, of course, very easily have been fancy) I thought that I detected once more that strange unwholesome smell.

"I forgot this again when we were both seated in front of a splendid fire in the library. Lunt had a very fine collection of books, and it was delightful to him, as it is to every book collector, to have somebody with him who could really appreciate them. We stood looking at one book after another and talking eagerly about some of the minor early English novelists who were my especial hobby—Bage, Godwin, Henry Mackenzie, Mrs. Shelley, Mat Lewis, and others—when once again he affected me most unpleasantly by putting his arm round my shoulders. I have all my life disliked intensely to be touched by certain people. I suppose we all feel like this. It is one of those inexplicable things; and I disliked this so much that I abruptly drew away.

"Instantly he was changed into a man of furious and ungovernable rage; I thought that he was going to strike me. He stood there quivering all over, the words pouring out of his mouth incoherently, as though he were mad and did not know what he was saying. He accused me of insulting him, of abusing his hospitality, of throwing his kindness back into his face, and of a thousand other ridiculous things; and I can't tell you how strange it was to hear all this coming out in that shrill, piping voice as though it were from an agitated woman, and yet to see with one's eyes that big, muscular frame, those immense shoulders, and that dark bearded face.

"I said nothing. I am, physically, a coward, I dislike, above anything else in the world, any sort of quarrel. At last, I brought out, 'I am very sorry. I didn't mean anything. Please forgive me,' and then hurriedly turned to leave the room. At once he changed again; now he was almost in tears. He implored me not to go; said it was his wretched temper, but that he was so miserable and unhappy, and had for so long now been alone and desolate that he hardly knew what he was doing. He begged me to give him another chance, and if I would only listen to his story, I would perhaps be more patient with him.

"At once, so oddly is man constituted, I changed in my feelings towards him. I was very sorry for him. I saw that he was a man on the edge of his nerves, and that he really did need some help and sympathy, and would be quite distracted if he could not get it. I put my hand on his shoulder to quieten him and to show him that I bore no malice, and I felt that his great body was quivering from head to foot. We sat down again, and in an odd, rambling manner he told me his story. It amounted to very little, and the gist of it was that, rather to have some sort of companionship than from any impulse of passion, he had married some fifteen years before the daughter of a neighbouring clergyman. They had had no very happy life together, and at the last, he told me quite frankly, he had hated her. She had been mean, overbearing, and narrow-minded; it had been, he confessed, nothing but a relief to him when, just a year ago, she had suddenly died from heart failure. He had thought, then, that things would go better with him, but they had not; nothing had gone right with him since. He hadn't been able to work, many of his friends had ceased to come to see him, he had found it even difficult to get servants to stay with him, he was desperately lonely, he slept badly—that was why his temper was so terribly on edge. He had no one in the house with him save the old man, who was, fortunately, an excellent cook, and a boy—the old man's grandson.

"'Oh, I thought,' I said, 'that that excellent meal tonight was cooked by your housekeeper.'

"'My housekeeper?' he answered. 'There's no woman in the house.'

"'Oh, but one came to my room,' I replied, 'this evening—an old, ladylike-looking person in a black silk dress.'

"'You were mistaken,' he answered in the oddest voice, as though he were exerting all the strength that he possessed to keep himself quiet and controlled.

"'I am sure that I saw her,' I answered. 'There couldn't be any mistake.' And I described her to him.

"'You were mistaken,' he repeated again. 'Don't you see that you must have been when I tell you there is no woman in the house?'

"I reassured him quickly lest there should be another outbreak of rage. Then there followed the oddest kind of appeal. Urgently, as though his very life depended upon it, he begged me to stay with him for a few days. He implied, although he said nothing definitely, that he was in great trouble, that if only I would stay for a few days all would be well, that if ever in all my life I had had a chance of doing a kind action I had one now, that he couldn't expect me to stop in so dreary a place, but that he would never forget it if I did. He spoke in a voice of such urgent distress that I reassured him as I might a child, promising that I would stay and shaking hands with him on it as though it were a kind of solemn oath between us."

II

"I am sure that you would wish me to give you this incident as it occurred, and if the final catastrophe seems to come, as it were, accidentally, I can only say to you that that was how it happened. It is since the event that I have tried to put two and two together, and that they don't altogether make four is the fault that mine shares, I suppose, with every true ghost story.

"But the truth is that after that very strange episode between us I had a very good night. I slept the sleep of all justice, cosy and warm, in my four-poster, with the murmur of the sea beyond the windows to rock my slumbers. Next morning, too, was bright and cheerful, the sun sparkling down on the snow, and the snow sparkling back to the sun as though they were glad to see one another. I had a very pleasant morning looking at Lunt's books, talking to him, and writing one or two letters. I must say that, after all, I liked the man. His appeal to me on the night before had touched me. So few people, you see, had ever appealed to me about anything. His nervousness was there and the constant sense of apprehension, yet he seemed to be putting the best face on it, doing his utmost to set me at my ease in order to induce me to stay, I suppose, and to give him a little of that company that he so terribly needed. I dare say if I had not been so busy about the books, I would not have been so happy. There was a strange eerie silence about that house if one ever stopped to listen; and once, I remember, sitting at the old bureau writing a letter, I raised my head and looked up, and caught Lunt watching as though he wondered whether I had heard or noticed anything. And so I listened, too, and it seemed to me as though someone were on the other side of the library door with their hand raised to knock; a quaint notion, with nothing to support it, but I could have sworn that if I had gone to the door and opened it suddenly someone would have been there.

"However, I was cheerful enough, and after lunch quite happy. Lunt asked me if I would like a walk, and I said I would; and we started out in the sunshine over the crunching snow towards the sea. I don't remember of what we talked; we seemed to be now quite at our ease with one another. We

crossed the fields to a certain point, looked down at the sea—
smooth now, like silk—and turned back. I remember that I was
so cheerful that I seemed suddenly to take a happy view of all
my prospects. I began to confide in Lunt, telling him of my
little plans, of my hopes for the book that I was then writing,
and even began rather timidly to suggest to him that perhaps
we should do something together; that what we both needed
was a friend of common taste with ourselves, I know that I was
talking on, that we had crossed a little village street, and were
turning up the path towards the dark avenue of trees that led
to his house, when suddenly the change came.

"What I first noticed was that he was not listening to me;
his gaze was fixed beyond me, into the very heart of the black
clump of trees that fringed the silver landscape. I looked too,
and my heart bounded. There was, standing just in front of the
trees, as though she were waiting for us, the old woman whom
I had seen in my room the night before. I stopped.

"'Why, there she is!' I said. 'That's the old woman of whom
I was speaking—the old woman who came to my room.'

"He caught my shoulder with his hand. 'There's nothing
there,' he said. 'Don't you see that that's shadow? What's the
matter with you? Can't you see that there's nothing?'

"I stepped forward, and there was nothing, and I wouldn't,
to this day, be able to tell you whether it was hallucination or
not. I can only say that, from that moment, the afternoon
appeared to become dark. As we entered into the avenue of
trees, silently, and hurrying as though someone were behind
us, the dusk seemed to have fallen so that I could scarcely see
my way. We reached the house breathless. He hastened into his
study as though I were not with him, but I followed and,
closing the door behind me, said, with all the force that I had at
command: 'Now, what is this? What is it that's troubling you?
You must tell me! How can I help you if you don't?'

"And he replied, in so strange a voice that it was as though he had gone out of his mind: 'I tell you there's nothing! Can't you believe me when I tell you there's nothing at all? I'm quite all right ... Oh, my God! my God! ... don't leave me! ... This is the very day—the very night she said ... But I did nothing, I tell you —I did nothing—it's only her beastly malice....' He broke off. He still held my arm with his hand. He made strange movements, wiping his forehead as though it were damp with sweat, almost pleading with me; then suddenly angry again, then beseeching once more, as though I had refused him the one thing he wanted.

"I saw that he was truly not far from madness, and I began myself to have a sudden terror of this damp, dark house, this great, trembling man, and something more that was worse than they. But I pitied him. How could you or any man have helped it? I made him sit down in the armchair beside the fire, which had now dwindled to a few glimmering red coals. I let him hold me close to him with his arm and clutch my hand with his, and I repeated, as quietly as I might: 'But tell me; don't be afraid, whatever it is you have done. Tell me what danger it is you fear, and then we can face it together.'

"'Fear! fear!' he repeated; and then, with a mighty effort which I could not but admire, he summoned all his control. 'I'm off my head,' he said, 'with loneliness and depression. My wife died a year ago on this very night. We hated one another. I couldn't be sorry when she died, and she knew it. When that last heart attack came on, between her gasps she told me that she would return, and I've always dreaded this night. That's partly why I asked you to come, to have anyone here, anybody, and you've been very kind—more kind than I had any right to expect. You must think me insane going on like this, but see me through tonight and we'll have splendid times together. Don't desert me now—now, of all times!'

"I promised that I would not. I soothed him as best I could. We sat there, for I know not how long, through the gathering dark; we neither of us moved, the fire died out, and the room was lit with a strange dim glow that came from the snowy landscape beyond the uncurtained windows. Ridiculous, perhaps, as I look back at it. We sat there, I in a chair close to his, hand in hand, like a couple of lovers; but, in real truth, two men terrified, fearful of what was coming, and unable to do anything to meet it.

"I think that that was perhaps the strangest part of it; a sort of paralysis that crept over me. What would you or anyone else have done—summoned the old man, gone down to the village inn, fetched the local doctor? I could do nothing, but see the snow shine move like trembling water about the furniture and hear, through the urgent silence, the faint hoot of an owl from the trees in the wood.

III

"Oddly enough, I can remember nothing, try as I may, between that strange vigil and the moment when I myself, wakened out of a brief sleep, sat up in bed to see Lunt standing inside my room holding a candle. He was wearing a nightshirt, and looked huge in the candlelight, his black beard falling intensely dark on the white stuff of his shirt. He came very quietly towards my bed, the candle throwing flickering shadows about the room. When he spoke, it was in a voice low and subdued, almost a whisper.

"'Would you come,' he asked, 'only for half an hour—just for half an hour?' he repeated, staring at me as though he didn't know me. 'I'm unhappy without somebody—very unhappy.'

"Then he looked over his shoulder, held the candle high

above his head, and stared piercingly at every part of the room. I could see that something had happened to him, that he had taken another step into the country of Fear—a step that had withdrawn him from me and from every other human being.

"He whispered: 'When you come, tread softly; I don't want anyone to hear us.'

"I did what I could. I got out of bed, put on my dressing gown and slippers, and tried to persuade him to stay with me. The fire was almost dead, but I told him that we would build it up again, and that we would sit there and wait for the morning; but no, he repeated again and again: 'It's better in my own room; we're safer there.'

"'Safe from what?' I asked him, making him look at me. 'Lunt, wake up! You're as though you were asleep. There's nothing to fear. We've nobody but ourselves. Stay here and let us talk, and have done with this nonsense.'

"But he wouldn't answer; only drew me forward down the dark passage, and then turned into his room, beckoning me to follow. He got into bed and sat hunched up there, his hands holding his knees, staring at the door, and every once and again shivering with a little tremor. The only light in the room was that from the candle, now burning low, and the only sound was the purring whisper of the sea.

"It seemed to make little difference to him that I was there. He did not look at me, but only at the door, and when I spoke to him, he did not answer me nor seem to hear what I had said. I sat down beside the bed and, in order to break the silence, talked on about anything, about nothing, and was dropping off, I think, into a confused doze, when I heard his voice breaking across mine.

"Very clearly and distinctly he said: 'If I killed her, she deserved it; she was never a good wife to me, not from the first; she shouldn't have irritated me as she did—she knew what my temper was. She had a worse one than mine, though. She can't touch me; I'm as strong as she is.'

"And it was then, as clearly as I can now remember, that his voice suddenly sank into a sort of gentle whisper, as though he were almost glad that his fears had been confirmed.

"He whispered: 'She's there!'

"I cannot possibly describe to you how that whisper seemed to let Fear loose like water through my body. I could see nothing—the candle was flaming high in the last moments of its life—I could see nothing; but Lunt suddenly screamed, with a shrill cry like a tortured animal in agony: 'Keep her off me, keep her away from me, keep her off—keep her off!'

"He caught me, his hands digging into my shoulders; then, with an awful effect of constricted muscles, as though rigor had caught and held him, his arms slowly fell away, he slipped back on to the bed as though someone were pushing him, his hands fell against the sheet, his whole body jerked with a convulsive effort, and then he rolled over.

"I saw nothing; only, quite distinctly, in my nostrils was that same fetid odour that I had known on the preceding evening. I rushed to the door, opened it, shouted down the long passage again and again, and soon the old man came running. I sent him for the doctor, and then could not return to the room, but stood there listening, hearing nothing save the whisper of the sea, the loud ticking of the hall clock. I flung open the window at the end of the passage; the sea rushed in with its precipitant roar; some bells chimed the hour. Then at last, beating into myself more courage, I turned back towards the room...."

"Well?" I asked as Runciman paused. "He was dead, of course?"

"Dead, the doctor afterwards said, of heart failure."

"Well?" I asked again.

"That's all." Runciman paused. "I don't know whether you can even call it a ghost story. My idea of the old woman may have been all hallucination. I don't even know whether his wife was like that when she was alive. She may have been large and fat. Lunt died of an evil conscience."

"Yes," I said.

"The only thing," Runciman added at last, after a long pause, "is that on Lunt's body there were marks—on his neck especially, some on his chest—as of fingers pressing in, scratches and dull blue marks. He may, in his terror, have caught at his own throat...."

"Yes," I said again.

"Anyway." Runciman shivered. "I don't like Cornwall— beastly county. Queer things happen there—something in the air...."

"So I've heard," I answered. "And now have a drink. We both will."

MUNITIONS OF WAR
ARTHUR MACHEN

There was as thick fog, acrid and abominable, all over London when I set out for the West. And at the heart of the fog, as it were, was the shudder of the hard frost that made one think of those winters in Dickens that had seemed to have become fabulous. It was a day on which to hear in dreams the iron ring of the horses' hoofs on the Great North Road, to meditate the old inns with blazing fires, the coach going onward into the darkness, into a frozen world. A few miles out of London the fog lifted. The horizon was still vague in a purple mist of cold, but the sun shone brilliantly from a pale clear sky of blue, and all the earth was a magic of whiteness. White fields stretched to that dim violet mist far away, white hedges divided them, and the trees were all snowy white with the winter blossom of the frost. The train had been delayed a little by the thick fog about London; now it was rushing at a tremendous speed through this strange white world.

My business with the famous town in the West was to attempt to make some picture of it as it faced the stress of war, to find out whether it prospered or not. From what I had seen in other large towns, I expected to find it all of a bustle on the Saturday, its shops busy, its streets thronged and massed with people. Therefore, it was with no small astonishment that I found the atmosphere of Westpool wholly different from anything I had observed at Sheffield or Birmingham. Hardly anybody seemed to leave the train at the big station, and the broad road into the town wore a shy, barred-up air; it reminded one somewhat of the streets by which the traveller passes into forgotten places, little villages that once were great cities. I remember how in the town of my birth, Caerleon-on-Usk, the doctor's wife would leave the fire and run to the window if a step sounded in the main street outside; and strangely I was reminded of this as I walked from the Westpool station. Save for one thing: at intervals there were silent parties huddled together as if for help and comfort, and all making for the outskirts of the city.

There is a fair quarter of an hour's walk between Westpool station and the centre of the town. And here I would say that though Westpool is one of the biggest and busiest cities in England, it is also, in my judgment, one of the most beautiful. Not only on account of the ancient timbered houses that still overhang many of its narrower streets, not only because of its glorious churches and noble old traditions of splendour—I am known to be weak and partial where such things are concerned —but rather because of its site. For through the very heart of the great town a narrow, deep river runs, full of tall ships, bordered by bustling quays; and so you can often look over your garden wall and see a cluster of masts, and the shaking out of sails for a fair wind. And this bringing of deep-sea business into the middle of the dusty streets has always seemed to me an enchantment; there is something of Sinbad and Basra and Baghdad and the Nights in it. But this is not all the delight of Westpool; from the very quays of the river the town rushes up to great heights, with streets so steep that often they are flights of steps as in St Peter Port, and ladder-like ascents. And as I came to Middle Quay in Westpool that winter day the sun hovered over the violet mists, and the windows of the houses on the heights flamed and flashed red, vehement fires.

But the slight astonishment with which I had noted the shuttered and dismal aspect of the station road now became bewilderment. Middle Quay is the heart of Westpool, and all its business. I had always seen it swarm like an anthill. There were scarcely half a dozen people there on Saturday afternoon; and they seemed to be hurrying away. The Vintry and the Little Vintry, those famous streets, were deserted. I saw in a moment that I had come on a fool's errand: in Westpool assuredly there was no hurry or rush of war business, no swarm of eager shoppers for me to describe. I had an introduction to a well-known Westpool man.

"Oh no," he said, "we are very slack in Westpool. We are doing hardly anything. There's an aeroplane factory out at Oldham, and they're making high explosives by Portdown, but that doesn't affect us. Things are quiet, very quiet."

I suggested that they might brighten up a little at night.

"No," he said, "it really wouldn't be worth your while to stay on; you wouldn't find anything to write about, I assure you."

I was not satisfied. I went out and about the desolate streets of the great city; I made inquiries at random, and always heard the same story—"Things were very slack." And I began to receive an extraordinary impression: that the few I met were frightened, and were making the best of their way, either out of the town, or to the safety of their own bolted doors and barred shutters. It was only the very special mention of a friendly commercial traveller of my acquaintance that got me a room for the night at the Pineapple on Middle Quay, overlooking the river. The landlord assented with difficulty, after praising the express to town.

"It's a noisy place, this," he said, "if you're not used to it."

I looked at him. It was as quiet as if we were in the heart of the forest or the desert.

"You see," he said, "we don't do much in munitions, but there's a lot of night transport for the docks at Portdown. You know those climbing motors that they use in the Army, caterpillars or whatever they call them. We get a lot of them through Westpool; we get all sorts of heavy stuff, and I expect they'll wake you at night. I wouldn't go to the window, if I were you, if you do wake up. They don't like anybody peering about."

And I woke up in the dead of night. There was a thundering and a rumbling and a trembling of the earth such as I had never heard. And shouting too; and rolling oaths that sounded like judgement. I got up and drew the blind a little aside, in spite of the landlord's warning, and there was that desolate Middle Quay swarming with men, and the river full of great ships, faint and huge in the frosty mist, and sailing-ships too. Men were rolling casks by the hundred down to the ships.

"Hurry up, you lazy lubbers, you damned sons of guns, damn ye," said a great voice. "Shall the King's Majesty lack powder?"

"No, by God, he shall not," roared the answer, "I rolled it aboard for old King George, and young King George shall be none the worse for me."

"And who the devil are you to speak so bold?"

"Blast ye, bos'n; I fell at Trafalgar."

THE ROCKING HORSE WINNER
D. H. LAWRENCE

There was a woman who was beautiful, who started with all the advantages, yet she had no luck. She married for love, and the love turned to dust. She had bonny children, yet she felt they had been thrust upon her, and she could not love them. They looked at her coldly, as if they were finding fault with her. And hurriedly she felt she must cover up some fault in herself. Yet what it was that she must cover up she never knew. Nevertheless, when her children were present, she always felt the centre of her heart go hard. This troubled her, and in her manner, she was all the more gentle and anxious for her children, as if she loved them very much. Only she herself knew that at the centre of her heart was a hard little place that could not feel love, no, not for anybody.

Everybody else said of her: "She is such a good mother. She adores her children."

Only she herself, and her children themselves, knew it was not so. They read it in each other's eyes.

There were a boy and two little girls. They lived in a pleasant house, with a garden, and they had discreet servants, and felt themselves superior to anyone in the neighbourhood.

Although they lived in style, they felt always an anxiety in the house. There was never enough money. The mother had a small income, and the father had a small income, but not nearly enough for the social position which they had to keep up. The father went into town to some office. But though he had good prospects, these prospects never materialized. There was always the grinding sense of the shortage of money, though the style was always kept up.

At last, the mother said, "I will see if *I* can't make something." But she did not know where to begin. She racked her brains, and tried this thing and the other, but could not find anything successful. The failure made deep lines come into her face. Her children were growing up, they would have to go to school. There must be more money, there must be more money. The father, who was always very handsome and expensive in his tastes, seemed as if he never would be able to do anything worth doing. And the mother, who had a great belief in herself, did not succeed any better, and her tastes were just as expensive.

And so the house came to be haunted by the unspoken phrase: *There must be more money! There must be more money!* The children could hear it all the time, though nobody said it aloud. They heard it at Christmas, when the expensive and splendid toys filled the nursery. Behind the shining modern rocking horse, behind the smart doll's house, a voice would start whispering: "There *must* be more money! There *must* be more money!"

And the children would stop playing, to listen for a moment. They would look into each other's eyes, to see if they had all heard. And each one saw in the eyes of the other two that they, too, had heard.

"There *must* be more money! There *must* be more money!"

It came whispering from the springs of the still-swaying rocking horse, and even the horse, bending his wooden, champing head, heard it. The big doll, sitting so pink and smirking in her new pram, could hear it quite plainly, and seemed to be smirking all the more self-consciously because of it. The foolish puppy, too, that took the place of the teddy bear, he was looking so extraordinarily foolish for no other reason but that he heard the secret whisper all over the house: "There *must* be more money."

Yet nobody ever said it aloud. The whisper was everywhere, and therefore no one spoke it. Just as no one ever says: "We are breathing!" in spite of the fact that breath is coming and going all the time.

"Mother!" said the boy Paul one day. "Why don't we keep a car of our own? Why do we always use Uncle's, or else a taxi?"

"Because we're the poor members of the family," said the mother.

"But why *are* we, mother?"

"Well—I suppose," she said slowly and bitterly, "it's because your father has no luck."

The boy was silent for some time.

"Is luck money, Mother?" he asked, rather timidly.

"No, Paul! Not quite. It's what causes you to have money."

"Oh?" said Paul vaguely. "I thought when Uncle Oscar said *filthy lucker*, it meant money."

"*Filthy lucre* does mean money," said the mother. "But it's lucre, not luck."

"Oh!" said the boy. "Then what *is* luck, Mother?"

"It's what causes you to have money. If you're lucky you have money. That's why it's better to be born lucky than rich. If you're rich, you may lose your money. But if you're lucky, you will always get more money."

"Oh! Will you! And is Father not lucky?"

"Very unlucky, I should say," she said bitterly.

The boy watched her with unsure eyes.

"Why?" he asked.

"I don't know. Nobody ever knows why one person is lucky and another unlucky."

"Don't they? Nobody at all? Does *nobody* know?"

"Perhaps God! But He never tells."

"He ought to, then. And aren't you lucky either, Mother?"

"I can't be, if I married an unlucky husband."

"But by yourself, aren't you?"

"I used to think I was, before I married. Now I think I am very unlucky indeed."

"Why?"

"Well—never mind! Perhaps I'm not really," she said.

The child looked at her, to see if she meant it. But he saw, by the lines of her mouth, that she was only trying to hide something from him.

"Well, anyhow," he said stoutly, "I'm a lucky person."

"Why?" said his mother, with a sudden laugh.

He stared at her. He didn't even know why he had said it.

"God told me," he asserted, brazening it out.

"I hope He did, dear!" she said, again with a laugh, but rather bitter.

"He did, Mother!"

"Excellent!" said the mother, using one of her husband's exclamations.

The boy saw she did not believe him; or rather, that she paid no attention to his assertion. This angered him somewhere, and made him want to compel her attention.

He went off by himself, vaguely, in a childish way, seeking for the clue to "luck."

Absorbed, taking no heed of other people, he went about

with a sort of stealth, seeking inwardly for luck. He wanted luck, he wanted it, he wanted it. When the two girls were playing dolls, in the nursery, he would sit on his big rocking horse, charging madly into space, with a frenzy that made the little girls peer at him uneasily. Wildly the horse careered, the waving dark hair of the boy tossed, his eyes had a strange glare in them. The little girls dared not speak to him.

When he had ridden to the end of his mad little journey, he climbed down and stood in front of his rocking horse, staring fixedly into its lowered face. Its red mouth was slightly open, its big eye was wide and glassy bright.

"Now!" he would silently command the snorting steed. "Now take me to where there is luck! Now take me!"

And he would slash the horse on the neck with the little whip he had asked Uncle Oscar for. He *knew* the horse could take him to where there was luck, if only he forced it. So he would mount again, and start on his furious ride, hoping at last to get there. He knew he could get there.

"You'll break your horse, Paul!" said the nurse.

"He's always riding like that! I wish he'd leave off!" said his elder sister Joan.

But he only glared down on them in silence. Nurse gave him up. She could make nothing of him. Anyhow he was growing beyond her.

One day his mother and his Uncle Oscar came in when he was on one of his furious rides. He did not speak to them.

"Hallo! you young jockey! Riding a winner?" said his uncle.

"Aren't you growing too big for a rocking horse? You're not a very little boy any longer, you know," said his mother.

But Paul only gave a blue glare from his big, rather close-set eyes. He would speak to nobody when he was in full tilt. His mother watched him with an anxious expression on her face.

At last, he suddenly stopped forcing his horse into the mechanical gallop, and slid down.

"Well, I got there!" he announced fiercely, his blue eyes still flaring, and his sturdy long legs straddling apart.

"Where did you get to?" asked his mother.

"Where I wanted to go to," he flared back at her.

"That's right, son!" said Uncle Oscar. "Don't you stop till you get there. What's the horse's name?"

"He doesn't have a name," said the boy.

"Gets on without all right?" asked the uncle.

"Well, he has different names. He was called Sansovino last week."

"Sansovino, eh? Won the Ascot. How did you know his name?"

"He always talks about horse races with Bassett," said Joan.

The uncle was delighted to find that his small nephew was posted with all the racing news. Bassett, the young gardener who had been wounded in the left foot in the war, and had got his present job through Oscar Cresswell, whose batman he had been, was a perfect blade of the "turf." He lived in the racing events, and the small boy lived with him.

Oscar Cresswell got it all from Bassett.

"Master Paul comes and asks me, so I can't do more than tell him, sir," said Bassett, his face terribly serious, as if he were speaking of religious matters.

"And does he ever put anything on a horse he fancies?"

"Well—I don't want to give him away—he's a young sport, sir. Would you mind asking him himself? He sort of takes a pleasure in it, and perhaps he'd feel I was giving him away, sir, if you don't mind."

Bassett was serious as a church.

The uncle went back to his nephew, and took him off for a ride in the car.

"Say, Paul, old man, do you ever put anything on a horse?" the uncle asked.

The boy watched the handsome man closely.

"Why, do you think I oughtn't to?" he parried.

"Not a bit of it! I thought perhaps you might give me a tip for the Lincoln."

The car sped on into the country, going down to Uncle Oscar's place in Hampshire.

"Honour bright?" said the nephew.

"Honour bright, son!" said the uncle.

"Well, then, Daffodil."

"Daffodil! I doubt it, sonny. What about Mirza?"

"I only know the winner," said the boy. "That's Daffodil!"

"Daffodil, eh?"

There was a pause. Daffodil was an obscure horse comparatively.

"Uncle!"

"Yes, son?"

"You won't let it go any further, will you? I promised Bassett."

"Bassett be damned, old man! What's he got to do with it?"

"We're partners! We've been partners from the first! Uncle, he lent me my first five shillings, which I lost. I promised him, honour bright, it was only between me and him: only you gave me that ten-shilling note I started winning with, so I thought you were lucky. You won't let it go any further, will you?"

The boy gazed at his uncle from those big, hot, blue eyes, set rather close together. The uncle stirred and laughed uneasily.

"Right you are, son! I'll keep your tip private. Daffodil, eh! How much are you putting on him?"

"All except twenty pounds," said the boy. "I keep that in reserve."

The uncle thought it a good joke.

"You keep twenty pounds in reserve, do you, you young romancer? What are you betting, then?"

"I'm betting three hundred," said the boy gravely. "But it's between you and me, Uncle Oscar! Honour bright?"

The uncle burst into a roar of laughter.

"It's between you and me all right, you young Nat Gould," he said, laughing. "But where's your three hundred?"

"Bassett keeps it for me. We're partners."

"You are, are you! And what is Bassett putting on Daffodil?"

"He won't go quite as high as I do, I expect. Perhaps he'll go a hundred and fifty."

"What, pennies?" laughed the uncle.

"Pounds," said the child, with a surprised look at his uncle. "Bassett keeps a bigger reserve than I do."

Between wonder and amusement, Uncle Oscar was silent. He pursued the matter no further, but he determined to take his nephew with him to the Lincoln races.

"Now, son," he said, "I'm putting twenty on Mirza, and I'll put five for you on any horse you fancy. What's your pick?"

"Daffodil, Uncle!"

"No, not the fiver on Daffodil!"

"I should if it was my own fiver," said the child.

"Good! Good! Right you are! A fiver for me and a fiver for you on Daffodil."

The child had never been to a race meeting before, and his eyes were blue fire. He pursed his mouth tight, and watched.

A Frenchman just in front had put his money on Lancelot. Wild with excitement, he flayed his arms up and down, yelling "*Lancelot! Lancelot!*" in his French accent.

Daffodil came in first, Lancelot second, Mirza third. The child, flushed and with eyes blazing, was curiously serene. His uncle brought him five five-pound notes: four to one.

"What am I to do with these?" he cried, waving them before the boy's eyes.

"I suppose we'll talk to Bassett," said the boy. "I expect I have fifteen hundred now: and twenty in reserve: and this twenty."

His uncle studied him for some moments.

"Look here, son!" he said. "You're not serious about Bassett and that fifteen hundred, are you?"

"Yes, I am. But it's between you and me, Uncle! Honour bright!"

"Honour bright all right, son! But I must talk to Bassett."

"If you'd like to be a partner, Uncle, with Bassett and me, we could all be partners. Only you'd have to promise, honour bright, Uncle, not to let it go beyond us three. Bassett and I are lucky, and you must be lucky, because it was your ten shillings I started winning with...."

Uncle Oscar took both Bassett and Paul into Richmond Park for an afternoon, and there they talked.

"It's like this, you see, sir," Bassett said. "Master Paul would get me talking about racing events, spinning yarns, you know, sir. And he was always keen on knowing if I'd made or if I'd lost. It's about a year since, now, that I put five shillings on Blush of Dawn for him: and we lost. Then the luck turned, with that ten shillings he had from you: that we put on Singhalese. And since that time, it's been pretty steady, all things considering. What do you say, Master Paul?"

"We're all right when we're *sure*," said Paul. "It's when we're not quite sure that we go down."

"Oh, but we're careful then," said Bassett.

"But when are you *sure*?" smiled Uncle Oscar.

"It's Master Paul, sir," said Bassett, in a secret, religious voice. "It's as if he had it from heaven. Like Daffodil now, for the Lincoln. That was as sure as eggs."

"Did you put anything on Daffodil?" asked Oscar Cresswell.

"Yes, sir. I made my bit."

"And my nephew?"

Bassett was obstinately silent, looking at Paul.

"I made twelve hundred, didn't I, Bassett? I told Uncle I was putting three hundred on Daffodil."

"That's right," said Bassett, nodding.

"But where's the money?" asked the uncle.

"I keep it safe locked up, sir. Master Paul, he can have it any minute he likes to ask for it."

"What, fifteen hundred pounds?"

"And twenty! And *forty*, that is, with the twenty he made on the course."

"It's amazing!" said the uncle.

"If Master Paul offers you to be partners, sir, I would, if I were you: if you'll excuse me," said Bassett.

Oscar Cresswell thought about it, "I'll see the money," he said.

They drove home again, and sure enough, Bassett came round to the garden house with fifteen hundred pounds in notes. The twenty pounds reserve was left with Joe Glee, in the Turf Commission deposit.

"You see, it's all right, Uncle, when I'm *sure*! Then we go strong, for all we're worth. Don't we, Bassett?"

"We do that, Master Paul."

"And when are you sure?" said the uncle, laughing.

"Oh, well, sometimes I'm *absolutely* sure, like about Daffodil," said the boy; "and sometimes I have an idea; and sometimes I haven't even an idea, have I, Bassett? Then we're careful, because we mostly go down."

"You do, do you! And when you're sure, like about Daffodil, what makes you sure, sonny?"

"Oh, well, I don't know," said the boy uneasily. "I'm sure, you know, Uncle; that's all."

"It's as if he had it from heaven, sir," Bassett reiterated.

"I should say so!" said the uncle.

But he became a partner. And when the Leger was coming on, Paul was "sure" about Lively Spark, which was a quite inconsiderable horse. The boy insisted on putting a thousand on the horse, Bassett went for five hundred, and Oscar Cresswell two hundred. Lively Spark came in first, and the betting had been ten to one against him. Paul had made ten thousand.

"You see," he said, "I was absolutely sure of him."

Even Oscar Cresswell had cleared two thousand.

"Look here, son," he said, "this sort of thing makes me nervous."

"It needn't, Uncle! Perhaps I shan't be sure again for a long time."

"But what are you going to do with your money?" asked the uncle.

"Of course," said the boy, "I started it for Mother. She said she had no luck, because Father is unlucky, so I thought if I was lucky, it might stop whispering."

"What might stop whispering?"

"Our house! I *hate* our house for whispering."

"What does it whisper?"

"Why—why," the boy fidgeted. "Why, I don't know! But it's always short of money, you know, Uncle."

"I know it, son, I know it."

"You know people send Mother writs, don't you, Uncle?"

"I'm afraid I do," said the uncle.

"And then the house whispers like people laughing at you behind your back. It's awful, that is! I thought if I was lucky—"

"You might stop it," added the uncle.

The boy watched him with big, blue eyes, that had an uncanny cold fire in them, and he said never a word.

"Well then!" said the uncle. "What are we doing?"

"I shouldn't like Mother to know I was lucky," said the boy.

"Why not, son?"

"She'd stop me."

"I don't think she would."

"Oh!" And the boy writhed in an odd way. "I *don't* want her to know, Uncle."

"All right, son! We'll manage it without her knowing."

They managed it very easily. Paul, at the other's suggestion, handed over five thousand pounds to his uncle, who deposited it with the family lawyer, who was then to inform Paul's mother that a relative had put five thousand pounds into his hands, which sum was to be paid out a thousand pounds at a time, on the mother's birthday, for the next five years.

"So she'll have a birthday present of a thousand pounds for five successive years," said Uncle Oscar. "I hope it won't make it all the harder for her later."

Paul's mother had her birthday in November. The house had been "whispering" worse than ever lately, and even in spite of his luck, Paul could not bear up against it. He was very anxious to see the effect of the birthday letter, telling his mother about the thousand pounds.

When there were no visitors, Paul now took his meals with his parents, as he was beyond the nursery control. His mother went into town nearly every day. She had discovered that she had an odd knack of sketching furs and dress materials, so she worked secretly in the studio of a friend who was the chief "artist" for the leading drapers. She drew the figures of ladies in furs and sequins for the newspaper advertisements. This young woman artist earned several thousand pounds a year, but Paul's mother only made several hundreds, and she was again dissatisfied. She so wanted to be first in something, and she did not succeed, even in making sketches for drapery advertisements.

She was down to breakfast on the morning of her birthday. Paul watched her face as she read her letters. He knew the lawyer's letter. As his mother read it, her face hardened and became more expressionless. Then a cold, determined look came on her mouth. She hid the letter under the pile of others, and said not a word about it.

"Didn't you have anything nice in the post for your birthday, Mother?" said Paul.

"Quite moderately nice," she said, her voice cold and absent.

She went away to town without saying more.

But in the afternoon Uncle Oscar appeared. He said Paul's mother had had a long interview with the lawyer, asking if the whole five thousand could not be advanced at once, as she was in debt.

"What do you think, Uncle?" said the boy.

"I leave it to you, son."

"Oh, let her have it, then! We can get some more with the other," said the boy.

"A bird in the hand is worth two in the bush, laddie!" said Uncle Oscar, "But I'm sure to *know* for the Grand National; or the Lincolnshire; or else the Derby. I'm sure to know for *one* of them," said Paul.

So Uncle Oscar signed the agreement, and Paul's mother touched the whole five thousand. Then something very curious happened. The voices in the house suddenly went mad, like a chorus of frogs on a spring evening. There were certain new furnishings, and Paul had a tutor. He was *really* going to Eton, his father's school, in the following autumn. There were flowers in the winter, and a blossoming of the luxury Paul's mother had been used to. And yet the voices in the house, behind the sprays of mimosa and almond-blossom, and from under the piles of iridescent cushions, simply trilled and screamed in a sort of ecstasy: "There *must* be more money! Oh-h-h! There *must* be more money! Oh, now, now-w! now-w-w— there *must* be more money!—more than ever! More than ever!"

It frightened Paul terribly. He studied away at his Latin and Greek with his tutors. But his intense hours were spent with Bassett. The Grand National had gone by: he had not 'known,' and had lost a hundred pounds. Summer was at hand. He was in agony for the Lincoln. But even for the Lincoln he didn't "know," and he lost fifty pounds. He became wild-eyed and strange, as if something were going to explode in him.

"Let it alone, son! Don't you bother about it!" urged Uncle Oscar. But it was as if the boy couldn't really hear what his uncle was saying.

"I've got to know for the Derby! I've *got* to know for the Derby!" the child reiterated, his big, blue eyes blazing with a sort of madness.

His mother noticed how overwrought he was.

"You'd better go to the seaside. Wouldn't you like to go now to the seaside instead of waiting? I think you'd better," she said, looking down at him anxiously, her heart curiously heavy because of him.

But the child lifted his uncanny blue eyes.

"I couldn't possibly go before the Derby, Mother!" he said. "I couldn't possibly!"

"Why not?" she said, her voice becoming heavy when she was opposed. "Why not? You can still go from the seaside to see the Derby with your Uncle Oscar, if that's what you wish. No need for you to wait here. Besides, I think you care too much about these races. It's a bad sign. My family has been a gambling family, and you won't know till you grow up how much damage it has done. But it has done damage. I shall have to send Bassett away, and ask Uncle Oscar not to talk racing to you, unless you promise to be reasonable about it: go away to the seaside and forget it. You're all nerves!"

"I'll do what you like, Mother, so long as you don't send me away till after the Derby," the boy said.

"Send you away from where? Just from this house?"

"Yes," he said, gazing at her.

"Why, you curious child, what makes you care about this house so much, suddenly? I never knew you loved it!"

He gazed at her without speaking. He had a secret within a secret, something he had not divulged, even to Bassett or to his Uncle Oscar.

But his mother, after standing undecided and a little bit sullen for some moments, said:

"Very well, then! Don't go to the seaside till after the Derby, if you don't wish it. But promise me you won't let your nerves go to pieces! Promise you won't think so much about horse racing and *events*, as you call them!"

"Oh no!" said the boy, casually, "I won't think much about them, Mother. You needn't worry. I wouldn't worry, Mother, if I were you."

"If you were me and I were you," said his mother, "I wonder what we *should* do!"

"But you know you needn't worry, Mother, don't you?" the boy repeated.

"I should be awfully glad to know it," she said wearily.

"Oh, well, you can, you know. I mean you *ought* to know you needn't worry!" he insisted.

"Ought I? Then I'll see about it," she said.

Paul's secret of secrets was his wooden horse, that which had no name. Since he was emancipated from a nurse and a nursery governess, he had had his rocking horse removed to his own bedroom at the top of the house.

"Surely you're too big for a rocking horse!" his mother had remonstrated.

"Well, you see, Mother, till I can have a *real* horse, I like to have some *sort* of animal about," had been his quaint answer.

"Do you feel he keeps you company?" she laughed.

"Oh yes! He's very good, he always keeps me company, when I'm there," said Paul.

So the horse, rather shabby, stood in an arrested prance in the boy's bedroom.

The Derby was drawing near, and the boy grew more and more tense. He hardly heard what was spoken to him, he was very frail, and his eyes were really uncanny. His mother had sudden strange seizures of uneasiness about him. Sometimes, for half an hour, she would feel a sudden anxiety about him that was almost anguish. She wanted to rush to him at once, and know he was safe.

Two nights before the Derby, she was at a big party in town, when one of her rushes of anxiety about her boy, her firstborn, gripped her heart till she could hardly speak. She fought with the feeling, might and main, for she believed in common sense. But it was too strong. She had to leave the dance and go downstairs to telephone to the country. The children's nursery governess was terribly surprised and startled at being rung up in the night.

"Are the children all right, Miss Wilmot?"

"Oh yes, they are quite all right."

"Master Paul? Is he all right?"

"He went to bed as right as a trivet. Shall I run up and look at him?"

"No!" said Paul's mother reluctantly. "No! Don't trouble.

It's all right. Don't sit up. We shall be home fairly soon." She did not want her son's privacy intruded upon.

"Very good," said the governess.

It was about one o'clock when Paul's mother and father drove up to their house. All was still. Paul's mother went to her room and slipped off her white fur cloak. She had told her maid not to wait up for her. She heard her husband downstairs, mixing a whisky and soda.

And then, because of the strange anxiety at her heart, she stole upstairs to her son's room. Noiselessly she went along the upper corridor. Was there a faint noise? What was it?

She stood, with arrested muscles, outside his door, listening. There was a strange, heavy, and yet not loud noise. Her heart stood still. It was a soundless noise, yet rushing and powerful. Something huge, in violent, hushed motion. What was it? What in God's Name was it? She ought to know. She felt that she *knew* the noise. She knew what it was.

Yet she could not place it. She couldn't say what it was. And on and on it went, like a madness.

Softly, frozen with anxiety and fear, she turned the door handle.

The room was dark. Yet in the space near the window, she heard and saw something plunging to and fro. She gazed in fear and amazement.

Then suddenly she switched on the light, and saw her son, in his green pyjamas, madly surging on his rocking horse. The blaze of light suddenly lit him up, as he urged the wooden horse, and lit her up, as she stood, blonde, in her dress of pale green and crystal, in the doorway.

"Paul!" she cried. "Whatever are you doing?"

"It's Malabar!" he screamed, in a powerful, strange voice. "It's Malabar!"

His eyes blazed at her for one strange and senseless second, as he ceased urging his wooden horse. Then he fell with a crash to the ground, and she, all her tormented motherhood flooding upon her, rushed to gather him up.

But he was unconscious, and unconscious he remained, with some brain fever. He talked and tossed, and his mother sat stonily by his side.

"Malabar! It's Malabar! Bassett, Bassett, I *know*: it's Malabar!"

So the child cried, trying to get up and urge the rocking horse that gave him his inspiration.

"What does he mean by Malabar?" asked the heart-frozen mother.

"I don't know," said the father stonily.

"What does he mean by Malabar?" she asked her brother Oscar.

"It's one of the horses running for the Derby," was the answer.

And, in spite of himself, Oscar Cresswell spoke to Bassett, and himself put a thousand on Malabar: at fourteen to one.

The third day of the illness was critical: they were watching for a change. The boy, with his rather long, curly hair, was tossing ceaselessly on the pillow. He neither slept nor regained consciousness, and his eyes were like blue stones. His mother sat, feeling her heart had gone, turned actually into a stone.

In the evening, Oscar Cresswell did not come, but Bassett sent a message, saying could he come up for one moment, just one moment? Paul's mother was very angry at the intrusion, but of second thoughts she agreed. The boy was the same. Perhaps Bassett might bring him to consciousness.

The gardener, a shortish fellow with a little brown moustache and sharp little brown eyes, tiptoed into the room, touched his imaginary cap to Paul's mother and stole to the bedside, staring with glittering, smallish eyes at the tossing, dying child.

"Master Paul!" he whispered. "Master Paul! Malabar came in first all right, a clean win. I did as you told me. You've made over seventy thousand pounds, you have; you've got over eighty thousand. Malabar came in all right, Master Paul."

"Malabar! Malabar! Did I say Malabar, Mother? Did I say Malabar? Do you think I'm lucky, Mother? I knew Malabar, didn't I? Over eighty thousand pounds! I call that lucky, don't you, Mother? Over eighty thousand pounds! I knew, didn't I know I knew? Malabar came in all right. If I ride my horse till I'm sure, then I tell you, Bassett, you can go as high as you like. Did you go for all you were worth, Bassett?"

"I went a thousand on it, Master Paul."

"I never told you, Mother, that if I can ride my horse, and *get there*, then I'm absolutely sure—oh, absolutely! Mother, did I never tell you? I *am* lucky!"

"No, you never did," said the mother.

But the boy died in the night.

And even as he lay dead, his mother heard her brother's voice saying to her: "My God, Hester, you're eighty-odd thousand to the good, and a poor devil of a son to the bad. But, poor devil, poor devil, he's best gone out of a life where he rides his rocking horse to find a winner."

"A RECLUSE"

WALTER DE LA MARE

Which of the world's wiseacres, I wonder, was responsible for the aphorism that "the best things in life are to be found at its edges?" It is too vague, of course. So much depends on what you mean by the "best" and the "edges." And in any case, most of us prefer the central. It has been explored; it is safe; you know where you are; it has been amply, copiously corroborated. But, "Amusing? Well, hardly. Quite so!" as my friend, Mr. Bloom, would have said. But then, Mr. Bloom has now ventured beyond the utmost borderline. He has passed over. He is, I imagine, interested in edges no longer.

I have been reminded of him again—as if there were any need of it!—by an announcement in *The Times.* His "mansion," Montrésor, is for sale by auction. The auctioneers are enthusiastic: "This singularly charming freehold residential property ... n all about thirty-eight acres ... the Matured Pleasure Grounds of unusual beauty." I don't deny it. But was it discreet of them to describe the house itself as an *imposing* mansion? A pair of slippers in my possession prompts this query. But how answer it? I can only make my record as full, concise, and definite as possible.

It was an afternoon towards the end of May—a Thursday. I had been to see a friend who, after a dangerous illness, was now apparently convalescent. We sat talking awhile, he propped up on his pillow, his eyes fixed on the green branches beyond his window, and that bleak, hungry look on his face one knows so well. It was pathetic to watch his greedy admiration of the flowers I had brought him, though he could scarcely more than whisper his pleasure. We discussed the weather, a new novel or two. He told me of his plans—in the most matter-of-fact fashion.

But when we fell silent, and the nurse covertly looked in, I rose with an almost indecent readiness, clasped his cold, bony hand in mine, and bade him goodbye.

It is always a relief to leave a sick room—to breathe freely again after that drugged and stagnant atmosphere. The medicine bottles, the stuffiness, the dulcet optimism: dismal reminders! I confess I found myself softly whistling as I climbed back into my cosy two-seater again. A lime-tree bower her garage was: the flickering leafy evening sunshine gilding the dust on her bonnet. I released the brake; she leapt to life again.

And what wonder? Flora and her nymphs might at any moment turn the corner of this sequestered country road. I felt adventurous. It would be miserably unenterprising to go back by the way I had come. I should *find* my way home.

Early evening is, with dawn, day's most seductive hour; and how entrancing is any scene on earth after even a fleeting glance into the valley of shadows. The woods and meadows were almost absurdly gay in their new green coats and garlands—the looping, wild-flowered lanes, the buttercup hollows, the parsleyed nooks and dusky coppices, the amorous birds and butterflies. Nothing lovely can long endure. The sweet and sickly blossom of the hawthorns hinted at that. Drowsy, lush, tepid, inexhaustible—an English evening.

And as I bowled idly on, I overtook a horseman. So far as I can see he has nothing whatever to do with what comes after —no more, at most, than my poor thin-nosed, gasping friend. I put him in because he put himself in. And in an odd way too. For at first sight (and at a distance) I mistook the creature for a bird—a large, strange, ungainly bird. It was the cardboard box he was carrying accounted for that.

Many shades lighter than his clothes and his horse, it lay on his back cornerwise, suspended about his neck with a piece of rope. As he trotted along, he bumped in the saddle, and his box bumped too. Meanwhile, odd mechanical creature, he beat time to his bumping on his animal's shoulder blade with a little leafy switch he carried. I glanced up into his face as I passed him—a greyish, hairy, indefinite face, like a miller's. To mistake a cardboard box for a bird! He amused me, I burst out laughing; never dreaming but that he was gone forever.

Five or six miles farther on, after passing a huddle of derelict Tudor cottages and a duckpond, I caught my first glimpse of the house, of Montrésor; and I defy anybody with eyes in his head to pass that house unheeded. And as I sat looking at it through its wrought-iron gates, I heard presently the beating of a horse's hoofs in the dust. Even before I glanced over my shoulder, I knew what I should see, my man on horse-back. He had taken the high road, I the low.

> There rode a Miller on a horse,
> A jake on a donkey could do no worse—
> With a Hey, and a Hey, hollie, ho!
> Meal on his chops and his whiskers too—

The devil sowed tares where the tare-crop grew—
With a Hey, and a Hey, hollie, ho!

Up he bumped, down he bumped, and his leafy switch kept time. When he drew level, I twisted my head round, and yelled up at him a question about the house. The curmudgeon never so much as paused. He merely pushed that indiscriminately hairy face a half-foot or so towards me, and flung up his hand with the switch. Maybe the poor fellow was dumb; his raw-boned horse had coughed, as if in sympathy. But anyhow his gesture seemed clearly to intimate—though with unnecessary violence—that Montrésor wasn't worth asking questions about, that I had better "move on." And, naturally, it intensi-fied my interest. I watched him out of sight. Why I have mentioned him I scarcely know, except that there he was, for an instant, at those gates. And as soon as he was gone, I turned to enjoy another look at the house—a prolonged look too.

To all appearance it was vacant; but if so, it could not have been vacant long. The drive was sadly in need of weeding: it was green with moss; but the lawns had been recently mown. High-grown forest trees towered round about it, over-topping its roof—chiefly chestnuts, their curved lower branches drooping so close to the turf that they almost brushed its surface. They were festooned from crown to root with branching candelabra-like spikes of blossom. Imagine them on a still, pitch-black night, their every cup of blossom upholding a tiny, phosphoric taper!

Not that Montrésor (or rather the two-thirds of its facade within sight) was a particularly old or beautiful house. It looked to have been built about 1750 and—like the character-istic work of that period, from furniture to verse—was of pleasant proportions. But it had "atmosphere." It wore a look of reticence, rather than of mystery. It seemed to be holding back from the interloper's scrutiny; to be positively taking advantage of the cover afforded by those widespread, blossoming branches.

"I could an' I would," it whispered, as do certain human faces; though no doubt the queer gesture and the queerer looks of my cardboard-boxed gentleman on horseback accounted for something of its effects.

A thin haze of cloud had spread over the sky, paling its blue. The sun had set; and a diffused light hung over its walls and roof. It suited the house—as powder may suit a pale face. Even Nature appeared to be condoning these artifices—those hollowish lawns, the honeyed azaleas, those stagnant chestnuts.

How absurd are one's little hesitations. All this while I had been debating whether to approach nearer on foot or to drive boldly in. I think I chose the second alternative with the faint notion in my mind that it would ensure me, if necessary, a speedier retreat. But then, premonitions are apt to display themselves a little clearer in retrospect! Anyhow, if I had *walked* up to the house, that night would not have been spent with Mr. Bloom. Mine is a quiet little car. I put her into gear, and glided gently in under the spreading chestnut trees towards the entrance: and there came to a standstill.

A wide, low porch supported by four slender stone columns sheltered the beautiful doorway. The metalwork of its fanlight, like that of the gates, was adorned with the device of the pelican feeding her young. Mr. Bloom's crest, no doubt. But in spite of the simplicity of the porch, it was not in keeping, and may have been a later addition to the house. Its echoings stilled, I sat on in the car, idly surveying the scene around me, and almost without conscious thought of it. What state of mind can be more serene—or more active?

No notice whatever seemed to have been taken of my

intrusion. Silence, silence remained. Indeed, considering the abundant cover around me, there was curiously little bird song —only a faraway thrush calling faintly, "Ahoy! Ahoy! Ahoy! Come to tea! Come to tea!" After all it was the merry month of May, and still early. But near at hand, not even a wren sounded. So presently I got out of the car, and mooned off to the end of the shallow, stone-vased terrace, stepping deliberately from tuft to tuft of grass and moss. Only a dense shrubbery beyond: yew, ilex, holly; a dampish winding walk. But on this north side of the house there were blinds to the windows, and curtains too—faded but pleasant in colour.

What few live things may have spied out the intruder had instantly withdrawn. I sighed, and turned away. The forsaken pierces quicker to the heart than by way of the mind. My car looked oddly out of place—even a little homesick!—under the porch, and was as grey with dust as my pseudo-miller's whiskers. I had come to the conclusion quite wrongly—that for the time being the place was unoccupied; though possibly at any moment caretaker or housekeeper might reappear.

Indeed, my foot was actually on the step of the car, when, as if at a definite summons, I turned my head and discovered not only that the door was now open, but that a figure—Mr. Bloom's—was standing a pace or so beyond the threshold, his regard steadily fixed on myself. Mr. Bloom—a memorable figure. He must have been well over six feet in height, but carried his heavy head and shoulders with a pronounced stoop. He was both stout and fat, but his clothes now hung loosely upon him, as if made to old measurements—a wide, black morning-coat and waistcoat, and brown cloth trousers. I noticed in particular his elegant boots. They were adorned with what I then supposed was an obsolete device—imitation laces. A well-cut pair of boots from a good maker's. His head was bald on the crown above a fine lofty forehead—but it wore a superfluity of side hair, and his face was bushily bearded. With head drawn back a little, he was surveying me from under very powerful magnifying spectacles, his left hand resting on the inside handle of the door.

He had taken me so much by surprise that for the moment I was speechless. We merely looked at one another; he, with a more easily justifiable intentness than I. He seemed, as the saying goes, to be sizing me up; to be fitting me in; and it was his voice that at length set the porch echoing again—a voice, as might have been inferred from the look of him, sonorous but muffled, as if his beard interfered with its resonance.

"I see you are interested in the appearance of my house," he was saying.

The greeting was courteous enough; and yet extraordinarily impersonal. I made the lamest apologies, adding some trivial comment on the picturesqueness of the scene, and the general "evening effects." But of this I am certain: the one thing uppermost in my mind, even at this stage in our brief acquaintance, was the desire not to continue the interview. Mr. Bloom had somehow exhausted my interest in his house. I wanted to shake him off, to go away. He was an empty-looking man in spite of his domed brow. His house had suggested vacancy, so did he—not of human inmate, that is, but of pleasing interest! Far from countenancing this inclination, he was inviting me to continue my survey. He was welcoming the interloper. After a slow comprehensive glance to left and right, he actually stepped out under the porch, and—with a peculiar tentative gesture—thrust out a well-kept, fleshy hand in my direction, as if with the intention of putting me entirely at my ease. He then stood solemnly scrutinizing my tiny car.

At a loss for any alternative, I withdrew a few paces, and took another long look at the facade—the blank windows, their red-brick mouldings, the peeping chimney-stacks, the simple, serene sufficiency of it all. There was a sorry little array, I remember, of abandoned martins' nests plastered up under the narrow jutting of the roof. But this craning attitude was fatiguing, and I returned to the porch.

Mr. Bloom had not stirred. He looked like a provincial statue of some forgotten Victorian notability—his feet set close together in those neat, polished, indoor boots, his right hand on his watch-chain.

And now he seemed to be smiling at me out of his bluish-grey, rather prominent eyes, from under those thick distorting lenses. He was suggesting that I should "come in." It was an invitation innocent of warmth, but more pressing than its mere words implied. The wreathing, seductive odour of toasted cheese—before the actual trap comes into sight—must be similar in effect. There was a suppressed eagerness in the eyes behind those glasses. They had rolled a little in their sockets. And yet, even so, why should I have distrusted him? It would be monstrous to take this world solely on its face value! I was on the point of blurting out a churlish refusal when he stepped back and pushed the door open. The glimpse beyond decided me.

For the hall within was peculiarly attractive. Not very lofty, but of admirable proportions, it was panelled in light wood, the carving on its cornice and pilasters tinged in here and there with gilt. From its roof hung three chandeliers of greenish-grey glass—entrancing things resembling that mysterious exquisite ice that comes only from Waterford. The evening light swam softly in through the uncurtained windows, as if upon the still-ness of a dream.

Empty, it would have been a fascinating room; but just now it was grotesquely packed with old furniture—beautiful, costly things in themselves, but, in this hugger-mugger, robbed of charm and grace. Only the narrowest alleyway had been left unoccupied—an alleyway hardly wide enough to enable a human being to come and go without positively mounting up off the floor, as in the Land-and-Water game beloved of children. It might have been some antique furniture dealer's interior, prepared for "a moonlight flit."

Having thus enticed me in under his roof, Mr. Bloom rapidly motioned me on, not even turning his head to see if I were following him. For so cumbersome a man he was agile, and at the dusky twist of the corridor I found him already awaiting me, his hand on an inner door.

"This is the library," he informed me, with a suavity that suggested my being a wealthy visitor to whom he wished to dispose of the property. "One moment," he added hurriedly, "I think I neglected to shut the outer door."

A library is often in effect little better than a mausoleum; but on a sunny morning this room must have been as gay as a beautiful young heiress's boudoir. It was evening now. Faded Persian rugs lay on the floor; there was a large writing table. The immense armchairs were covered with red Morocco leather, and the walls, apart from a few engravings and mezzotints, were lined with books. On one side the books had been removed and lay stacked up in portable bundles beneath the shelves on which they had stood. On the other was a lofty chimney-piece of carved stone. And once again the self-sacrificing pelican showed in the stone—engaged in feeding her brood.

I was looking out of the French windows when Mr. Bloom reappeared. He still seemed to be smiling in his non-committal fashion, and treated me to yet another slow scrutiny, the most conspicuous feature of his person, apart from his spectacles, being at such moments the spade guinea that dangled from his watch-chain. Brown trousers, my friend, I was thinking to myself, why brown? And why not wear clothes that fit?

"You are a lover of books?" he was murmuring, in that flat, muffled voice of his; and we were soon conversing amiably enough on the diversions of literature. He led me steadily from shelf to shelf; but for the time being he was only making conversation. He was detaining me for his own purposes, and successfully staved off every opportunity I attempted to seize of extricating myself from his company. At last, I bluntly held out my hand, and in spite of his protestations—so insistent that he began stuttering—I made my way out of the room.

Daylight was fading now, and the spectacle of that hoard of furniture in the gloaming was oddly depressing.

Mr. Bloom had followed me out, cooing, as he came on, his protestations and regrets that I could spare him no more time —"The upper rooms ... the garden ... my China."

I persisted, nevertheless, and myself opened the outer door; and there in the twilight, with as disconsolate an appearance as a cocker spaniel that has wearied of waiting for its mistress, sat my car.

I had actually taken my seat in it—having omitted to shake hands with Mr. Bloom—when I noticed that the little Yale gear key was missing. Misadventures like this are absolutely disconcerting. I searched my pockets; leapt out of the car and searched them again; and not only in vain, but without the faintest recollection in my mind of having removed the key. It was a ridiculous, a mortifying situation. With eyes fixed, in an effort to recall my every movement, I gazed out over the wide, green turf beneath the motionless chestnut trees, and then at last turned again, and looked at Mr. Bloom.

With plump hands held loosely and helplessly a little in front of him, and head on one side, he was watching my efforts with an almost paternal concern.

"I have mislaid the key," I almost shouted at him, as if the old man were hard of hearing.

"Is it anything of importance? Can I get you anything? Water? A little grease?"

That one word, grease, was accompanied with so ridiculous a trill that I lost patience.

"It's the gear key," I snapped at him. "She's fixed, immovable, useless! I wish to heaven I—" I began aimlessly, fretfully searching the porch, the turf beyond. Mr. Bloom watched me with the solicitude of a mother. "I ought to have been home an hour ago," I stuttered over my shoulder.

"Most vexatious! Dear me! I am distressed. But my memory too ... absentmindedness. Do you think by any chance, Mr. Dash, you can have put the key in your *pocket*?"

I stared at him. The suggestion was little short of imbecile; and yet he had evidently had the sagacity to look for my name on my handbag! "What is the nearest town?" I all but shouted.

"The nearest," he echoed; "ah, the nearest! Now, let me see! The nearest *town*—garage, of course. A nice question. Come in again. We must get a map; yes, a map, don't you think? That will be our best course: an excellent plan."

I thrust my hand into the leather pocket of the car, and produced my own. But only the eyes of an owl could have read its lettering in that light, and somehow it did not occur to me in this tranquil dusky scene to switch on the lamps. There was no alternative. I followed Mr. Bloom into the house again, and on into his study. He lit a couple of candles; we sat down together at the writing table and examined the map. It was the closest I ever got to him.

The position was ludicrous. Montrésor was a good four miles from the nearest village of any size; seven from the nearest railway station—and that on a branch line. And here was this old man peppering me with futile advice and offers of assistance, and yet obviously beaming with satisfaction at my dilemma. There was not even a servant in the house to take a telegram to the village—if a telegram had been of the slightest use. I hastily folded up my map—folded it up wrong, of course —and sat glooming. He was breathing a little rapidly after this exercise of intelligence.

"But why be disturbed?" he entreated me. "Why? A misadventure; but of no importance. Indeed not. You will give me the pleasure of being my guest for the night—nothing but a happiness, I assure you. Say no more. It won't incommode me in the slightest degree. This old house ... a most unfortunate accident. They should make larger, heavier keys. Ridiculous! But then I am no mechanic."

He stooped round at me—the loose, copious creature— and was almost coy. "Frankly, my dear young sir, I cannot regret an accident that promises me more of your company. We bookish people, you understand."

I protested, stood up, and once more began searching my pockets! His head jerked back into its habitual posture.

"Ah! I see what is in your mind. Think nothing of it. Yes, yes, yes. Comforts, conveniences curtailed, I agree. But my good housekeeper always prepares a meal sufficient for two— mere habit, Mr. Dash, almost animal habit. And besides—why not? I will forage for myself. A meal miscellaneous, perhaps, but not unsatisfying." He beamed. "Why not take a look at the garden meanwhile before it is dark?" The tones had fallen still flatter; the face had become immobile.

I was cornered. It was useless to protest—it would have been atrociously uncivil. He himself thrust open the windows for me. Fuming within, I stumped out on to the terrace while he went off to "forage." I saw in fancy those thick spectacles eyeing the broken meats in the great larder. What was wrong with the man? What made him so extortionately substantial, and yet in effect, so elusive and unreal? What indeed constitutes the reality of a fellow creature in himself? The something, the someone within, surely, not the mere physical frame.

In Mr. Bloom's company that physical frame seemed to be mainly a kind of stalking horse. If so, the fowler was exquisitely intent on not alarming his prey. Those honeyed decoynotes. But then, what conceivably could he want of *me*? Whom had he been waiting for, skulking there at some convenient window? Why was he alone in this great house? Only Mr. Bloom could answer these questions: and owing to some odd scruple of manners or what-not, I couldn't put them to him. Absurd!

My mind, by this time, wearied of these vexations, had begun to follow my eyes. I was looking northward—a clear lustre as of glass now in the heavens. It had been a calm but almost colourless sunset, and westward the evening star floated like a morsel of silver in a dove-grey fleece of cloud drawn gently across the blue of the horizon. The countryside lay darkly purple and saturnine, and about a hundred yards away in this direction was a wide stretch of water dead-white under the sky—a lake; wild-fowl; yet not so much as a peewit crying.

In front of me, the garden was densely walled in with trees, and an exceedingly skillful topiarist had been at work on the nearer yews. Year after year he must have been clipping his birds and arches and vast mushrooms and even an obelisk. They were now in their freshest green. Mr. Bloom's servants cannot have forsaken him in a batch. They were gone, though. Not a light showed in the dusk; no movement; no sound except out of the far distance presently the faint dreamlike *churring* of a nightjar. It is the bird of wooded solitude. Well, there would be something of a moon that night, I knew. She would charm out the owls, and should at least ensure me a lullaby. But why this distaste, this sense of inward disquietude?

And suddenly I wheeled about at the sound, as I thought, of a footstep. But no; I was alone. Mr. Bloom must still be busy foraging in his back quarters or his cellarage. And yet (is it credible?) once more in a last forlorn hope I began to search my pockets for the missing key! But this time Mr. Bloom interrupted the operation. He came out sleeking his hands together in front of him and looking as amiably hospitable as a churchwarden at a parochial conversazione. He led me in, volubly explaining the while that since he had been alone in the house, he had all but given up the use of the upper rooms.

"As a matter of fact, I am preparing to leave," he told me, "As soon as it is—convenient. Meanwhile I camp on the ground floor. There is many a novelty in the ordinary routine of life, Mr. Dash, that we seldom enjoy. It amused my secretary, this system of picnicking, poor fellow, for a while!"

He came to a standstill on the threshold of the room into which he was leading me. A cluster of candles burned on the long oak table set out for our evening meal, but otherwise the room—not very much smaller than the study, and containing almost as many books—was thickly curtained and in darkness.

"I must explain," he was saying, and he laid the four fingers of his left hand very gently on my shoulder, "that my secretary has left me. He has left me for good. He is dead." With owl-like solemnity he scrutinized the blank face I turned on him, as if he were expectant of sympathy. But I had none to give. You can't even feign sympathy without preparation.

Mr. Bloom glanced over his shoulder into the corridor behind us. "He has been a great loss," he added. "I miss him. On the other hand," he added more cheerfully, "we mustn't allow our personal feelings to interfere with the enjoyment of what I am afraid even at best is an extremely modest little meal."

Again Mr. Bloom was showing himself incapable of facing

facts. It was by no means a modest little meal. Our cold bouillon was followed by a pair of spring chickens, the white sauce on their delicate breasts adorned in the most elegant design with fragments of cucumber, radish, truffle and mushroom. There was an asparagus salad, so cold to the tongue as to suggest ice; and neighbouring it were a dish of meringues and an amber-coloured wine jelly, richly clotted with cream. Champagne was our wine; and it was solely owing to my abstemiousness that we failed to finish the second bottle.

Between his mouthfuls Mr. Bloom indulged in general conversation—of the exclamatory order. It covered a pretty wide autobiographical field. He told me of his boyhood in Montrésor. The estate had been in his family for close on two centuries. These last few years he had shared it with an only sister.

"She's there!" he exclaimed, pointing an instant with uplifted fork at a portrait that hung to the right of the chimney-piece. I glanced up at Miss Bloom; but she was looking in the other direction, and our real and painted eyes did not meet. It seemed incredible that these two could ever have been children, have played together, giggled, quarrelled, and made it up. Even if I could imagine the extinguished lady in the portrait as a little girl, no feat of fancy could convert Mr. Bloom into a small boy—a sufferable one, I mean.

By the time I had given up the attempt, and, having abandoned the jelly, we had set to work on the Camembert cheese, Mr. Bloom's remarks about his secretary had become almost aggrieved.

"He was of indispensable use to me in my literary work— modest enough in itself—I won't trouble you with that—only an obscure by-way of interest. Indispensable. We differed in our views, of course: no human beings ever see perfectly eye to eye on such a topic. In a word, the occult. But he had an unusual *flair.*" He laid his left hand on the table. "I am not denying that for one moment. We succeeded in attaining the most curious and interesting results from our little experiments. I could astonish you."

I tried in vain to welcome the suggestion; but the light even of four candles is a little stupefying when one has to gaze through them at one's host, and Mr. Bloom was sitting immediately opposite to me on the other side of the table.

"My own personal view," he explained, "is that his ill health was in no way due to these investigations. Indeed, it was against my wish that he should continue them on his own account, Flatly, two heads, two wills, two cautions even, I might say, are better than one in such matters. Dr. Ponsonby— I should explain that Dr. Ponsonby is my medical adviser; he attended my poor sister in her last illness—Dr. Ponsonby, unfortunately, lives at some little distance, but he did not hesitate to sacrifice all the time he could spare. On the other hand, as far as I can gather, he was not in the least surprised that when the end came, it came suddenly. My secretary, Mr. Dash, was found dead in his bed—that is, in his bedroom. Speaking for myself, I should"—back went his head again, and once more his slightly bolting eyes gazed out at me like polished agates across the silvery lustre of the candlelight—"speaking for myself"—his voice muffled itself almost to the inarticulate beneath his beard—"I should prefer to go quickly when I have to go at all."

The white plump hand replenished his glass with champagne. "Not that I intend to imply that I have any immediate desire for that. You, yourself," he added almost merrily, "having enjoyed only a third of my experience in this world, must desire that consummation even less."

"You mean, to die, Mr. Bloom?" I put it to him. His chin

lowered itself into his collar again; the eyelids descended over his eyes.

"Precisely. Though it is as well to remember there is more than one way of dying. There is first the body to be taken into account; and there is next, what remains: though nowadays, of course—well, I leave it to you."

Mr. Bloom was a peculiar conversationalist. Like an astute letter writer, he ignored questions in which he was not interested, or did not wish to answer; and with the agility of a chimpanzee in its native wilds would swing off from a topic not to his liking to another that up to that point had not even been hinted at. Quite early in our *tête-à-tête* meal I began to suspect that the secret of his welcome to a visitor who had involuntarily descended on him out of the blue, was a desire to indulge in talk. Events proved this to be true only in part. But in the meantime, it became pretty evident why Mr. Bloom should be in want of company; I mean of ordinary human company. He seemed to have wearied of his secretary some little time before that secretary had been summoned away.

"You will agree, my dear sir, that to see eye to eye with an invalid for any protracted period is a severe strain. Illness breeds fancies, not all of them considerate. Not a happy youth, *ever*: introspective—an 'introvert' in the cant of our time. But still meaning well; and oh yes, endeavouring not to give way when—when in company. My sister never really liked him. But then, she was the prey of conventions that are yet for some, maybe, a safeguard. We shared the same interests, of course—he and I. Our arrangement was based on that. He had his own views, but at times, oh yes"— he filled his glass again—"exceedingly obstinate about them. He had little *staying* power. He began to fumble, to hesitate, to question, to fluster himself—and me, too, for that matter—just when we were arriving at an excessively interesting juncture.

"You know the general process, of course?" He had glanced up over his food at me, but not in order to listen to any answer I might have given. "It is this,"—and he forthwith embarked on a long and tedious discourse concerning the sweet uses of the planchette, of automatic writing, table-rapping, the hidden slate, ectoplasm, and all the other—to me rather disagreeable —paraphernalia of the spiritualistic séance, Nothing I could say or do, not even unconcealed and deliberate yawning, had the least effect upon Mr. Bloom's fluency. Lung trouble appeared to have been the primary cause of his secretary's final resignation. But if the unfortunate young man had night after night been submitted to the experience that I was now enduring, exasperation and boredom alone would have accounted for it. How on earth indeed, I asked myself, could he have endured Mr. Bloom so long.

I ceased to listen. The cascade of talk suddenly came to an end. Mr. Bloom laid his hands on either side of his plate and once more fixed me in silence under his glasses. "You, yourself, have possibly dabbled a little in my hobby?" he inquired.

I had indeed. In my young days my family had possessed an elderly female friend—a Miss Altogood. She had been one of my mother's bridesmaids, and it was an unwritten law in the household that every possible consideration and affection should be shown to her in all circumstances. The poor soul— she had come down in the world—lived on the top floor in lodgings in Westbourne Park. She was tall, gaunt, dark, and affectionate; and she had a consuming interest in the other world. I hear her now: "On the other side, my dear Charles."— "Another plane, Charles."—"When I myself pass over."

For old sake's sake, and I am afraid for very little else, I used to go to tea with her occasionally. And we would sit together, the heat welling up out of the sun-struck street outside her window; and she would bring out the hateful little round Victorian table, and the wine glass and the cardboard alphabet; and we'd ask questions of the unseen, the mischievous, the half-crazy, the unknowable; and she would grow flushed and excited and full of trepidations and misgivings and triumphs. And though I can honestly say I never deliberately tampered with that execrable little wine glass in its wanderings over the varnished table; and though she herself never deliberately cooked the messages it spelt out for us; we enjoyed astonishing revelations.

Those "spiritualistic" answers to our cross-examination were at the same time so unintelligibly intelligent, and so unutterably silly and futile, that my mind had been cured once and for all of the faintest interest in the "other side." If anything, in fact, the experience had even a little tarnished the side Mr. Bloom now shared with me.

For this reason alone, his first mention of the subject had almost completely taken away my appetite for his cold chicken, his asparagus, his jelly, his champagne. After all, that "other side's" borderline from which, according to the poet, no traveller returns, must be a good many miles longer even than the wall of China, and not *all* its gates can lead to plains of peace or paradise or even human endurableness.

I explained at last to Mr. Bloom that my interest in spiritualism was of the tepidest variety. Those prominent stone-blue eyes of his, faintly illuminated by the concentrated candlelight, incited me to be more emphatic than I intended. I told him I detested the whole subject.

"It is my conviction," I assured him, "that if the messages, results, whatever you like to call them, are anything else than the babblings of subconsciousness—a deadly dubious term, in itself—then they are probably the work of something or somebody even more 'sub' than that."

I *knew* very little at firsthand about the subject, but ignorance, of course, gives one strength. "Whatever I have heard," I told him, "from *that* source, of the future that awaits us when we get out of this body of ours, Mr. Bloom, fills me with nothing but regret that this life is not the end of everything. I don't say that you get *no*where, and I don't say that you mayn't get further someday than you intend, but," I stupidly blustered on, "my own personal opinion is that the whole business, so conducted, is a silly and dangerous waste of time."

His eyes never wavered; he lowered his head by not the fraction of an inch.

"All that you are saying, my dear Mr. Dash," he replied, "amuses me. Extraordinary! Most amusing! Illuminating! Quite so! Quite so! Capital! You tell me that you know nothing about the subject. Oh yes! And that it is silly and dangerous. Ah, yes! And why not? Dangerous! Well, one word in your ear. Here, my dear sir, we are in the very thick of it; a positive hot bed. But if there is one course I should avoid"—his eyes withdrew themselves, and the thick glasses blazed into the candlelight once more—"it would be that of taking any personal steps to initiate you into—into our mysteries. No. I shall leave matters completely to themselves."

His intonation had been equable; his expression had never wavered; only his thick fingers trembled a little on the tablecloth. But he was grey with rage. It seemed even that the scalp of his head had a little raised the hair on its either side, so intense was his resentment.

"A happy state—ignorance, Mr. Dash? That of our first parents?"

And then, like a fool, I flared up and mentioned Miss Altogood. He listened, steadily smiling.

"I see; a professional medium," he insinuated at last with a shrug of his great heavy shoulders. "Pooh! Banal!"

I hotly defended my well-meaning sentimental old friend.

"Ah, indeed, a retired governess!" and once more his rage nearly mastered him. "Have no fear, Mr. Dash, she is not on my visiting list. There are deeps, and vasty deeps."

With that he thrust out a hand and caught up the chicken bone that had long lain discarded on my plate.

"Come out there!" he called baldly. "Here, you!" His head dipped out of sight as he stooped; and a yellowish dog—with a white-gleaming sidelong eye—of which up to the present I had seen or heard no symptom, came skulking out from under a chair in the corner of the room to enjoy its evening meal. For awhile, only the crunching of teeth on bones broke the silence.

"You greedy! You glutton!" Mr. Bloom was cajoling him. "Aye, but where's Steve? An animal's intelligence, Mr. Dash"—his voice floated up to me from under the other side of the table—"is concentrated in his belly. And even when one climbs up to human prejudices one usually finds the foundation as material."

For an instant I could make no reply to this pleasantry. He took advantage of the pause to present me with a smile.

"There, there: I refuse to disagree," he was saying. "Your company has been very welcome to me; and well—one should never embark on one's little private preserves without encouragement. My own in particular meet with very scant courtesy usually. That animal could tell a tale." The crunching continued. "Couldn't yer, you old rascal? Where's Steve; where's Steve? Now get along back!" The scrunching ceased. The yellowish dog retreated into its corner.

"And now, Mr. Dash," declared Mr. Bloom, "if you have sufficiently refreshed yourself, let us leave these remains. These last few years I have detested being encumbered with servants in the house. A foreign element. They are further away from us, I assure you, in all that really matters than that rascal, Chunks, there in the corner. Eh, you old devil?" he called at his pet, "ain't it so? Now, let me see,"—he took out a worn gold watch—"nine o'clock; h'm; h'm; h'm! Just nine! We have a long evening before us. Believe me, I am exceedingly grateful for your company, and regret that—but there, I see you have already forgiven an old man's edginess."

There was something curiously aimless, even pathetic in the tones of that last remark. He had eaten with excellent appetite, and had accounted for at least four-fifths of our champagne. But he rose from the table looking more dejected than I should have supposed possible, and shuffled away in his slippers, as if the last ten minutes had added years to his age.

He was leading the way with the candelabrum in his hand, but, to avoid their guttering, I suppose, had blown out three of its candles. A dusky moonlight loomed beyond the long French windows of his study. The faint earthy scent of spring and night saturated the air, for one of them was open. He paused at sight of it, glancing about him.

"If there is an animal I cannot endure," he muttered over his shoulder at me, "it is the cat—the feline cat. They have a history; they retreat into the past; we meet them in far other circumstances. Yes, yes."

He had closed and bolted the window, drawn shutters and curtains, while he was speaking.

"And now, bless my soul, Mr. Dash, how about your room!" With feet close together he stood looking at me. "My secretary's, now?—would that meet the case? He was a creature of comfort. But one has fancies, reluctances, perhaps. As I say, the upper rooms are all dismantled, though we might put up a camp-bed up there; and—and water in the bathroom. I myself sleep in here."

He stepped across and drew aside a curtain hung between the bookcases. But there was not light enough to see beyond it.

"The room I propose is also on this floor, so we should not, if need be, be far apart. Eh? Now come this way."

He paused. Once more he led me out, and stopped at the third door of the corridor on the left-hand side. So long was the pause, one might have supposed he was waiting for permission to enter. I followed him in. It was a lofty room—a bed-sitting room; its curtains and upholstery of a pale purple. Its window was shut, the air stuffy and faintly sweet. The bed was in the further corner to the left of the window; and there again the dusky moonlight showed.

I sat looking at the mute inanimate things around me in that blending of the two faint lights. No doubt if I had been ignorant that the owner, or user of the room, had made his last exit there, I should have noticed little unusual in its stillness, its vacant calm. And yet, well, I had left a friend only that afternoon still a little breathless after his scramble up the nearer bank of the Jordan. And now, this was the last place on earth—these four walls, these colours, this bookcase, that table, that window—which Mr. Bloom's secretary had set eyes on before setting out, not to return.

My host watched me. He would, I think, have pulled the curtains over these windows too, if I had given him an opportunity.

"You think you—I hesitate to press the matter—but in fact, Mr. Dash, it is the only room I *can* offer you."

I thanked him, assuring him that I should be comfortable.

"Capital!" cried Mr. Bloom. "Excellent! My only apprehension—well, you know how sensitive people may be. You will find me in the study, and I can assure you that one little theme shall not intrude on us again. The bee may buzz, but I will keep my bonnet on! The fourth door on the right—after turning to your right down the corridor. Ah! I am leaving you no light."

He lit the candles on his secretary's dressing table and withdrew.

I myself stood for a while gazing stupidly out of the window. Apart from his extraordinary fluency, Mr. Bloom, I realized, was an exceedingly secretive old man. I had known all along that it was not my beautiful eyes he was after! nor even my mere company. The old creature—admirable mask though his outward appearance might be—was on edge. He was detesting his solitude, though until recently, at any rate, it had been the one aim of his life. It had even occurred to me that he was not much "missing" his secretary. Quite the reverse. He had spoken of him with contempt. There were two things unforgiven in Mr. Bloom's mind indeed: some acute disagreement between them and the fact that Mr. Champneys had left him without due notice—unless inefficient lungs constitute due notice.

I took one of the candles and glanced at the books. They were chiefly of fiction and a little poetry. There was a complete row of manuscript books with pigskin backs labelled *Proceedings*. I turned to the writing table. Little there of interest—a stopped clock, a dried-up inkwell, a tarnished silver cup, and one or two books: *The Sentimental Journey*, a *Thomas à Kempis*, bound in limp maroon leather. I opened the *Thomas à Kempis*, and read the spidery inscription on the flyleaf: "To darling Sidney, with love from Mother." It startled me, as if I had been caught in a theft.

"Life surely should never come to that," some secret voice within piped out of the void.

I shut the book up.

The drawer beneath contained only envelopes and letter paper—*Montrésor*, in large pale-blue letters on a Silurian background—and a thick black exercise book, with a label *Diary: S. S. Champneys*. I glanced up, then turned to the last entry—

dated only six weeks ago—just a few scribbled words: "Not me, at any rate: not me. And even if I could get away for—" the ink was smudged and had left its ghost on the blank page opposite it. A mere scrap of feminine handwriting and that poor hasty smudge of ink—they resembled an incantation; Mr. Bloom's secretary himself seemed to be sharing his secrets with me. I shut up that book too, and turned away.

To my astonishment a log fire was handsomely burning in the grate when I returned to the study, and Mr. Bloom, having drawn up two of his voluminous armchairs in front of it, was now deeply and amply encased in one of them. He had taken off his spectacles, and appeared to be asleep. But his eyes opened at my footstep. He had been merely "resting" perhaps.

"I hope," was his greeting, "you found everything needful, Mr. Dash? In the circumstances ..."

He called this up at me as if I were at a distance, but his tone subsided again. "But there's just one little matter we missed, eh?—night attire! Not that you wouldn't find a complete trousseau to choose from in the wardrobe. My secretary, in fact, was inclined to be foppish. No blame; no blame: fine feathers, Mr. Dash."

It is, thank heaven, an unusual experience to be compelled to share an evening as the guest of a stranger one distrusts. It was not only that Mr. Bloom's manner was obviously a mask, but even the occasional stupidity of his remarks seemed to be an affectation—and one of a rare and dangerous kind. As for Montrésor—it was the simplest and happiest of things. It shared its quiet, eighteenth-century charm with its every door plate and moulding. One fell in love with it at first sight, as with an open, charming face. But then—a look in the eyes! It reeked of the dubious and distasteful. But how can one produce definite evidence for such sensations as these? They lie outside the tests even of mighty Science—as must a good many other things that don't conform with the norm of human evidence.

Mr. Bloom's company at a dinner party or a reception might have proved refreshingly droll. He did his best to make himself amusing. He had read widely—and out-of-the way books, too; and had an unusual range of interests. We discussed music and art—and he brought out portfolio after portfolio of drawings and etchings to illustrate some absurd theory he had of the one, and play a scrap or two of Debussy and Ravel to prove some far-fetched little theory of his own about the other. We talked of Chance and Dreams and Disease and Heredity, edged on to Woman, and skated rapidly away. He dismissed life as "an episode in disconcerting surroundings," and scuttled off from a eulogy of Fabre to the problem of pain.

"Mr. Dash, we *fear* pain too much—and the giving of it. The very mention of the word stifles me. And how unchristian!"

The look he peeked down at me at this was proof enough that he was intent only on decoying me on and drawing me out. But I was becoming a little more cautious, and suggested that that kind of philosophy best begins at home.

"Aye, indeed! A retort, a retort. With Charity on the other side of the hearth in a mobcap and carpet slippers, I suppose. I see the dear creatures: I see them! Still, you will agree, even *you* will agree that once, Mr. Dash, the head loses its way in the heart, one's brainpan might as well be a basin of soap bubbles. A man of feeling by all means—but just a trace, a soupçon of rationality, well, it serves! Eh?"

A few minutes afterwards, in the midst of a discourse on

the progress of thought, he suddenly inquired if I cared for the game of backgammon.

"And why not? or draughts, Mr. Dash?—a grossly underestimated amusement."

But all this fluency, these high spirits were clearly an elaborate disguise. He was "keeping it up" merely to keep *me* up; and maybe, to keep himself up. Much of it was automatic—mere mental antics. Like a Tibetan praying-wheel, his mind went round and round. And his attention was divided. One at least of those long, narrow ears was cocked in another direction. And at last, the question that had been on my tongue throughout most of the evening popped out almost automatically. I asked if he were expecting a visitor. At the moment his round black back was turned; he was rummaging in a corner cupboard for glasses to accompany the decanter of whisky he had produced; his head turned slyly on his heavy shoulders.

"A visitor? You astonish me. Here? Now? As if, my dear Mr. Dash, this rural retreat were Bloomsbury or Mayfair. You amuse me. Callers! Thank heaven, not so. Be candid with me. Let us go back an hour or two. You came, you saw, but you did not *expect* a welcome. The unworthy tenant of Montrésor took you by surprise. Confess it! So be it. And why not? What if you yourself were my looked-for visitor? What then? There are surmises, intuitions, forebodings—to give a pleasant tinge to the word. Yes, yes, I agree. I was on the watch; patiently, *patiently*. In due time your charming little car appears at my gate. You pause: I say to myself, here he is. Company at last; discussion; powwow; even controversy perhaps. Why not? We are sharing the same hemisphere. Plain as a pikestaff. I foresaw your decision as may the shepherd in contemplation of a red sunrise foresee the deluge. I step downstairs; and here we are!"

My reply came a little more warmly than I intended. I assured Mr. Bloom that if it had not been for the loss of my key,

I shouldn't have stayed five minutes. "I prefer *not* to be expected in a strange house." It was unutterably *gauche*.

He chuckled; he shrugged his shoulders; he was vastly amused. "Ah, but are we not forgetting that such little misadventures are merely part and parcel of the general plan? The end-shaping process, as the poet puts it?"

"What general plan?"

"Mr. Dash, when you fire out your inquiries at me like bullets out of the muzzle of a gun, I am positively disconcerted, I can scarcely keep my wits together. Pray let us not treat each other like witnesses in the witness box, or even"—a catlike smile crept into his face "like prisoners in the dock. Have a little whisky? Pure malt; a tot? It may be whimsical, but for me one of the few exasperating things about my poor secretary, Mr. Champneys, was his aversion to 'alcohol!' £300 a year— Mr. Dash. No less. And everything 'found.' No expenses except fiction, pyjamas, tooth powder and petrol—a motor bicycle, in fact, now *hors de combat*. And 'alcohol,' if you please! What a word! What a libel! These specialists! Soda water or Apollinaris?"

In sheer chagrin I drank the stuff, and rose to turn in. Not a bit of it! With covert glances at his watch, Mr. Bloom kept me there by hook and by crook until it was long past midnight, and try as he might to conceal it, the disquietude that had peeped out earlier in the evening became more and more apparent. The only effect of this restlessness on his talk, however, was to increase its volume and incoherence. If Mr. Bloom had been play-acting, and had been cast for his own character, his improvisation could not have been more masterly. He hardly made any pretence now of listening to my small part in this display: and when he did, it was only in order to attend to some other business he had in mind. Ever and again, as if to emphasize his point, he would haul himself up out of his deep-bottomed chair, and edge off towards the door —with the pretence maybe of looking for a book. He would pause there for but an instant—and the bumbling muffled voice would once again take up his strain. Once, however, he came to a dead stop, raised his hand and openly stood listening.

"A nightingale certainly; if not two," he murmured *sotto voce*, "but tell me, Mr. Dash," he called softly out across the room, "was I deceived into thinking I heard a distant knocking? In a house large as this; articles of some value perhaps; we read even of violence. You never can tell."

I asked him with clumsy irony if there would be anything remarkable in that. "Don't your friends ever volunteer even a rap or two on their own account? I should have supposed it would be the least they could offer."

"A signal; m'm; a rap or two;" he echoed me blandly. "How that?"

"From 'the other side.'"

"Eh? Eh?" he suddenly broke off, his cheek whitening; the sole cause of his dismay being merely a scratching at the door panel, announcing that his faithful pet had so much wearied of solitude in the dining room that he had come seeking even his master's company. But Mr. Bloom did not open the door.

"Be off!" he called at the panel. "Away, sir! To your mat! That dog, Mr. Dash, is more than human—or shall we say, less than human." The words were jovial enough, but the lips that uttered them trembled beneath his beard.

I had had enough, and this time got my way. He accompanied me to the door of the study but not further, and held out his hand.

"If by any chance," he scarcely more than murmured, "you should want anything in the night, you will know, of course, where to find me; I am in there." He pointed. "On the other hand, Mr. Dash,"—he laid his hand again on my arm, deprecatingly, almost as if with shy affection—"I am an exceedingly poor sleeper. And occasionally I find a brief amble round proves a sedative. Follow me up. By all means. I should welcome it. But tonight, I expect—nothing."

He closed the door again. "Have you ever tried that particular remedy for insomnia? Mere cold air? Or perhaps a hard biscuit, just to humour the circulation. But a young man—no: the machine comparatively new. My housekeeper returns at six: breakfast, I hope, at eight-thirty. A most punctual woman; a treasure. But then, servants! I detest the whole race of them. Goodnight; goodnight. And none of those *Proceedings*, I warn you!"

But even now I had not completely shaken him off. He hastened after me, puffing as he came, and clutched at my coat sleeve.

"What I was meaning, Mr. Dash, is that I have never attempted to make converts—a fruit, let me tell you, that from being incredibly raw and unwholesome, rapidly goes rotten. Besides, my secretary had very little talent for marshalling facts. That's why I mentioned the *Proceedings*. A turn for *writing*, maybe, but no method. Just that. And now, of course, you *must* go. Our evening is at an end. But who knows? Of course. Never matter. What must come, comes."

At last, I was free, though his whisper presently pursued me down the corridor. "No need for caution, Mr. Dash, should you need me. No infants, no invalids; sleep well."

Having put my candlestick on the table, shut the door of Mr. Champneys's bedroom, and very softly locked it, I sat down on the bed to think things over. Easier said than done! The one thing in my mind was relief at finding myself alone again, and of distaste (as I wound my watch) at the recollection of how many hours still remained before dawn. I opened the window, and looked out. The porch was out of sight. Mr. Bloom's nightingales, if not creatures of his imagination, had ceased to lament. A ground mist lay like a lake of milk beneath the chestnut trees, soundlessly lapping their boughs.

I drew in. The draught had set my candle guttering. Almost automatically I opened one of the long drawers in Mr. Champneys's chest. It was crammed with his linen. Had he no relatives, then, I wondered, or had Mr. Bloom succeeded to his property? These pyjamas would grace an Arabian prince; of palest blue silk with 'S.S.C.' in beautiful scarlet lettering. It was fastidious perhaps, but I left them undisturbed.

There were a few photographs above the chimney piece; but photographs of the relatives and friends of a deceased stranger are not exhilarating company. Mr. Champneys himself being dead, these, too, seemed to be tinged with the same eclipse. One of them was a snapshot of a tall, dark, young man, in tennis clothes. He was smiling; he had a longish nose; a racket was under his arm; and a tiny strip of maroon and yellow ribbon had been glued to the frame. Another Champneys, a brother, perhaps. I stood there, idly gazing at it for minutes together, as if in search of inspiration.

No talker had ever more completely exhausted me than Mr. Bloom. Even while I was still deep in contemplation of the photograph, I was seized suddenly with a series of yawns almost painful in their intensity. I turned away. My one longing was for the bathroom. But no—Mr. Bloom had failed to show me the way there, and any attempt to find it for myself might involve me in more talk. It is embarrassing to meet anyone after farewells have been said—but *that* one: no. Half dressed, and having hunted in vain for a second box of matches, I lay down on the bed, drew its purple quilt over me —after all, Mr. Bloom's secretary had not died in it!—and blew out my candle.

I must have at once fallen asleep—a heavy and, maybe, dreamless sleep; but woke softly, instantly, as if at an inward signal. Night had gone; the creeping grey of dawn was at the window, its coldish, mist-burdened airs filled the room. I lay awhile inert, sharply scrutinizing my surroundings, realizing precisely where I was, and at the same time that something was radically and inexplicably wrong with them. What?

It is difficult to suggest; but it was as if a certain *aspect* of the room, its walls, angles, furniture had been peculiarly intensified. Whatever was naturally grotesque in it was now more grotesque—and less real. Matter seldom advertises the precariousness imputed to it by the physicist. But now, every object around me seemed to be proclaiming its own transitoriness. With a conviction that thrilled me like an unexpected contact with ice, I suddenly realized that this is how Mr. Champneys's room would appear to anyone who had become for some reason or another intensely afraid. It may sound wildly preposterous, but I stick to it. I myself was *not* afraid—there was as yet nothing to be afraid of; and yet everything I saw seemed to be dependent on that most untrustworthy but vivid condition of consciousness. Once I let my mind, so to speak, accept the evidence of my senses, then I should be as helpless as the victim of a drug or of the wildest nightmare. I sat there, stiff and cold, eyeing the door.

And then I heard the sound of voices: the faint, hollow, incoherent sound that voices make at a distance in a large house. At that, I confess, a deadly chill came over me. As gingerly as a cat I stepped down to the floor, put on the rest of my clothes, and over them a floral dressing gown that hung on the door hook. Thus attired, I was disguised, but ready for action. It took me half a minute to unlock the door; caution is snail-slow. I was shivering a little, but that may have been due to the cold May morning. The voices were more distinct now;

one of them, I fancied, was Mr. Bloom's. But there was a curious similarity between them; so much so that I may have been playing eavesdropper to Mr. Bloom talking to himself. The sound was filtering down from an upper room; my corridor beneath being as still as a drop scene in a theatre, the footlights out.

I listened, but could detect no words. And then the talking ceased. There came a sort of thump at the *other* end of the house, and then overhead, the sound as of someone retreating towards it—heavily, unaccustomedly, but at a pretty good pace. Inaction is unnerving; and yet, I hesitated, detesting the thought of meeting Mr. Bloom again (and especially if he had company). But that little risk had to be taken; there was no help for it. I tiptoed along the corridor and entered his study.

The curtain at the further end of the room was drawn aside. A deep-piled Turkey carpet adorned the floor of his study; I crossed it, and looked in. The light here was duskier than in my own room, and at first, after one comprehensive glance, I saw nothing unusual except that near at hand was a sofa, half-covered by a travelling rug; and standing beside it, a familiar pair of boots. Unmistakable, ludicrous, excellent boots! Empty as only boots can be, they squatted there side by side, like creatures, by no means mute, yet speechless. And towards the head of the sofa, on a little round table drawn up beside it, lay the miscellaneous contents, obviously, of Mr. Bloom's pockets. The old gold watch and the spade guinea, a notecase, a pocketbook, a pencil case, a scrap of carved stained ivory, an antique silver toothpick, a couple of telegram envelopes, a bunch of keys, a heap of loose money—I see them all, but I see even more distinctly—and it was actually hobnobbing with the spade guinea—a solitary Yale key. Why Mr. Bloom emptied his pockets at night, I cannot guess—a habit possibly from childhood. His black morning coat had been thrown over a chair; no other clothes were visible. But I made no search.

The crux was that key. There is, I suppose, no limit to human stupidity. Never once had it occurred to me that Mr. Bloom himself had been responsible for its loss. I stole nearer, and examined it. Yale keys at a casual glance are as like one another as leaves on a tree. Was this mine? I was uncertain. I must risk it. The footsteps seemed now to be dully thumping down a remote flight of wooden stairs, and it was unmistakably Mr. Bloom's voice that I heard booming back at me, but with all its manlier resonances and its gusto gone.

"Yes, yes: coming, coming!" and the footsteps stumped on.

Well; I had no wish to interfere with any assignation. I had long since suspected that Mr. Bloom's activities might have proved responsible for guests even more undesirable than myself. Like attracts like, I assume, in *any* sphere. My blame, moreover, if my raw prejudices were unfair to his chosen methods of spiritistic investigation. He seemed to have pressed on a little further than most. That is all: a pioneer.

What I was not prepared for was the spectacle of Mr. Bloom's bed. When I entered the room, I am perfectly certain there had been nothing abnormal about that—except that it had not been slept in. True, the light had meanwhile increased a little, but not much. No—the bed then had been empty.

Not so now. The lower part of it was all but entirely flat, the white coverlid over it was drawn almost as neat and close from side to side of it as the cover of a billiard table. But on the pillow, the beard protruding over the turned-down sheet, now showed what appeared to be the head and face of Mr. Bloom. With head jerked back, I watched that face steadily, transfixedly. It was a flawless facsimile, waxen, motionless; but it was not a real face and head. It was a hallucination. How induced is quite another matter. No spirit of life, no livingness had ever stirred those soap-like, stagnant features. It was a travesty utterly devoid—whatever its intention—of the faintest hint of humour. It was merely a mask, a lifelike mask (past even the dexterity of a Chinese artist to rival), and—though I hardly know why—it was inconceivably shocking.

Even when I made them, my remarks about indiscriminate spiritualism the evening before had been inadequate. At this moment, they seemed to be grotesquely inadequate. This house was not haunted, it was infested. Catspaw, poor young Mr. Champneys may have been, but he had indeed helped with the chestnuts. A horrible weariness and nausea swept over me. Without another glance at the bed, I made my way as rapidly as possible to the outer door. I broke into a run.

Still thickly muffled with her last journey's dust—except for the fingerprints I afterwards noticed on her bonnet—my car faithfully awaited me in the innocent blue of dawn beneath the porch. My heart literally stood still as I inserted the key—but, thank heaven, I had not been mistaken. The first burring of the engine was accompanied by the sound of a window being flung violently open. It was above and behind me, beyond the porch. I turned my head, and detected a vague greyish figure standing a little within cover of the hollies and ilexes—a short man, about twenty or thirty yards away, not looking at me. But he too may have been pure illusion, hallucination. When I looked again, he was gone. There was no sunshine yet; the garden was as still as a mechanical panorama, but the hubbub, the babbling was increasing overhead.

In an instant I had shot out from under the porch, and dignity forgotten, was on my way helter-skelter round the semi-circular drive. But to my utter confusion the gates at this end of it were heavily pad-locked. I all but stripped the gears in my haste to retreat, but succeeded none the less; and then, without so much as turning my head towards the house, I drove clean across the lawn, the boughs of the blossom-burdened trees actually brushing the hood of the car as I did so. In five minutes I must have been nearly four miles from Mr. Bloom's precincts.

It was fortunate perhaps the day was so early; even the most phlegmatic of rural constables might look a little askance at a motorist in a purple dressing gown and red Morocco slippers. But I was innocent of robbery, for in exchange for these articles I had left behind me as valuable a jacket and a pair of brown leather shoes. I wonder what they will fetch at the sale? I wonder if Mr. Bloom would have offered me Mr. Champneys's full £300 per annum if I had consented to stay? He was sorely in need, I think, of human company. A less easily prejudiced stranger than I might have been of crucial help to him in his extreme circumstances. But *I* ran away.

And it is now too late to make amends. He has gone home —as we all shall—and taken his wages. But what really troubles me, and now and then with acute misgivings, is the thought of Miss Altogood. She was so simple and so silly a Thomasina Tiddler. She dabbled in those obscure waters as heedlessly and as absorbedly as some little dark intense creature on the banks of the Serpentine over a gallipot of "tiddlers." I hate to think of any of "them" taking her seriously; of the possibility someday, too—when she is groping her way through that other world, for she never really found it in this— the possibility of her meeting Mr. Bloom. I would like to warn her against that, if I could—those dark, affectionate, saddened, hungry eyes: and yet I know of no harm he *did*.

THE CORNER SHOP
C. L. RAY

Peter Wood's executors found their task a very easy one. He had left his affairs in perfect order. The only surprise yielded by his tidy writing table was a sealed envelope on which was written, "Not wishing to be bothered by well-meaning Research Societies, I have never shown the enclosed to anyone, but after my death all are welcome to read what is, to the best of my knowledge, a true story."

The manuscript bears a date three years previous to the death of the writer, and is as follows:

I have long wished to write down an experience of my youth. I shall not attempt any diagnosis as to its nature. I draw no conclusions. I merely record certain facts; at least, as such these incidents presented themselves to my consciousness.

One evening, shortly after I had been called to the Bar, I was rather dejectedly returning to my lodgings, wishing I could afford a theatre ticket, when my attention was drawn to the brightly lit window of a shop. Having an uneducated love of bric-à-brac, and remembering an unavoidable wedding present, I grasped the handle of the door which, opening with one of those cheerful clanking bells, admitted me into large rambling premises thickly crowded with all the traditional litter of a curiosity shop. Fragments of armour, pewter pots, dark, distorting mirrors, church vestments, flower pictures, brass kettles, chairs, tables, chests, chandeliers—all were here! But in spite of the heterogeneous confusion, there was none of the dingy, dusty gloom one associates with such collections. The room was brightly lit and a crackling fire leapt up the chimney. The atmosphere was warm and cheerful. Very agreeable I found it after the cold dank fog outside.

At my entrance, a young woman and a child—by their resemblance obviously sisters—had risen from two armchairs. Bright, bustling, gaily dressed, they were curiously unlike the type of person who usually presides over that particular sort of wares. A flower shop would have seemed a more appropriate setting.

How wonderful of them to keep their premises so clean, I thought, as I wished them good evening.

Their smiling faces made a very pleasing impression on me, one of comfortable, serene well-being, and, though the grown-up sister was most courteous in showing me the crowded treasures and displayed knowledge and appreciation, she struck me as quite indifferent as to whether I made any purchase or not. Her manner was really more that of a custodian than of a saleswoman.

Finding a beautiful piece of Sheffield plate very moderately priced, I decided that here was the very present for my friend. The child deftly converted my purchase into a brown paper parcel. Explaining to her elder sister that I was without sufficient cash, I asked if she would take a cheque.

"Certainly," she answered, briskly producing pen and ink. "Will you please make it out to the 'Corner Curio Shop?'"

It was with conscious reluctance that I set out into the saffron fog.

"Good evening, sir. Always pleased to see you at any time," rang out the girl's pleasant voice, a voice so agreeable that I left almost with a sense of having made a friend.

I suppose it must have been about a week later that, as I walked home one very cold evening—fine powdery snow brushing against my face, and a cutting wind tearing down the streets, I remembered the welcoming warmth of the cheerful Corner Curio Shop, and determined to revisit it. I found myself to be in the very street, and there—yes—there was the very corner. It was with a sense of disappointment, out of all proportion to the event, that I found the shop to be wearing that baffling—so to speak—shut-eyed appearance, and saw that a piece of cardboard, on which was printed the word "Closed," hung from the handle.

A bitter gust of wind whistled round the corner; my wet trousers flapped dismally against my chapped ankles. I longed for the warmth and glow within, and felt annoyingly thwarted. Rather childishly—for I was certain the door was locked—I grasped the handle and shook it. To my surprise the handle turned in my hand, but not in answer to its pressure. The door was pulled open from inside, and I found myself peering into the dimly-lit countenance of a very old and frail-looking little man.

"Please to come in, sir," said a gentle, rather tremulous voice, and soft footsteps shuffled away in front of me.

It is impossible to describe the altered aspect of the place. I assumed that the electric light had fused, for the darkness of the large room was only thinned by two guttering candles, and in the dim wavering light, the jumble of furniture, formerly brightly lit, now loomed towering and mysterious, and cast weird, almost menacing shadows. The fire was out, only one faintly glowering ember told that any had lately been alive. Other evidence there was none, for the grim cold of the atmosphere was such as I had never experienced. The phrase "it struck chill" is laughably inadequate. In retrospect the street seemed almost agreeable; in its biting cold there had at least been something exhilarating. The atmosphere was now as gloomy as it had previously been genial. I felt a strong impulse to leave immediately, but the surrounding darkness thinned, and I saw that the old man was busily lighting candles here and there.

"Anything I can show you, sir?" he quavered, as he spoke approaching me with a lighted taper in his hand. I now saw him comparatively distinctly, and his appearance made an indescribable impression on me. Rembrandt flitted through my mind. Who else could have suggested the strange shadows on that time-worn face? Tired is a word we lightly use. Never had I known what the word might mean, till I stared at that exhausted countenance. The ineffable, patient weariness of the withered face, the eyes—which seemed as extinct as the fire, save for a feeble glow as of some purpose. And the wan frailty of the figure!

The words "dust and ashes, dust and ashes," strayed through my brain.

On my first visit, you may remember that I had been impressed by the incongruous cleanliness of the place. The queer fancy now struck me that this old man was like an accumulation of all the dust one might have expected to see scattered over such precincts. In truth, he looked scarcely more solid than a mere conglomeration of dust that might be dispersed at a breath or a touch.

What a queer old creature to be employed by those healthy, well-to-do-looking girls!

He must, I thought, *be some old retainer kept on out of charity.*

"Anything I can show you, sir?" repeated the old man. His voice had little more body than the tearing of a cobweb, and yet there was a curious, almost pleading, insistence in it, and his eyes were fixed on me in a wan yet devouring. stare. I wanted to leave. Definitely I wanted to go.

The proximity of this pitiable old man depressed me; I felt wretchedly dispirited, but, involuntarily murmuring "Thank you, I'll look round," I found myself following his frail form and absentmindedly inspecting various objects temporarily illuminated by his trembling taper.

The chill silence only broken by the tired shuffle of his carpet slippers got on my nerves. "Very cold night, isn't it?" I hazarded.

"Cold, is it? Cold, cold, yes, I dare say." In his grey voice was the apathy of extreme initiation.

"Been at this job long?" I asked, dully peering at an old four-poster bed.

"A long, long time." The answer came softly as a sigh, and as he spoke Time seemed no longer a matter of days, weeks, months, years, but something that stretched immeasurably. I resented the old man's exhaustion and melancholy, the infection of which was so unaccountably weighing down my own spirits.

"How long, O Lord, how long?" I said as jauntily as possible —adding, with odious jocularity—"Old age pension about due, what?" No response.

In silence we moved across to the other side of the room.

"Quaint piece that," said my guide, picking up a little grotesque frog that was lying on a shelf amongst numerous other small objects.

It seemed to be made of some substance similar to jade and, rather struck by its uncouth appearance, I took it from the old man's hand. It was strikingly cold.

"I think it's rather fun," I said. "How much?"

"Half a crown, sir," whispered the old man, glancing up at my face. His voice had no more body than the sliding of dust, but in his eyes there was an unmistakable gleam of eagerness.

"Is that all? I'll have it," said I. "Don't bother to pack up old Anthony Roland. I'll put him in my pocket. Half a crown, did you say? Here it is."

In giving the old man the coin, I inadvertently touched his extended palm. I could scarcely suppress a start. I have said the frog struck cold, but its substance was tepid compared to that desiccated skin. I cannot describe the chill sensation received in that second's contact.

Poor old fellow! I thought, *he's not fit to be about in this cold, lonely place. I wonder at those kind-looking girls allowing such an old wreck to struggle on.*

"Goodnight," I said.

"Goodnight, sir; thank you, sir," quavered the feeble old voice. He closed the door behind me.

Turning my head as I breasted the driving snow, I saw his form, scarcely more solid than shadow, outlined against the candlelight. His face was pressed against the big glass pane. I imagined his tired, patient eyes peering after his vanishing customer.

Somehow, I was unable to dismiss the thought of that old man from my mind. Long, long after I was in bed and courting sleep I saw that maze of wrinkles, his ravaged face and his great initiated eyes like lifeless planets, staring, staring at me, and in their steady stare there seemed a sort of question. Yes, I was unaccountably perturbed by his personality, and even after I achieved sleep my dreams were full of my strange acquaintance.

Haunted, I suppose, by a sense of his infinite tiredness, in my dream I was trying to force him to rest—to lie down. But no sooner did I succeed in laying his frail form on the four-poster bed I had noticed in the shop (only now it seemed more like a grave than a bed, and the brocade coverlet had turned into sods of turf) —than he would slip from my grasp and totteringly set forth on his rambles around the shop. On and on I chased him, down endless avenues of weird furniture, but still he eluded me, and now the dim shop seemed to stretch on and on immeasurably— to merge into an infinity of sunless, airless space until at length I myself sank breathless and exhausted on to the four-poster grave.

The next morning, I received an urgent summons to my mother's sick bed, and in the anxiety of the ensuing week the episode of the Corner Curio Shop was banished from my mind. As soon as the invalid was declared out of danger, I returned to my dreary lodging. Dejectedly engaged in adding up my petty household accounts and wondering where on earth I was to find the money to pay next quarter's rent, I was agreeably surprised by a visit from an old schoolfellow—at that time practically the only friend I possessed in London. He was employed by one of the best-known firms of fine art dealers and auctioneers.

After a few minutes' conversation, he rose in search of a light. My back was turned to him. I heard the sharp scratch of a match, followed by propitiating noises to his pipe. These were suddenly broken off by an exclamation.

"Good God, man!" he shouted. "Where, in the name of trade, did you get this?"

Turning round, I saw that he had snatched up my purchase of the other night, the funny little frog, whose presence on my mantelpiece I had practically forgotten.

He was holding it under the gas jet, closely scrutinizing it through a small magnifying glass, and his hands were shaking with excitement. "Where did you get this?" he repeated. "Have you any idea what it is?"

Briefly I told him that, rather than leave a shop empty-handed, I had bought the frog for half a crown.

"For half a crown?" he echoed. "My dear fellow, I can't swear to it, but I believe you've had one of those amazing pieces of luck one hears about. Unless I'm very much mistaken, this is a piece of jade of the Hsia Dynasty."

To my ignorance these words conveyed little. "Do you mean it's worth money?"

"Worth money? Phew!" he ejaculated. "Look here. Will you leave this business to me? Let me have the thing for my firm to do the best they can by you. Today's Monday. I shall be able to get it into Thursday's auction."

Knowing I could implicitly trust my friend, I readily agreed to his proposal. Carefully enwrapping the frog in cotton wool, he departed.

Friday morning, I received the shock of my life. Shock does not necessarily imply bad news, and I can assure you that for some seconds after opening the one envelope lying on my dingy breakfast-tray, the room spun round and round me. The envelope contained an invoice from Messrs. Spunk, fine art dealers and auctioneers:

To sale of Hsia jade, £2,000, less 10 per cent commission £1,800

... and there, neatly folded, made out to Peter Wood, Esq, was Messrs. Spunk's cheque for £1,800. For some time, I was completely bewildered. My friend's words had raised hopes; hopes that my chance purchase might facilitate the payment of next quarter's rent—might even provide for a whole year's rent—but that so large a sum was involved had never even crossed my mind. Could it be true, or was it some hideous joke? Surely it was—in the trite phrase—much, much too good to be true! It was not the sort of thing that happened to oneself.

Still feeling physically dizzy, I rang up my friend. The normality of his voice and the heartiness of his congratulations convinced me as to the truth of my astounding fortune. It was no joke—no dream. I, Peter Wood, whose bank account was at present £20 overdrawn, and who possessed no securities save shares to the extent of £150, by a sheer fluke, now held in my hand a piece of paper convertible into 1,800 golden sovereigns. I sat down to think—to try to realize to readjust. From a jumble of plans, problems, and emotions one fact emerged crystal clear. Obviously, I could not take advantage of the girl's ignorance or of her poor old caretaker's incompetence. I could not accept this amazing gift from Fate, simply because I had bought a treasure for half a crown.

Clearly I must return at least half of the sum to my unconscious benefactors. Otherwise, I should feel I had robbed them almost as much as though I had broken into their shop like a thief in the night. I remember their pleasant open countenances. What fun to astonish them with the wonderful news! I felt a strong impulse to rush to the shop, but having for once a case in court, I was obliged to go to the Temple. Endorsing Messrs. Spunk's cheque, I addressed it to my bankers, and, consulting the flyleaf of my chequebook, made out one to the Corner Curio Shop for £900. This I placed in my pocket, determined to call at the Corner Shop on my way home.

It was late before I was free to leave the Law Courts, and on arriving at the shop, though somewhat disappointed, I was not greatly surprised to find that it was again shut, with the notice "Closed" slung over the handle. Even supposing the old caretaker be on duty, there was no particular point in seeing him. My business was with his mistress. So, deciding to postpone my visit to the following day, I was just on the point of hurrying home, when—as though I was expected—the door opened, and there on the threshold stood the old man peering out into the darkness.

"Anything I can do for you, sir?"

His voice was even queerer than before. I now realized that I had dreaded re-encountering him, but I felt irresistibly compelled to enter. The atmosphere was as grimly cold as on my last visit. I found myself actually shivering. Several candles, obviously only just lit, were burning, and by their glimmering light I saw the old man's grey gaze questioningly fixed upon me. What a face! I had not exaggerated its weirdness. Never had I seen so singular, so striking a being. No wonder I had dreamt of him. I wished he hadn't opened the door.

"Anything I can show you tonight, sir?" he rather tremulously inquired.

"No, thanks. I have come about that thing you sold me the other day. I find it's of great value. Please tell your mistress that I will pay her a proper price for it tomorrow."

As I spoke there spread over the old man's face the most wonderful smile. "Smile" I use for lack of a better word; but how convey any idea of the beauty of the indefinable expression that now transfigured that time-worn face? Tender triumph, gentle rapture! It was frost yielding to sunshine. Never before have I witnessed the thawing of thickly frozen grief—the dawn radiance of attainment. For the first time I had some inkling of the meaning of the word "beatitude."

Impossible to describe the impression made on me by that transfigured face. The moment, as it were, brimmed over. Time ceased, and I became conscious of infinite things. The silence of the shop was now broken by that gathering sound of an old clock about to break into speech. I turned my head towards one of those wonderful pieces of medieval workmanship—a

Nuremberg grandfather clock. From a recess beneath its exquisitely painted face, quaint figures emerged, and while one struck a bell, others daintily stepped through a minuet. My attention was riveted by the pretty spectacle, and not till the last sounds had trembled into silence did I turn my head.

I found myself alone.

The old man had disappeared. Surprised at his leaving me, I looked all round the large room. Oddly enough, the fire, which I had supposed to be dead, had flared into unexpected life, and was now casting a cheerful glow. But neither fire nor candlelight showed any trace of the old caretaker. He had vanished.

"Hullo! Hullo!" I called out interrogatively.

No answer. No sound, save the loud ticking of clocks and the busy crackling of the fire. I walked all round the room. I even looked into the four-poster bed of which I had dreamt. I then saw that there was a smaller adjoining room, and, seizing a candle, I resolved to explore it. At the far end I discerned a small staircase obviously leading up to a sort of gallery that surrounded the room. The old man must have withdrawn into some upstairs lair, I would follow him. I groped my way to the foot of the stairs, and began to ascend, but the steps creaked beneath my feet, I had a feeling of crumbling woodwork, my candle went out: cobwebs brushed against my face. To continue was most uninviting. I desisted.

After all, what did it matter? Let the old man hide himself. I had given my message. Best be gone. But the main room to which I had returned had now become quite warm and cheerful. How could I ever have thought it sinister? And it was with a distinct sense of regret that I left the shop. I felt balked. I would have liked to see more of that irradiating smile. Dear, strange, old man! How could I ever have fancied that I feared him?

The next Saturday I was free to go straight to the shop.

On the way there my mind was agreeably occupied in anticipating the cordial welcome the grateful sisters were sure to give me. As the clank of the bell announced my opening of the door, the two girls, who were busily dusting their treasures, turned their heads to see who came at so unusually early an hour. Recognizing me, to my surprise they bowed pleasantly, but quite casually, as though to a mere acquaintance.

With the fairy-tale bond between us, I had expected quite a different sort of greeting. I at once guessed that they had not yet heard the astounding news, and when I said, "I've brought the cheque!" I saw that my surmise was correct. Their faces expressed blank incomprehension.

"Cheque?" echoed the grown-up sister. "What cheque?"

"For the frog I bought the other day."

"The frog? What frog? I only remember you buying a piece of Sheffield plate."

I saw they knew nothing, not even of my second visit to their shop! By degrees I told them the whole story. They were bewildered with astonishment. The elder sister seemed quite dazed.

"But I can't understand it! I can't understand it!" she repeated. "Holmes isn't even supposed to admit anyone in our absence—far less to sell things. He just comes here as caretaker on the evenings when we leave early, and he's only supposed to stay till the night policeman comes on to his beat. I can't believe he let you in and never even told us he'd sold you something. It's too extraordinary! What time was it?"

"Round about seven, I should think," I answered.

"He generally leaves about half past six," said the girl. "But I suppose the policeman must have been late."

"It was later when I came yesterday."

"Did you come again yesterday?" she asked.

Briefly I told her of my visit and the message I had left with the caretaker.

"What an incredible thing!" she exclaimed. "I can't begin to understand it; but we shall soon hear his explanation. I'm expecting him in at any moment now. He comes in every morning to sweep the floors."

At the prospect of meeting the remarkable old man again, I felt an appreciable thrill of excitement. How would he look in the strong daylight? Would he smile again?

"He's very old, isn't he?" I hazarded.

"Old? Yes, I suppose he is getting rather old; but it's a very easy job. He's a good, honest fellow. I can't understand his doing this sort of thing on the sly. I'm afraid we've been rather slack in our cataloguing lately. I wonder if he's been selling odds and ends for himself? Oh no, I can't bear to think of it! By the way, can you remember whereabouts this frog was?"

I pointed to the shelf from which the caretaker had picked up the piece of jade.

"Oh, from that assortment? It's a lot I bought the other day for next to nothing, and I haven't sorted or priced them yet. I can't remember seeing a frog. Oh, what an incredible thing to happen!"

At this moment the telephone rang. She raised the receiver to her ear, and spoke down the instrument.

"Hullo! Hullo!" I heard her voice. "Yes, it's Miss Wilton speaking. Yes, Mrs. Holmes, what do you want?" There was a few seconds' pause, and then in startled tones her voice went on: "*Dead?* Dead? But how? Why? Oh, I *am* sorry!"

After a few more words she replaced the receiver and turned to us, her eyes full of tears.

"Fancy," she said. "Poor old Holmes, the caretaker, is dead. When he got home yesterday evening he complained of pain, and he died in the middle of the night. Heart failure. No one had any idea there was anything the matter with him. Oh, poor Mrs. Holmes! What will she do? We must go round and see her at once!"

Both girls were very much upset and, saying that I would soon return, I thought it best to leave. That hauntingly singular old man had made so vivid an impression upon me that I felt deeply moved by the news of his sudden death. How strange that I should have been, except for his wife, the last person to speak with him. No doubt the fatal pain had seized him in my very presence, and that was why he had left me so abruptly and without a word. Had Death already brushed against his consciousness? That ineffable, irradiating smile? Was that the beginning of the Peace that passes all understanding?

I returned to the Corner Curio Shop the next day. I told them all the details of the sale of the fabulous frog, and presented the cheque I had drawn out. Here I met with unexpected opposition. The sisters showed great unwillingness to accept the money. It was—they said—all mine, and they had no need of it.

"You see," explained Miss Wilton, "my father had a flare for this business amounting to a sort of genius, and made quite a large fortune. When he became too old to carry on the shop, we kept it open out of sentiment and for the sake of occupation; but we don't need to make any profit out of it."

At last, I prevailed upon them to accept the money, if only to spend it on the various charities in which they were interested. It was a relief to my mind when the matter was thus settled.

The strange coincidence of the frog was a bond between us, and in the course of our amicable arguments we had become very friendly. I got into the way of dropping in quite often. In fact, I grew rather to rely on the sympathetic companionship of these two bright girls and became quite at my ease with them.

I never forgot the impression made on me by the old man, and often questioned the girls about their poor caretaker, but they had nothing of much interest to tell me. They just described him as an "old dear" who had been in their father's service as long as they could remember. No further light was thrown on his sale of the frog. Naturally, they didn't like to question his widow.

One evening, when I had been having tea in the inner room with the elder sister, I picked up an album of photographs. Turning over its pages, I came on a remarkably fine likeness of the old man. There, before me, was the strange, striking countenance; but, obviously, this photograph had been taken many years before I saw him. The face was much fuller and had not yet acquired the wearied, fragile look I so vividly remembered. But what magnificent eyes he had! Certainly, there was something extraordinarily impressive about the man. I stared at the faded photograph.

"What a splendid photograph of poor old Holmes!" I said.

"Photograph of Holmes? I'd no idea there was one," she answered. "Let's see."

As I approached with the open book the younger sister looked in through the open door.

"I'm off to the movies now," she called out. "Father's just rung up to say he'll be round in about a quarter of an hour to have a look at that Sheraton sideboard."

"All right. I'll be here, and very glad to have his opinion," said Miss Wilton, taking the album from my hand. There were several photographs on the page at which I had opened the book.

"I don't see anything of old Holmes," she said.

I pointed out the photograph.

"*That!*" she exclaimed. "Why, that's my dear father!"

"Your *father?*" I gasped.

"Yes, I can't imagine two people much more unlike. It must have been very dark in the shop when you saw Holmes!"

"Yes, yes; it was very dark," I quickly said to gain time in which to think; for I felt quite bewildered with surprise. No degree of darkness could account for any such mistake. I had no moment's doubt as to the identity of him I had taken for the caretaker with the man whose photograph I now held in my hand. But what an amazing, unaccountable affair!

Her *father*? Why on earth should he have been in the shop unknown to his daughters, and for what possible purpose had he concealed his sale of the frog? And when he heard of its fabulous value, why leave the girls under the impression that it was Holmes, the dead caretaker, who had sold it?

Had he been ashamed to confess his own inadvertence? Or was it possible that the girls had never told him, wishing perhaps to keep their sudden wealth a secret? What strange family intrigue was this into which I had stumbled? If the father had determined thus to keep his actions in the dark, I had better not precipitate any exposure. Instinct bade me hold my tongue. The younger sister had announced his approaching visit. Would he recognize me?

"It's a splendid face," I said, resolving on reserve.

"Isn't it?" she said with pleased eagerness. "Isn't it clever and strong? Yes, I remember when that photograph was taken. It was just before he got religion." The girl spoke as though she regarded "religion" as a regrettable indisposition.

"Did he suddenly become very religious?"

"Yes," she said reluctantly. "Poor Father! He made friends with a priest, and he became so changed. He was never the same again."

From the sort of break in the girl's voice, I guessed she thought her father's reason had been affected. Did not this explain the whole affair? On the two occasions when I saw him, was he not wandering in mind as well as in body?

"Did his religion make him unhappy?" I ventured to ask, for I was anxious to get more light on the strange being before I re-encountered him.

"Yes, dreadfully." The girl's eyes were full of tears. "You see ... it was ..." She hesitated, and after a glance at me went on. "There's really no reason why I shouldn't tell you. I've come to regard you as a real friend. Poor Father got to think he had done very wrong. He couldn't quiet his conscience. You remember my telling you of his extraordinary flare? Well, his fortune was really founded on three marvellous strokes of business. He had the same sort of luck you had here the other day—that's why I'm telling you. It seems such an odd coincidence." She paused.

"Please go on," I urged.

"Well, you see, on three separate occasions he bought, for a few shillings, objects that were of immense value. Only— unlike you—he knew what he was about. The money he realized on their sale came as no surprise to him ... Unlike you, he did not then see any obligation to make it up to the ignorant people who had thrown away fortunes. After all, most dealers wouldn't, would they?" she almost angrily asked.

"Well, Father grew richer and richer. Years after, he met this priest, and then he seemed to go all sort of morbid. He came to think that our wealth was founded on what was really no better than theft. Bitterly he reproached himself for having taken advantage of those three men's ignorance and allowed them to chuck away their fortunes. Unfortunately, in each case he succeeded in discovering what had ultimately happened to those he called his 'victims.' Most unfortunately, all three men had died in destitution. This discovery made him incurably miserable. Two of these men had died without leaving any children, and no relations could be found.

"He traced the son of the third to America; but there he had died, leaving no family. So poor Father could find no means of making reparation. That was what he longed for—to make reparation. This preyed and preyed on him, until in my opinion —his poor dear mind became unhinged. As religion took stronger and stronger hold on him, he got a queer sort of notion into his head—a regular obsession—a 'complex' they would call it now. 'The next best thing to doing a good action,' he would say, '*is to provide someone else with the opportunity for doing one.*' To give him his cue, so to speak. 'In our sins Christ is crucified afresh.' I must be the cause of three good actions corresponding to my own bad ones. In no other way can I expiate my crimes against Christ, for crimes they were—' In vain we argued with him, saying he had only done as nearly all men would have done. It had no effect. 'Other men must judge for themselves. I have done what I know to be wrong,' he would mournfully repeat. He got more and more fixed in his idea. Real religious mania it became!

"Being determined to find three human beings who would, by their good actions, as it were, *cancel* the pain caused to Divinity by what he considered his three crimes, he now busied himself in finding insignificant-looking treasures which he would offer to the public for a few shillings. Poor old Father! I shall never forget his joy when one day a man returned a piece of porcelain he had bought for five shillings and discovered to be worth five hundred pounds, saying: 'I think you must have made a mistake.' Just as you did, bless you!

"Five years later a similar thing occurred, and he was, oh, so radiant! Two of Humanity's crimes cancelled, he felt. Then came years and years of weary disappointment. 'I shall never rest until I find the third,' was what he always said." Here the girl began to cry, hiding her face behind her hands and murmuring something about "Too late, too late!"

I heard the doorbell ring.

"How he must have suffered!" I said. "I'm so glad I had the luck to be the third."

She withdrew her hands from her face and stared at me.

"And I'm so glad I'm going to meet him again," I said, as I heard footsteps approaching.

"Meet him!" she echoed in amazement, as the footsteps drew near.

"Yes, I may stay, mayn't I? I heard your sister say he was coming round now."

"Oh, I see!" she ejaculated. "*Her* father! We are only step-sisters. My father died seven years ago."

TWO TRIFLES
OLIVER ONIONS

THE ETHER HOGS

1

With one foot thrust into an angle to brace himself against the motion of the ship, the twin telephone receivers about his head, and one hand on the transmitting key, while the other hovered over screws and armatures, the young wireless operator was trying to get into tune. He had had the pitch, but had either lost it again, or else something had gone wrong on the ship from which that single urgent call had come. The pear-shaped incandescent light made cavernous shadows under his anxiously drawn brows; it shone harshly on dials and switch-boards, on bells and coils, and milled screws and tubes; and the whole white-painted room now heeled slowly over this way, and then steeved as violently back the other, as the liner rolled to the storm.

The operator seemed to be able to get any ship except the one he wanted. As a keyed-up violin string answers to tension after tension, or as if a shell held to the ear should sing, not one Song of the Sea, but a multitude, so he fluctuated through level after level of the diapason of messages that the installation successfully picked up. They were comically various, had the young operator's face not been so ghastly anxious and set. "Merry Christmas ... the *Doric* ... buy Erie Railroads ... Merry Christmas ... overland from Marseilles ... closing price copper ... goodnight ... Merry Christmas"—the night hummed with messages as a telephone exchange hums; and many decks overhead, and many scores of feet above that again, his own antennae described vast loops and arcs in the wintry sky, and from time to time spoke with a roar that gashed the night.

But of all the confusion of intercourse about him, what follows is a Conference that the young wireless operator did *not* hear.

The spirits of the Special Committee on Ethereal Traffic and Right of Way were holding an Extraordinary General Meeting. They were holding it because the nuisance had finally become intolerable. Mortal messages tore great rents through space with such a reckless disregard of the Ethereal Regulations that not a ghost among them was safe. A spectre would be going peacefully about his haunting; there would come one of these radio-telegraphic blasts; and lo! his essence would be shattered into fragments, which could only be reassembled after the hideous racket had passed away.

And by haunting they meant, not merely the old-fashioned terrorizing by means of white sheets and clanking fetters, nor yet only the more modern forms of intimidation that are independent of the stroke of midnight and the crowing of the first cock, but also benigner suggestions—their gentle promptings to the poets of the world, their whispered inspirations to its painters, their care for the integrity of letters, their impulses to kindliness, their spurs to bravery, and, in short, any other noble urging that earth dwellers know, who give their strength and labour for the unprofitable things they believe without ever having seen them.

A venerable spirit with a faint aura of silver beard still clinging about him spoke.

"I think we are agreed something must be done," he said. "Even now, one of the most amiable junior ghosts of my acquaintance, on his way with a *motif* to a poor tired musician, was radio'd into flinders, and though his own essence is not permanently harmed, his inspiration was shocked quite out of him, and may never be recovered again."

"That is so," another bore witness. "I happened to be projecting myself not far from the spot, and saw the whole occurrence—poor fellow! he had no chance whatever to escape. It was one of these 'directive' messages, as they call them, and no ghost of his grade could have stood up for a moment against it."

"But it is the universal messages, sent out equally in all directions, that are the most serious menace to our state," another urged.

"Quite so. We have a chance of getting out of the way of the directive ones, but the others leave us no escape."

"Look—there goes one now," said another, suddenly pointing; "luckily it's far enough away."

There was an indignant clamour.

"Vandals!"

"Huns!"

"Hooligans!"

"Shame!"

Then a female spirit spoke. It was known that she owed her condition to a motor accident on earth.

"I remember a name the grosser ones used to have for those who exceeded the speed limit in their motor cars. They were called road hogs. In the same way the creators of these disturbances ought to be called ether hogs."

There was applause at this, which the young wireless operator, still seeking his pitch, mistook for the general radio commotion about him.

"Yes," the female spirit went on (she had always been a little garrulous under encouragement), "I was afflicted with deafness, and in that horrible instrument they call an Insurance Policy I had to pay an extra premium on that account; dear, dear, the number of times my heart jumped into my mouth as their cars whizzed by!"

But at this point two attendant spirits, whose office it was, gently but firmly "damped" her, that is, merged into her and rarefied her astral coherence; they had heard her story many, many times before. The deliberations continued.

Punitive measures were resolved on. With that the question arose, of whom were they to make an example?

"Take a survey," said the spirit with the aura of silver beard; and a messenger was gone, and immediately back again, with the tidings that at that very moment a young operator, in an admirably susceptible condition of nerves, was seeking to compass a further outrage.

"Good," said the venerable one, dismissing his minion again. "We have now to decide who shall haunt him. The Chair invites suggestions."

Now the selection of a haunter is always a matter for careful thought. Not every ghost can haunt everybody. Indeed, the superior attenuations have often difficulty in manifesting themselves at all, so that in practice a duller spirit becomes their deputy. Thus, it is only the less ghostly ghosts we of earth know, those barely yet weaned from the breast of the world, and that is the weakness of haunting from the ghostly point of view. The perfect message must go through the imperfect channel. The great ghosts may plan, but the coarser ones execute.

But as this is not unknown on earth also, we need hardly dwell on it.

Now the Committee had no more redoubtable haunter in certain respects than it had in the spirit of an old Scottish engineer, who had suffered translation in the middle days of steam. True, they had to watch him rather carefully, for he had more than once been suspected of having earthly hankerings and regrets; but that, a demerit in one sense, meant added haunting efficacy in another, and no less a spirit than Vanderdecken himself had recommended him for a certain class of seafaring commission. He was bidden to appear, and his errand was explained to him.

"You understand," they said a little severely when all had been made clear. "Your instructions are definite, remember, and you are not to exceed them."

"Ay, ay, sir," said that blunt ghost. "I kenned sail, and I kenned steam, and I ha' sairved on a cable ship. Ye canna dae better than leave a' tae me."

There was the ring, at any rate, of sincere intention in his tone, and they were satisfied.

"Very well," said the presiding spirit. "You know where to find him. Be off."

"Ay, ay, sir—dinna fash yersel'—I'll gi'e the laddie a twisting!"

But at that moment a terrific blast from the Cape Cod Station scattered the meeting as if it had been blown from the muzzle of a gun.

And you are to understand that the foregoing took no time at all, as earthly time is reckoned.

2

"Oh, get out of my way, you fool! I want the ship that called me five minutes ago—the *Bainbridge*. Has she called you? ... O Lord, here's another lunatic—wants to know who's won the prizefight! Are you the *Bainbridge*? Then buzz off! ... You there —have you had a call from the *Bainbridge*? Yes, five minutes ago; I think she said she was on fire, but I'm not sure, and I can't get her note again! You try—shove that Merry Christmas fool out—B-a-i-n ... No, but I think—I say I think—she said so —perhaps she can't transmit anymore...."

Dot, dash—dot, dash—dot, dash—

Again, he was running up and down the gamut, seeking the ship that had given him that flickering uncertain message, and then—silence.

A ship on fire somewhere.

He was almost certain she had said she was on fire—

And perhaps she could no longer transmit—

Anyway, half a dozen ships were trying for her now.

It was at this moment, when the whole stormy night throbbed with calls for the *Bainbridge*, that the ghost came to make an example of the young wireless operator for the warning of Ethereal Trespassers at large.

Indeed, the ships were making an abominable racket. The Morse tore from the antennae through the void, and if a home-less spectre missed one annihilating wavelength, he encountered another. They raged. What was the good of their being the Great Majority if they were to be bullied by a mortal minority with these devastating devices at its command?

Even as that ghostly avenger, in a state of imminent precip-itation, hung about the rocking operating-room, he felt himself racked by disintegrating thrills. The young operator's fingers were on the transmitting key again.

"Can't you get the *Bainbridge*? Oh, try, for God's sake ... Are you there? Nothing come through yet? ... *Doric*. Can't you couple...?"

Lurch, heave; crest, trough; a cant to port, an angle of forty-five degrees to starboard; on the vessel drove, with the antennae high overhead describing those dizzy loops and circles and rendering the night with the sputtering Morse.

Dot, dash—dot, dash—dot, dash—

But already that old ghost, who in his day had known sail and steam and had served on a cable-ship, had hesitated even on the brink of manifestation. He knew that he was only a low-grade ghost, charged rather than trusted with an errand, and their own evident mistrust of him was not a thing greatly to strengthen his allegiance to them. He began to remember his bones and blood, and his past earthly passion for his job. He had been a fine engineer, abreast of all the knowledge of his day, and what he now saw puzzled him exceedingly. By virtue of his instantaneousness and ubiquity, he had already taken a complete conspectus of the ship. Much that he had seen was new, more not. The engines were more powerful, yet essentially the same. In the stokeholds, down the interminable escalades, all was much as it had formerly been. Of electric lighting he had seen more than the beginnings, so that the staring incandescents were no wonder to him, and on the liner's fripperies of painted and gilded saloons and gymnasium and staterooms and swimming baths he had wasted little attention. And yet, even in gathering himself for visibility, he had hesitated. He tried to tell himself why he did so. He told himself that, formidable haunter as he was, it is no easy matter to haunt a deeply preoccupied man. He told himself that he would be able to haunt him all the more soundly did he hold off for awhile and find the hauntee's weak spot. He told himself that his superiors (a little condescending and sniffy always) had after all left a good deal to his discretion. He told himself that, did he return with his errand unaccomplished, they would at all events be no worse off than they had been before.

In a word, he told himself all the things that we mere mortals tell ourselves when we want to persuade ourselves that our inclinations and our consciences are one and the same thing.

And in the meantime, he was peering and prying about a little moving band of wires that passed round two wooden pulleys geared to a sort of clock, with certain coils of wire and a couple of horseshoe magnets, the whole attached to the telephone clasped about the young ether hog's head. He was tingling to know what the thing was for.

It was, of course, the Detector, the instrument's vital ear. Then the young man's finger began to tap on the transmitter key again.

"*Doric* ... Anything yet? ... You're the *Imperator*? ... Are you calling the *Bainbridge*?"

Now the ghost, who could not make head or tail of the Detector, nevertheless knew Morse; and though it had not yet occurred to him to squeeze himself in between the operator's ears and the telephone receiver, he read the transmitted message. Also, he saw the young man's strained and sweating face. He wanted some ship—the *Bainbridge*; from the corrugations of his brows, a grid in the glare of the incandescent, and the glassy set of his eyes, he wanted her badly; and so apparently did those other ships whose mysterious apparatus harrowed the fields of ether with long and short—

Moreover, on board a ship again that wistful old ghost felt himself at home—or would do so could he but grasp the operation of that tapping key, of that airwire that barked and oscillated overhead, and of that slowly-moving endless band that passed over the magnets and was attached to the receivers about the young ether hog's ears.

Whatever they thought of him who had sent him, he *had* been a person of no small account on earth, and a highly skilled mechanic into the bargain.

Suddenly he found himself in temptation's grip. He didn't want to haunt this young man. If he did, something might go wrong with that unknown instrument, and then they might not get this ship they were hunting through the night.

And if he could only ascertain *why* they wanted her so badly, it would be the simplest thing in space for a ghost to find her.

Then, as he nosed about the Detector, it occurred to him to insinuate a portion of his imponderable fabric between the receiver and the young man's ear.

The next moment he had started resiliently back again, as like pole repels like pole of the swinging needle. He was trembling as no radio message had ever set him trembling yet.

Fire! A ship on fire!

That was why these friendly young engineers and operators were blowing a lot of silly ghosts to smithereens!

The *Bainbridge*, on fire!

What did all the ghosts of the Universe matter if a ship was on fire?

That faithless emissary did not hesitate for an instant. The ghostly Council might cast him out, if they liked; he didn't care; they should be hogged till Domesday if, on all the seas of the world, a single ship was on fire! A ship on fire? He had once seen a ship on fire, and didn't want, even as a ghost, to see another.

Even while you have been reading this, he was off to find the *Bainbridge*.

Of course, he hadn't really to go anywhere to find her at all.

Low-class and ill-conditioned ghost as he was, he still had that property of ubiquity. An instantaneous double change in his own tension and he was there and back again, with the *Bainbridge's* bearings, her course, and the knowledge that it was still not too late. The operator was listening in an agony into the twin receivers; a thrill of thankfulness passed through the ghost that he had not forgotten the Morse he had learned on the cable-ship. Swiftly he precipitated himself into a point of action on the transmitter key.

Long, short—long, short—long, short—

The operator heard. He started up as if he had been hogged himself. His eyes were staring, his mouth horridly open. What was the matter with his instrument?

Long, short—long, short—long, short—

It was not in the telephone. The young man's eyes fell on his own transmitter key. It was clicking up and down. He read out "*Bainbridge*," and a bearing, and of course his instrument was spelling it out to the others,

Feverishly he grabbed the telephone.

Already the *Doric* was acknowledging. So was the *Imperator*.

He had sent no message—

Yet, though it made him a little sick to think of it, he would let it stand. If one ship was fooled, all would be fooled. At any rate he did not think he had dreamed that *first* call, that first horrifying call of "*Bainbridge*—fire!"

He sprang to the tube and called up the bridge.

They picked them up from the *Bainbridge's* boats towards the middle of Christmas morning; but that unrepentant, old seafaring spectre, returning whence he had come, gave little satisfaction to his superiors. Against all their bullying he was proof; he merely repeated doggedly over and over again, "The laddie's nairves o' steel! Ower and ower again I manifested mysel' tae him, but it made na mair impression on him than if I'd tried to ha'nt Saturn oot o' his Rings! It's my opeenion that being a ghaistie isna what it was. They hae ower mony new-fangled improvements in these days."

But his spectral heart was secretly sad because he had not been able to make head or tail of the Detector.

~

THE MORTAL

1

"Oh, Egbert," the White Lady implored, "let me beg of you to abandon this mad, wicked idea!"

Sir Egbert the Dauntless was in the act of passing himself through the wainscot of the North Gallery; he turned, half on this side of the panel, half already in the Priest's Hole in the thickness of the wall.

"No, Rowena," he replied firmly. "You saw fit to cast doubts upon my courage before all the Family Ancestors, and now I intend to do it. If anything happens to me my essence will be upon your head."

The Lady Rowena wailed. In her agitation she clasped her hands awry, so that they interpenetrated.

"Nay, Egbert, I did but jest! On earth you were known as the Dauntless; our descendants are proud of you; cannot you forget my foolish words?"

"No," replied Sir Egbert, sternly. "Though it cost me my Non-existence I will spend the night in a Human Chamber!"

"Egbert—Egbert—stay—not *that* one—*not* the Parson's! Think—should he exorcize you!"

"Too late; I have spoken!" said Sir Egbert, with an abrupt

wave of his hand. He vanished into the Fifth Dimension. No sooner had he done so than the general lamentation broke out.

"Oh, he'll Be, he'll Be, I *know* he'll Be!" the White Lady sobbed.

To be re-confined in Matter, so that there is no speech save with a tongue and no motion save with limbs—to be once more subject to the Three Dimensions of the grosser life—is the final menace to the spectral Condition.

"Poor chap—I fancied I detected a trace of Visibility about him already," grim Sir Hugo muttered.

"Oh, it's playing with Flesh!" another cried, with a shiver.

"Almost Human folly!"

"Already his glide isn't what it was," said the melancholy Lady Annice, who on Earth had been a famous attender at funerals.

"I shall never behold his dear Aura again," moaned the White Lady, already half opaque herself. "It will be the Existence of me!"

"If only it had not been a Parson's Chamber," said the Lady Annice, with mournful relish.

"Here—catch her quick—she's solidifying!" half a dozen of them cried at once.

It was with difficulty that they brought the White Lady even to a state of semi-evaporation again.

2

It was midnight, and the Parson snored. He turned uneasily in his sleep. Perhaps already he was conscious of Sir Egbert's presence.

Sir Egbert himself dared approach no nearer to the Mortal Bed than the lattice. Fear had given him the pink gossamer look that is the perilous symptom of veins and blood, and he knew that he received faintly the crisscrossed shadow of the lattice. To save his Nonentity he could not have glided up the shaft of moonlight that streamed in at the window.

Suddenly a violent Hertzian Wave passed through Sir Egbert's ether. He jumped almost clear out of his Dimension. The Parson had opened his eyes. To Be or not to Be? Had he seen him?

He had. His horrible embodied eyes were on the poor harmless Spectre. The two looked at one another, the one quailing in the moonlight, the other sitting in all the horror of Solidity bolt upright in bed.

Then the Mortal began to practise his fearsome devices.

First, he gave the hoarse cry that all ghosts dread, and Sir Egbert felt himself suddenly heavier by a pound. But he remembered his name—the Dauntless. He would not yield.

Then the Parson's teeth began to chatter. He gibbered, and Sir Egbert wondered whether this was the beginning of the Exorcism. If it was, he would never see the happy old Ancestral Gallery again, never hold his dear Rowena in perfect interpermeation again—never pass himself through a Solid again—never know again the jolly old lark of being nowhere and everywhere at once.

"Mercy, Mercy!" he tried to cry; and indeed, his voice all but stirred the palpable air.

But there was no mercy in that grisly Parson. His only reply was to shoot the hair up on his head, straight on end.

Then he protruded his eyes.

Then he grinned.

And then he began to talk as it were the deaf and dumb alphabet on his fingers.

Sir Egbert's semi-Substance was like reddish ground glass; it was the beginning of the agony. How near to the Mortal Precipitation he was he knew when suddenly he found himself thinking, almost with fright, of his own dear White Lady. *She was a Ghost.*

Then the Mortal began to gabble words. It was the Exorcism.

Oh, why—why—why had Sir Egbert not chosen a Layman?

The gabbling continued. Colour—warmth—weight—these settled down on Sir Egbert the Dauntless. He half Was. And as he continued steadily to Become, the words increased in speed. Sir Egbert's feet felt the floor; he cried; a faint windy moan came. The Parson bounded a foot up on the bed and tossed his pillow into the air.

Could nothing save Sir Egbert?

Ah, yes. They that lead a meek and blameless Nonexistence shall not be cast down; they shall not be given over at last to the terrors of the Solid and Known. From somewhere outside in the moonlight there came a shrill sound.

It was the crowing of a Cock.

The Parson had had a pillow over his face. It fell, and he looked again.

Nothing was there.

Sir Egbert, back in his comfortable Fourth Dimension, was of the loved indivisible texture of his dear White Lady again.

TWELVE O'CLOCK
CHARLES WHIBLEY

In 1779, the Year of his mysterious death, Thomas, Lord Lyttelton, had climbed the pinnacle of fame. Though he was but six and thirty, he was already known as "the wicked Lord Lyttelton." In what his wickedness consisted is not clear. Such reputations are seldom deserved, and are commonly founded upon flattery and vainglory. He is said to have had a great love of gambling, and was so unlucky in his youth that, more than once, he was compelled to leave his companions "abruptly" in far-off countries. But he presently became more artful and turned his sad experience to good account.

"The pigeon turned into a hawk," we are told, and at his death he had gained by play some £30,000. For the rest, he had practised with much success those vices in which Whiggish ministers in his day had full licence to excel. There is no evidence that he was a genuine rival in dissipation to Charles James Fox, for instance, of whom a partisan has confessed that when he returned to Eton from the Continent his "Parisian experiences ... produced a visible and durable change for the worse in the morals and habits of the place." In brains there was not much to choose between the two men. Dr Barnard, the Headmaster of Eton, who had had them both under his care, thought that the abilities of Lyttelton were vastly superior.

Whatever shape his legendary wickedness took, there is no doubt that he was shaped for nobler purposes. Fatigue is for rakes a better cure than repentance, and the years as they passed fashioned Thomas Lyttelton into a gravely ambitious statesman. Though he owned himself that his amendment was slow and progressive, it might be said of him, as was said of the great Rochester, whom he somewhat resembled, that "he seem'd to study nothing more than which way to make that great understanding God had given him most useful to his country." Like Rochester, too, he spoke in the House of Peers with general approbation. Men of all parties are agreed in his praise. Even his enemies were generous in extolling his gifts of eloquence and statesmanship. Sandwich, for instance, was no friend of Lyttelton. Lyttelton had attacked Sandwich with a bitter ferocity, and this is what Sandwich found to say about Lyttelton in 1776: "I think that so far from reprehension, the noble lord deserves commendation and thanks for so ably defending and asserting the rights of the British Parliament and the supreme legislative authority of the Mother Country. I think I never before heard such a speech delivered by anybody, and I am proud to testify my perfect approbation by affirming that it was the finest ever delivered within these walls."

The praise, if excessive, was disinterested, and that Sandwich was not alone in approbation is proved by Lyttelton's early promotion. At the age of thirty-two he was sworn of His Majesty's Privy Council, and made one of the Chief Justices in Eyre. As a politician he was energetically and consistently opposed to the rebels in America. His speeches breathe the true

spirit of patriotism, and had he been able to carry the adminis-
tration with him, England would not have been forced to
endure an unjust, unmerited disgrace. And by a freakish accident we remember less clearly how he lived than how he died.
His once famous dissipations are but a rumour; the speeches,
which were heard with a reluctant enthusiasm in the House of
Peers, are a vague echo from the past; the ghostly apparition,
which heralded his death, still holds the wonder of the world,
and is an incitement to controversy after a century and a half.

I have said so much about the man and his character,
because without some understanding of them the story of his
death might fail of its effect. He would not seem to be of those
who stand in awe of the invisible world. His hard, practical
sense, his determination to snatch from life whatever of pleasure it held, are not the qualities which we expect in those to
whom beckonings come from beyond the boundaries of the
world. Yet he had always been a dreamer of dreams and a seer
of visions. Not long before his death "I dreamt," said he, "that I
was dead, and was hurried away to the infernal regions, which
appeared as a large dark room, at the end of which was seated
Mrs. Brownrigg[1], who told me it was appointed for her to pour
red-hot bullets down my throat for a thousand years. The
resistance I endeavoured to make to her awakened me, but the
agitation of my mind when I awoke is not to be described, nor
can I get the better of it." So ugly a visitation as that of Mrs.
Brownrigg visited him but seldom. It was but the shadow cast
by a disordered fancy. Far more benign and amiable in aspect
was the apparition which foretold his death. The legend,
repeated by many and divers tongues, may be shaped into this:
On Wednesday, November 24th, 1779, Lyttelton, at his house in
Hill Street, saw, or dreamed that he saw, a bird fly into his
bedroom. He tried to clutch it, and found it, like Macbeth's

dagger, "of the mind, a false creation." Presently it turned into a woman, draped in white, and recalling by her ghostly features one whom Lyttelton had treated none too well. In a solemn voice, as from the grave, the voice with which spirits are said to intensify their effect, the disembodied woman told Lyttelton that he must die.

"I hope not soon," he murmured, "not in two months."

"In three days," said she.

In vain he attempted to speak to her.

She vanished from his sight, echoing as she went, "Three days, three days!"

Lyttelton was profoundly affected by this message from the other world. Like most men of a doubting temper, he was superstitious. He told those who lodged in his house what he had seen, and the vision lost nothing of terror and persuasiveness in the telling. His allotted span must come to an end, if the ghost spoke true, at midnight on Saturday. But even though he were credulous, Lyttelton would not allow meanwhile the fateful message to turn him from the paths of duty and pleasure. He went about his business with zeal and address. Before the House of Lords he delivered the best speech that ever he made. It was his swan song. For the first time he seceded openly from the Government, whose cowardly conduct in America and in Ireland he attacked with pitiless contempt and unrelenting logic. And all the while the visions of the dove and the white lady were before his eyes. When he said, in the solemn language which befitted the time and place, and which gained in solemnity after the event, "It is true I hold a place, but perhaps I shall not hold it long." The ministers laughed. From them the irony was concealed.

"The noble lords smile at what I say," he retorted: "let them turn their eyes on their own pusillanimity ... and then let them declare in their consciences which is most fitly the object of contempt, my thus openly and unreservedly speaking my sentiments in Parliament ... or their consenting, in a moment of difficulty and danger like the present, to pocket the wages of prostitution."

While they thought of the place which he would not hold long, he remembered that, of the three days given him by the ghost, one was all but at an end.

On Friday morning George Fortescue called upon him, and presently the two of them took the air together. Lyttelton was still reflecting upon an early death, when they crossed the churchyard of St James's Church.

"Now look at all the vulgar fellows," said he, pointing to the tombstones; "they die in their youth, at five and thirty. But you and I, who are gentlemen, shall live to a good old age."

A few hours later he went down to his house at Epsom, where he entertained a party, not such a party as the gossip of Walpole invented—"a caravan of nymphs," or "four virgins, whom he had picked up in the Strand"—but a party of ladies and gentlemen, whom he counted among his intimate friends. There was upon them all a certain foreboding, and when Saturday evening came, they thought of nothing but the ghost. Meanwhile, his friends all did their best to avert the depression, which settled upon Lyttelton, who, amid the shouting and the laughter of the others, exclaimed, "We shall jockey the ghost after all." A musician, named Russell, who had been summoned to entertain the company, noticed that despite the efforts of his friends, Lyttelton's melancholy still clung about him. So midnight drew on, the hour at which Lyttelton had been doomed to die by the ghost, and in spite of himself he kept an anxious eye upon the time. His valet, by an artful foresight, had put on the clock a quarter of an hour, in the hope that his master should not know when the foreordained minute came, and should not aid his death by a just fear. Slowly the seconds moved, and when Lyttelton saw that the clock marked the approach of midnight, he got up abruptly and bade goodnight to his guests. He had bilked the ghost, as he thought, and went upstairs to his bedroom with the light foot of a man reprieved. His thoughts were all of the morrow. He spoke to his servant with a cheerful voice, and "particularly enquired of him what care had been taken to provide good rolls for breakfast the next morning." He then bade the man prepare him a dose of medicine, and when he began to stir the medicine with a toothpick (or, according to another account, with a key), Lyttelton told him he was a dirty fellow, and bade him go downstairs and fetch a spoon. When the servant returned, he found his master speechless upon his pillow and in the last agony of death. The attempt to cheat the clock had failed, for Russell, the musician, records that at the moment when the servant came down to do his master's bidding, the clock of the parish church, which had not been tampered with, began slowly to strike the midnight hour.

Thus died Thomas, the second Lord Lyttelton, eminent alike in vice and virtue, renowned for eloquence in his life, most highly renowned for the manner of his death, which provided gossip for the malicious, and thought for the philosopher. Horace Walpole cut a new pen that he might share his contempt for the dead man with his friends. Samuel Johnson, the Commentator-General of his age, who heard the story with his own ears from Lyttelton's uncle, Lord Westcote, expressed at once his interest in it, and his faith.

"It is the most extraordinary thing," said he, "that has happened in my day ... I am so glad to have every evidence of the spiritual world, that I am willing to believe it."

1. Mrs. Brownrigg is the woman made immortal in *The Anti-Jacobin*:
    "Dost thou ask her crime?
    She whipped two female prentices to death,
    And hid them in the coal hole.
    ... For this act
    Did Brownrigg swing. Harsh laws!"

THE AMOROUS GHOST
ENID BAGNOLD

It was five o'clock on a summer morning. The birds, who had woken at three, had long scattered about their duties. The white, plain house, blinkered and green-shuttered, stood four-square to its soaking lawns, and up and down on the grass, his snow boots planting dark blots on the grey dew, walked the owner. His hair was uncombed, he wore his pyjamas and an overcoat, and at every turn at the end of the lawn he looked up at a certain window, that of his own and his wife's bedroom, where, as on every other window on the long front, the green shutters lay neatly back against the wall and the cream curtains hung down in heavy folds.

The owner of the house, strangely and uncomfortably on his lawns instead of in his bed, rubbed his chilly hands and continued his tramp. He had no watch on his wrist, but when the stable clock struck six, he entered the house and passing through the still hall he went up to his bathroom. The water was lukewarm in the taps from the night before, and he took a bath. As he left the bathroom for his dressing room he heard the stirring of the first housemaid in the living rooms below, and at seven o'clock he rang for his butler to lay out his clothes.

As the same thing had happened the day before, the butler was half prepared for the bell; yawning and incensed but ready dressed.

"Good morning," said Mr. Templeton rather suddenly. It was a greeting which he never gave, but he wished to try the quality of his voice. Finding it steady he went on, and gave an order for a melon from the greenhouse.

For breakfast he had very little appetite, and when he had finished the melon, he unfolded the newspaper. The door of the dining room opened, and the parlourmaid and housemaid came in and gave him their notice.

"A month from today, sir," repeated the parlourmaid to bridge the silence that followed.

"It's nothing to do with me," he said in a low voice. "Your mistress is coming home tonight. You must tell her of these things."

They left the room.

"What's the matter with those girls?" said Mr. Templeton to the butler who came in.

"They haven't spoken to me, sir," said the butler untruly; "but I gather there has been an upset."

"Because I chose to get up early on a summer morning?" asked Mr. Templeton with an effort.

"Yes, sir. And there were other reasons."

"Which were?"

"The housemaid," said the butler with detachment, as though he were speaking of the movements of a fly, "has found your bedroom, sir, strewn with clothes."

"With my clothes?" said Mr. Templeton.

"No, sir."

Mr. Templeton sat down. "A nightgown?" he said weakly, as though appealing for human understanding.

"Yes, sir."

"More than one?"

"Two, sir."

"Good God!" said Mr. Templeton, and walked to the window whistling shakily.

The butler cleared the table quietly and left the room.

"There's no question about it," said Mr. Templeton under his breath. "She was undressing ... behind the chair."

After breakfast he walked down his two fields and through a wood with the idea of talking to Mr. George Casson. But George had gone to London for the day, and Mr. Templeton, faced with the polish on the front door, the polish on the parlourmaid, and the sober look of the Morning Post folded on the hall table, felt that it was just as well that he had not after all to confide his incredible story. He walked back again, steadied by the air and exercise.

"I'll telephone to Hettie," he decided, "and make sure that she is coming tonight."

He rang up his wife, told her that he was well, that all was well, and heard with satisfaction that she was coming down that night after her dinner party, catching the eleven-thirty, arriving at twelve-fifteen at the station.

"There is no train before at all," she said. "I sent round to the station to see, and owing to the strike they run none between seven-fifteen and eleven-thirty."

"Then I'll send the car to the station and you'll be here at half past twelve. I may be in bed, as I'm tired."

"You're not ill?"

"No. I've had a bad night."

It was not until the afternoon, after a good luncheon and a

whisky and soda, that Mr. Templeton went up to his bedroom to have a look at it.

The cream curtains hung lightly blowing in the window. By the fireplace stood a high, wing, grandfather chair upholstered in patterned rep. Opposite the chair and the fireplace was the double bed, in one side of which Mr. Templeton had lain working at his papers the night before. He walked up to the chair, put his hands in his pocket, and stood looking down at it. Then he crossed to the chest of drawers and drew out a drawer. On the right-hand side were Hettie's vests and chemises, neatly pressed and folded. On the left was a pile, folded but not pressed, of Hettie's nightgowns. Mr. Templeton noted the crumples and creases on the silk.

"Evidence, evidence," he said, walking to the window, "that something happened in this room after I left it this morning. The maids believe they found a strange woman's nightgowns crumpled on the floor. As a matter of fact, they are Hettie's nightgowns. I suppose a doctor would say I'd done it myself in a trance."

"Two nights ago?" he thought, looking again at the bed. It seemed a week. The night before last as he lay working, propped up on pillows and cushions and his papers spread over the bed, he had glanced up, absorbed, at two o'clock in the morning and traced the pattern on the grandfather chair as it stood facing the empty grate with its back towards him, just as he had left it, when he had got into bed. It was then that he had seen the two hands hanging idly over the back of the chair as though an unseen owner were kneeling in the seat. His eyes stared, and a cold fear wandered down his spine. He sat without moving and watched the hands.

Ten minutes passed, and the hands were withdrawn quickly as though the occupant of the chair had silently changed its position.

Still, he watched, propped, stiffening, on his pillows, and as time went on, he fought the impression down.

"Tired," he said. "One's read of it. The brain reflecting something."

His heart quietened, and cautiously he settled himself a little lower and tried to sleep. He did not dare straighten the litter of papers around him, but with the light on he lay there till the dawn lit the yellow paint on the wall. At five he got up, sleepless, his eyes still on the back of the grandfather chair, and without his dressing gown or slippers he left the room. In the hall he found an overcoat and his warm snow boots behind a chest, and unbolting the front door he tramped the lawn in the dew.

On the second night (*last* night) he had worked as before. So completely had he convinced himself after a day of fresh air that his previous night's experience had been the result of his own imagination, his eyesight and his mind hallucinated by his work, that he had not even remembered (as he had meant to do) to turn the grandfather chair with its seat towards him. Now, as he worked in bed, he glanced from time to time at its patterned and concealing back, and wished vaguely that he had thought to turn it round.

He had not worked more than two hours before he knew that there was something going on in the chair.

"Who's there?" he called. The slight movement he had heard ceased for a moment, then he thought he saw a hand shoot out at the side, and once he could have sworn, he saw the tip of a mound of fair hair showing over the top. There was a sound of scuffling in the chair, and some object flew out and landed with a bump on the floor below the field of his vision. Five minutes went by, and after a fresh scuffle a hand shot up and laid a bundle, white and stiff, with what seemed a small arm hanging, on the back of the chair.

Mr. Templeton had had two bad nights and a great many hours of emotion. When he grasped that the object was a pair of stays with a suspender swinging from them, something bumped unevenly in his heart, a million black motes like a cloud of flies swam in his eyeballs; he fainted.

He woke up, and the room was dark, the light off, and he felt a little sick. Turning in bed to find comfort for his body, he remembered that he had been in the middle of a crisis of fear. He looked about him in the dark, and saw again the dawn on the curtains. Then he heard a chink by the washstand, several feet nearer to his bed than the grandfather chair. He was not alone; the thing was still in the room.

By the faint light from the curtains, he could just see that his visitor was by the washstand. There was a gentle clinking of China and a sound of water, and dimly he could see a woman standing.

"Undressing," he said to himself, "washing."

His gorge rose at the thought that came to him. Was it possible that the woman was coming to bed?

It was that thought that had driven him with a wild rush from the room, and sent him marching for a second time up and down his grey and dewy lawns.

"And now," thought Mr. Templeton as he stood in the neat bedroom in the afternoon light and looked around him, "Hettie's got to believe in the unfaithful or the supernatural."

He crossed to the grandfather chair, and taking it in his two hands, was about to push it on to the landing. But he paused.

I'll leave it where it is tonight, he thought, *and go to bed as usual. For both our sakes I must find out something more about all this.*

Spending the rest of the afternoon out of doors, he played golf after tea, and eating a very light dinner he went to bed. His head ached badly from lack of sleep, but he was pleased to notice that his heart beat steadily. He took a couple of aspirin tablets to ease his head, and with a light novel settled himself down in bed to read and watch. Hettie would arrive at half past twelve, and the butler was waiting up to let her in. Sandwiches, nicely covered from the air, were placed ready for her on a tray in a corner of the bedroom.

It was now eleven. He had an hour and a half to wait.

"She may come at any time," he said (thinking of his visitor). He had turned the grandfather chair towards him, so that he could see the seat.

Quarter of an hour went by, and his head throbbed so violently that he put the book on his knees and altered the lights, turned out the brilliant reading lamp, and switched on the light which illuminated the large face of the clock over the mantelpiece, so that he sat in shadow. Five minutes later he was asleep.

He lay with his face buried in the pillow, the pain still drumming in his head, aware of his headache even at the bottom of his sleep. Dimly he heard his wife arrive, and murmured a hope to himself that she would not wake him. A slight movement rustled around him as she entered the room and undressed, but his pain was so bad that he could not bring himself to give a sign of life, and soon, while he clung to his half sleep, he felt the bedclothes gently lifted and heard her slip in beside him.

Feeling chilly he drew his blanket closer round him. It was as though a draught was blowing about him in the bed, dispelling the mists of sleep and bringing him to himself. He felt a touch of remorse at his lack of welcome, and putting out his hand he sought his wife's beneath the sheet. Finding her wrist his fingers closed round it. She too was cold, strange, icy, and from her stillness and silence she appeared to be asleep.

A cold drive from the station, he thought, and held her wrist to warm it as he dozed again.

"She is positively chilling the bed," he murmured to himself.

He was awakened by a roar beneath the window and the sweep of a light across the wall of the room. With amazement he heard the bolts shoot back across the front door. On the illuminated face of the clock over the fireplace he saw the hands standing at twenty-seven minutes past twelve. Then Mr. Templeton, still gripping the wrist beside him, heard his wife's clear voice in the hall below.

MR. TALLENT'S GHOST
MARY WEBB

The first time I ever met Mr. Tallent was in the late summer of 1906, in a small, lonely inn on the top of a mountain. For natives, rainy days in these places are not very different from other days, since work fills them all, wet or fine. But for the tourist, rainy days are boring. I had been bored for nearly a week, and was thinking of returning to London, when Mr. Tallent came. And because I could not "place" Mr. Tallent, nor elucidate him to my satisfaction, he intrigued me. For a barrister should be able to sum up men in a few minutes.

I did not see Mr. Tallent arrive, nor did I observe him entering the room. I looked up, and he was there, in the small firelit parlour with its Bible, wool mats and copper preserving pan. He was reading a manuscript, slightly moving his lips as he read. He was a gentle, moth-like man, very lean and about six foot three or more. He had neutral-coloured hair and eyes, a nondescript suit, limp-looking hands and slightly turned-up toes. The most noticeable thing about him was an expression of passive and enduring obstinacy.

I wished him good evening, and asked if he had a paper, as he seemed to have come from civilization.

"No," he said softly, "no. Only a little manuscript of my own."

Now, as a rule I am as wary of manuscripts as a hare is of greyhounds. Having once been a critic, I am always liable to receive parcels of these for advice. So I might have saved myself and a dozen or so of other people from what turned out to be a terrible, an appalling, incubus. But the day had been so dull, and having exhausted Old Moore and sampled the Imprecatory Psalms, I had nothing else to read. So I said, "Your own?"

"Even so," replied Mr. Tallent modestly.

"May I have the privilege?" I queried, knowing he intended me to have it.

"How kind!" he exclaimed. "A stranger, knowing nothing of my hopes and aims, yet willing to undertake so onerous a task."

"Not at all!" I replied, with a nervous chuckle.

"I think," he murmured, drawing near and, as it were, taking possession of me, looming above me with his great height, "it might be best for me to read it to you. I am considered to have rather a fine reading voice."

I said I should be delighted, reflecting that supper could not very well be later than nine. I knew I should not like the reading.

He stood before the cloth-draped mantelpiece.

"This," he said, "shall be my rostrum." Then he read. I wish I could describe to you that slow, expressionless, unstoppable voice. It was a voice for which at the time I could find no comparison. Now I know that it was like the voice of the loud speaker in a dull subject. At first one listened, taking in even the sense of the words. I took in all the first six chapters, which were unbelievably dull. I got all the scenery, characters, undramatic events clearly marshalled. I imagined that something would, in time, happen. I thought the characters were going to develop, do fearful things or great and holy deeds. But they did nothing. Nothing happened. The book was flat, formless, yet not vital enough to be inchoate. It was just a meandering expression of a negative personality, with a plethora of muted, borrowed, stale ideas. He always said what one expected him to say. One knew what all his people would do. One waited for the culminating platitude as for an expected twinge of toothache. I thought he would pause after a time, for even the most arrogant usually do that, apologizing and at the same time obviously waiting for one to say: "Do go on, please."

This was not necessary in this case. In fact, it was impossible. The slow, monotonous voice went on without a pause, with the terrible tirelessness of a gramophone. I longed for him to whisper or shout—anything to relieve the tedium. I tried to think of other things, but he read too distinctly for that. I could neither listen to him nor ignore him. I have never spent such an evening. As luck would have it the little maidservant did not achieve our meal till nearly ten o'clock. The hours dragged on.

At last, I said: "Could we have a pause, just for a few minutes?"

"Why?" he inquired.

"For ... for discussion," I weakly murmured.

"Not," he replied, "at the most exciting moment. Don't you realize that now, at last, I have worked up my plot to the most dramatic moment? All the characters are waiting, attent, for the culminating tragedy."

He went on reading. I went on waiting the culminating tragedy. But there was no tragedy. My head ached abominably. The voice flowed on, over my senses, the room, the world. I felt as if it would wash me away into eternity. I found myself thinking, quite solemnly: *If she doesn't bring supper soon, I shall kill him.*

I thought it in the instinctive way in which one thinks it of an earwig or a midge. I took refuge in the consideration how to do it? This was absorbing. It enabled me to detach myself completely from the sense of what he read. I considered all the ways open to me. Strangling. The bread knife on the sideboard. Hanging. I gloated over them. I was beginning to be almost happy, when suddenly the reading stopped.

"She is bringing supper," he said. "Now we can have a little discussion. Afterwards I will finish the manuscript."

He did. And after that, he told me all about his will. He said he was leaving all his money for the posthumous publication of his manuscripts. He also said that he would like me to draw up this for him, and to be trustee of the manuscripts.

I said I was too busy. He replied that I could draw up the will tomorrow.

"I'm going tomorrow," I interpolated passionately.

"You cannot go until the carrier goes in the afternoon," he triumphed. "Meanwhile, you can draw up the will. After that you need do no more. You can pay a critic to read the manuscripts. You can pay a publisher to publish them. And I in them shall be remembered."

He added that if I still had doubts as to their literary worth, he would read me another.

I gave in. Would anyone else have done differently? I drew up the will, left an address where he could send his stuff, and left the inn.

"Thank God!" I breathed devoutly, as the turn of the lane hid him from view. He was standing on the doorstep, beginning to read what he called a pastoral to a big cattle dealer who had called for a pint of bitter. I smiled to think how much more he would get than he had bargained for.

After that, I forgot Mr. Tallent. I heard nothing more of him for some years. Occasionally I glanced down the lists of books to see if anybody else had relieved me of my task by publishing Mr. Tallent. But nobody had.

It was about ten years later, when I was in hospital with a "Blighty wound," that I met Mr. Tallent again. I was convalescent, sitting in the sun with some other chaps, when the door opened softly, and Mr. Tallent stole in. He read to us for two hours. He remembered me, and had a good deal to say about coincidence. When he had gone, I said to the nurse, "If you let that fellow in again while I'm here, I'll kill him."

She laughed a good deal, but the other chaps all agreed with me, and as a matter of fact, he never did come again. Not long after this I saw the notice of his death in the paper.

Poor chap! I thought, *he's been reading too much. Somebody's patience has given out. Well, he won't ever be able to read to me again.*

Then I remembered the manuscripts, realizing that, if he had been as good as his word, my troubles had only just begun.

And it was so.

First came the usual kind of letter from a solicitor in the town where he had lived. Next, I had a call from the said solicitor's clerk, who brought a large tin box.

"The relations," he said, "of the deceased are extremely angry. Nothing has been left to them. They say that the manuscripts are worthless, and that the living have rights."

I asked how they knew that the manuscripts were worthless.

"It appears, sir, that Mr. Tallent has, from time to time, read these aloud—"

I managed to conceal a grin.

"And they claim, sir, to share equally with the—er—manuscripts. They threaten to take proceedings, and have been getting legal opinions as to the advisability of demanding an investigation of the material you have."

I looked at the box. There was an air of Joanna Southcott about it.

I asked if it were full.

"Quite, sir. Typed manuscripts. Very neatly done."

He produced the key, a copy of the will, and a sealed letter.

I took the box home with me that evening. Fortified by dinner, a cigar, and a glass of port, I considered it. There is an extraordinary air of fatality about a box. For bane or for blessing, it has a perpetual fascination for mankind. A wizard's coffer, a casket of jewels, the alabaster box of precious nard, a chest of bridal linen, a stone sarcophagus—what a strange mystery is about them all! So when I opened Mr. Tallent's box, I felt like somebody letting loose a genie. And indeed, I was. I had already perused the will and the letter, and discovered that the fortune was moderately large. The letter merely repeated what Mr. Tallent had told me. I glanced at some of the manuscripts. Immediately the room seemed full of Mr. Tallent's presence and his voice. I looked towards the now dusky corners of the room as if he might be looming there. As I ran through more of the papers, I realized that what Mr. Tallent had chosen to read to me had been the best of them. I looked up Johnson's telephone number and asked him to come round. He is the kind of chap who never makes any money. He is a freelance journalist with a conscience. I knew he would be glad of the job.

He came round at once. He eyed the manuscripts with rapture. For at heart, he is a critic, and has the eternal hope of unearthing a masterpiece.

"You had better take a dozen at a time, and keep a record," I said. "Verdict at the end."

"Will it depend on me whether they are published?"

"*Which* are published," I said. "Some will have to be. The will says so."

"But if I found them all worthless, the poor beggars would get more of the cash? Damnable to be without cash."

"I shall have to look into that. I am not sure if it is legally possible. What, for instance, is the standard?"

"*I* shall create the standard," said Johnson rather haughtily. "Of course, if I find a masterpiece—"

"If you find a masterpiece, my dear chap," I said, "I'll give you a hundred pounds."

He asked if I had thought of a publisher. I said I had decided on Jukes, since no book, however bad, could make his reputation worse than it was, and the money might save his credit.

"Is that quite fair to poor Tallent?" he asked. Mr. Tallent had already got hold of him.

"If," I said as a parting benediction, "you wish you had never gone into it (as, when you have put your hand to the plough, you will), remember that at least they were never read aloud to you, and be thankful."

Nothing occurred for a week. Then letters began to come from Mr. Tallent's relations. They were a prolific family. They were all very poor, very angry, and intensely uninterested in literature. They wrote from all kinds of viewpoints, in all kinds of styles. They were, however, all alike in two things—the complete absence of literary excellence and legal exactitude.

It took an increasing time daily to read and answer these. If I gave them any hope, I at once felt Mr. Tallent's hovering presence, mute, anxious, hurt. If I gave no hope, I got a solicitor's letter by return of post. Nobody but myself seemed to feel the pathos of Mr. Tallent's ambitions and dreams. I was notified that proceedings were going to be taken by firms all over England. Money was being recklessly spent to rob Mr. Tallent of his immortality, but it appeared, later, that Mr. Tallent could take care of himself.

When Johnson came for more of the contents of the box, he said that there was no sign of a masterpiece yet, and that they were as bad as they well could be.

"A pathetic chap, Tallent," he said.

"Don't, for God's sake, my dear chap, let him get at you," I implored him. "Don't give way. He'll haunt you, as he's haunting me, with that abominable pathos of his. I think of him and his box continually just as one does of a life and death plea. If I sit by my own fireside, I can hear him reading. When I am just going to sleep, I dream that he is looming over me like an immense, wan moth. If I forget him for a little while, a letter comes from one of his unutterable relations and recalls me. Be wary of Tallent."

Needless to tell you that he did not take my advice. By the time he had finished the box, he was as much under Tallent's thumb as I was. Bitterly disappointed that there was no masterpiece, he was still loyal to the writer, yet he was emotionally harrowed by the pitiful letters that the relations were now sending to all the papers.

"I dreamed," he said to me one day (Johnson always says "dreamed," because he is a critic and considers it the elegant form of expression), "I dreamed that poor Tallent appeared to me in the watches of the night and told me exactly how each of his things came to him. He said they came like Kubla Khan."

I said it must have taken all night.

"It did," he replied. "And it has made me dislike a masterpiece."

I asked him if he intended to be present at the general meeting.

"Meeting?"

"Yes. Things have got to such a pitch that we have had to

call one. There will be about a hundred people. I shall have to entertain them to a meal afterwards. I can't very well charge it up to the account of the deceased."

"Gosh! It'll cost a pretty penny."

"It will. But perhaps we shall settle something. I shall be thankful."

"You're not looking well, old chap," he said. "Worn, you seem."

"I am," I said. "Tallent is ever with me. Will you come?"

"Rather. But I don't know what to say."

"The truth, the whole truth—"

"But it's so awful to think of that poor soul spending his whole life on those damned ... and that they should never see the light of day."

"Worse that they should. Much worse."

"My dear chap, what a confounded position!"

"If I had foreseen *how* confounded," I said, "I'd have strangled the fellow on the top of that mountain. I have had to get two clerks to deal with the correspondence. I get no rest. All night I dream of Tallent. And now I hear that a consumptive relation of his has died of disappointment at not getting any of the money, and his wife has written me a wild letter threatening to accuse me of manslaughter. Of course, that's all stuff, but it shows what a hysterical state everybody's in. I feel pretty well done for."

"You'd feel worse if you'd read the boxful."

I agreed.

We had a stormy meeting. It was obvious that the people did need the money. They were the sort of struggling, under-vitalized folk who always do need it. Children were waiting for a chance in life, old people were waiting to be saved from death a little longer, middle-aged people were waiting to set themselves up in business or buy snug little houses. And there was

Tallent, out of it all, in a spiritual existence, not needing beef and bread anymore, deliberately keeping it from them.

As I thought this, I distinctly saw Tallent pass the window of the room I had hired for the occasion. I stood up; I pointed; I cried out to them to follow him. The very man himself.

Johnson came to me.

"Steady, old man," he said. "You're overstrained."

"But I did see him," I said. "The very man. The cause of all the mischief. If I could only get my hands on him!"

A medical man who had married one of Tallent's sisters said that these hallucinations were very common, and that I was evidently not a fit person to have charge of the money. This brought me a ray of hope, till that ass Johnson contradicted him, saying foolish things about my career.

And a diversion was caused by a tremulous old lady calling out: "The Church! The Church! Consult the Church! There's something in the Bible about it, only I can't call it to mind at the moment. Has anybody got a Bible?"

A clerical nephew produced a pocket New Testament, and it transpired that what she had meant was, "Take ten talents."

"If I could take one, madam," I said, "it would be enough!"

"It speaks of that too," she replied triumphantly. "Listen! 'If any man have one talent ... Oh, there's everything in the Bible!"

"Let us," remarked one of the thirteen solicitors, "get to business. Whether it's in the Bible or not, whether Mr. Tallent went past the window or not, the legality or illegality of what we propose is not affected. Facts are facts. The deceased is dead. *You've* got the money. *We* want it."

"I devoutly wish you'd got it," I said, "and that Tallent was haunting you instead of me."

The meeting lasted four hours. The wildest ideas were put forward. One or two sporting cousins of the deceased suggested a decision by games—representatives of the would-be beneficiaries and representatives of the manuscript. They were unable to see that this could not affect the legal aspect. Johnson was asked for his opinion. He said that from a critic's point of view the manuscripts were balderdash. Everybody looked kindly upon him. But just as he was sunning himself in this atmosphere, and trying to forget Tallent, an immense lady, like Boadicea, advanced upon him, towering over him in a hostile manner.

"I haven't read the books, and I'm not going to," she said, "but I take exception to that word balderdash, sir, and I consider it libellous. Let me tell you, I brought Mr. Tallent into the world!"

I looked at her with awesome wonder. She had brought that portent into the world! But how ... whom had she persuaded?... I pulled myself up. And as I turned away from the contemplation of Boadicea, I saw Tallent pass the window again.

I rushed forward and tried to push up the sash. But the place was built for meetings, not for humanity, and it would not open. I seized the poker, intending to smash the glass. I suppose I must have looked rather mad, and as everybody else had been too intent on business to look out of the window, nobody believed that I had seen anything.

"You might just go round to the nearest chemist's and get some bromide," said the doctor to Johnson. "He's overwrought."

Johnson, who was thankful to escape Boadicea, went with alacrity.

The meeting was, however, over at last. A resolution was passed that we should try to arrange things out of court. We were to take the opinions of six eminent lawyers—judges preferably. We were also to submit what Johnson thought the best story to a distinguished critic. According to what they said we were to divide the money up or leave things as they were.

I felt very much discouraged as I walked home. All these opinions would entail much work and expense. There seemed no end to it.

"Damn the man!" I muttered, as I turned the corner into the square in which I live. And there, just the width of the Square away from me, was the man himself. I could almost have wept. What had I done that the gods should play with me thus?

I hurried forward, but he was walking fast, and in a moment, he turned down a side street. When I got to the corner, the street was empty. After this, hardly a day passed without my seeing Tallent. It made me horribly jumpy and nervous, and the fear of madness began to prey on my mind. Meanwhile, the business went on. It was finally decided that half the money should be divided among the relations. Now I thought there would be peace, and for a time there was —comparatively.

But it was only about a month from this date that I heard from one of the solicitors to say that a strange and disquieting thing had happened: two of the beneficiaries were haunted by Mr. Tallent to such an extent that their reason was in danger. I wrote to ask what form the haunting took. He said they continually heard Mr. Tallent reading aloud from his works. Wherever they were in the house, they still heard him. I wondered if he would begin reading to me soon. So far it had only been visions. If he began to read....

In a few months I heard that both the relations who were haunted had been taken to an asylum. While they were in the asylum, they heard nothing. But, sometime after, on being certified as cured and released, they heard the reading again, and had to go back. Gradually the same thing happened to others, but only to one or two at a time.

During the long winter, two years after his death, it began to happen to me.

I immediately went to a specialist, who said there was acute nervous prostration, and recommended a "home." But I refused. I would fight Tallent to the last. Six of the beneficiaries were now in "homes," and every penny of the money they had had was used up.

I considered things. "Bell, book, and candle" seemed to be what was required. But how, when, where to find him? I consulted a spiritualist, a priest, and a woman who has more intuitive perception than anyone I know. From their advice I made my plans. But it was Lesbia who saved me.

"Get a man who can run to go about with you," she said. "The moment *He* appears, let your companion rush round by a side street and cut him off."

"But how will that—?"

"Never mind. I know what I think."

She gave me a wise little smile.

I did what she advised, but it was not till my patience was nearly exhausted that I saw Tallent again. The reading went on, but only in the evenings when I was alone, and at night. I asked people in evening after evening. But when I got into bed, it began.

Johnson suggested that I should get married.

"What?" I said. "Offer a woman a ruined nervous system, a threatened home, and a possible end in an asylum?"

"There's one woman who would jump at it. I love my love with an L."

"Don't be an ass," I said. I felt in no mood for jokes. All I wanted was to get things cleared up.

· · ·

About three years after Tallent's death, my companion and I, going out rather earlier than usual, saw him hastening down a long road which had no side streets leading out of it. As luck would have it, an empty taxi passed us. I shouted.

We got in. Just in front of Tallent's ghost we stopped, leapt out, and flung ourselves upon him.

"My God!" I cried. "He's *solid*!"

He was perfectly solid, and not a little alarmed.

We put him into the taxi and took him to my house.

"*Now*, Tallent!" I said, "you will answer for what you have done."

He looked scared, but dreamy.

"Why aren't you dead?" was my next question. He seemed hurt.

"I never died," he replied softly.

"It was in the papers."

"I put it in. I was in America. It was quite easy."

"And that continual haunting of me, and the wicked driving of your unfortunate relations into asylums?" I was working myself into a rage. "Do you know how many of them are there now?"

"Yes, I know. Very interesting."

"Interesting?"

"It was in a great cause," he said. "Possibly you didn't grasp that I was a progressive psychoanalyst, and that I did not take those novels of mine seriously. In fact, they were just part of the experiment."

"In heaven's name, *what* experiment?"

"The plural would be better, really," he said, "for there were many experiments."

"But what for, you damned old blackguard?" I shouted.

"For my *magnum opus*," he said modestly.

"And what is your abominable *magnum opus*, you wicked old man?"

"It will be famous all over the world," he said complacently. "All this has given me exceptional opportunities. It was so easy to get into my relations' houses and experiment with them. It was regrettable, though, that I could not follow them to the asylum."

This evidently worried him far more than the trouble he had caused.

"So it was *you* reading, every time?"

"Every time."

"And it was you who went past the window of that horrible room when we discussed your will?"

"Yes. A most gratifying spectacle!"

"And now, you old scoundrel, before I decide what to do with you," I said, "what is the *magnum opus*?"

"It is a treatise," he said, with the pleased expression that made me so wild. "A treatise that will eclipse all former work in that field, and its title is—'An Exhaustive Enquiry, with numerous Experiments, into the Power of Human Endurance.'"

PARGITON AND HARBY
DESMOND MACCARTHY

Robert Harby and Thomas Pargiton had known each other well in youth; indeed, they had once been devoted to each other; then, for more than twenty years, their friendship had lapsed. On going down from Cambridge together they had shared lodgings in London. Both had had to make their way in the world, but while Harby dreaded the prospect and would have preferred a safe civil service or academic career, Pargiton had looked forward avidly to competitive adventure. At Cambridge Harby had envied his friend his ambitious temperament, but he soon began to deplore it. The toughmindedness he used to admire at the university showed up in London as unscrupulousness; and some of the transactions in the city in which Pargiton had become involved struck Harby as certainly mean, if not positively illegal. He had not been sorry when, one morning, Pargiton abruptly informed him that he could no longer afford to live at such "a bad address," and moved to an ostentatious flat in a fashionable part of London. After that Harby had seen less and less of Pargiton. At last, he only heard of him now and then; once he saw his name in the papers in connection with a commercial case which hinted blackmail.

Meanwhile, Robert Harby had gone quickly along the path which opportunity had first opened to him. He had been employed by a firm of map publishers which, thanks to the demand for new maps after the war, had prospered, and in course of time he had been taken into partnership. The firm had recently been putting on the market a series of guide-books, and this enterprise, which had proved lucrative, was in his particular charge. It necessitated frequent journeys abroad, and it was on one of these expeditions, which combined busi-ness and pleasure in proportions agreeable to his tempera-ment, that, after twenty years, he had met Pargiton again.

Harby had just arrived at Dieppe one wet February after-noon, when, looking out of his bedroom window, which faced the cobbled marketplace, he noticed a tall man in a brown coat buying sweets at one of the stalls below. His figure struck him as familiar, but when the man moved away to distribute what he had just bought among a group of children, Harby thought he must have been mistaken. The man in the brown coat walked with a heavy limp. He appeared now to be making for Harby's hotel. It was—no, was it?—Pargiton! The largess of sweets Harby had just witnessed was not at all like Pargiton, nor was it like him to be staying at a commercial hotel rather than at one of the glittering palaces on the seafront, and Pargiton was not lame. Still, in spite of that, in spite, too, of that painful, hitching gait, Harby felt sure that this was none other than his old friend; but it was curiosity rather than eagerness which the next moment made him descend the corkscrew stairs to meet him. Although he could not see the face of the man who had just entered, for the hall of the hotel was a mere passage and only lit by the open door, he went straight up to him and addressed him by name. It was Pargiton; and Pargiton was glad to see him—pathetically glad, so Harby reflected late that night while he undressed.

After meeting they had repaired at once to one of the cafés under the arches which face Dieppe harbour. There they sat and talked over *apéritifs*, dinner, and *cognacs*, watching, through the plate glass, craft of all sorts gently rocking on the dark water and now and then a train draw up, jangling and panting, on the quay. Harby was starting early next morning for Caen; meanwhile, for the sake of his company. Pargiton contentedly allowed the Newhaven boat to depart without him into the night.

Reviewing their conversation in the train next day, Harby was surprised to discover how little, after all, Pargiton had told him about the last twenty years. By tacit consent they had gone back to their pre-London memories, and Pargiton had touched him a little by saying, "I have always associated you with my better self," adding, "Now I have found you again, I don't mean to let you go."

His career had apparently been chequered, till he inherited, about two years ago, his elder brother's fortune and tea-broking business. Harby had also gathered that Pargiton's brother had been engaged to a widow at the time of his death, and that the widow's son was now being educated at Oxford at Pargiton's expense, and that it was his intention to soon hand over the business to him.

He had not spoken of his brother directly, but Harby gathered that it was not compulsion, but loyalty, which was actuating him in these matters. This rather astonished Harby, for it came back to him that the brothers had been on very indifferent terms in old days; "My ass of a brother," was a phrase which he remembered had often been on Pargiton's lips. Harby would have supposed that he was probably in love with the widow, had not a question elicited the fact that he had never seen her. As for his lameness (one leg was decidedly shorter than the other), about that, too, Pargiton had been decidedly laconic: he had had a fall on the ice and smashed his thigh near the hip joint. What was past was, thank Heaven, past; he had suffered incessant and awful pain for nine months; now his leg only troubled him sometimes. He was living in a little house at Greenwich to save money, as he would soon have to give up the business to the boy. Harby must come to see him often, very often. He was lonely and hated new friends, but old friends were different. It was at this point in their talk that Pargiton had touched him by saying, with an almost frightened earnestness, "I have always associated you with my better self." He was certainly changed, very much changed.

Harby's tour in France lasted some months, during which he had several letters from Pargiton. Near the end of the time a telegram announced that Pargiton would join him at once, but it was followed next day by another, "All well. No need to bother you now. Look forward to your return."

Harby had no idea that Pargiton had ever had "any need" of him. Perhaps he had missed a letter while on the move? Two days later he received one which, though it mystified him still more, at least cleared up that point:

DEAR ROBERT,

I am afraid you must have thought from my last letter [so there had been another letter] either that I was making an absurd fuss about nothing or that I was going off my head. I wrote in great agitation. The fact is, I have experienced symptoms of the same kind before, but never before so late in the year. January is my bad month, and I thought it was well over, when I suddenly discovered that someone had been marking my books, an annoyance which preceded last time that feeling of never being alone which I told you in my last letter I dreaded. I happened to take down Newman's "Apologia." (*He has changed!* thought Harby.) You remember, perhaps, the passage in which he tells how on one of his solitary walks the Provost of Oriel quoted as he bowed and passed, "*Nunquam minus solus, quam cum solus.*" Well, *in my copy these words were underlined in a brownish, deep-red ink.* You will say I must have done it myself and forgotten. But I never mark my books, and I have never had red ink in the house. "Never less alone than when alone!" You can imagine how these words alarmed me. I hurriedly pulled out another book. (I must tell you that on occasions I believe my hand is strangely guided.) There was nothing marked in it. I turned over every page. In the third and fourth I examined I also found nothing, but in my Wordsworth, opposite the line, "That inward eye which is the bliss of solitude," was written —in my own hand—the word, "Bliss!" with an ironical exclamation mark after it. You will say that the fact that the writing was exactly like my own proves that I must have done it myself—perhaps in my sleep or in some strange state of unconsciousness. Of course, I gave that explanation full weight, but listen. It was Saturday afternoon; I felt I could not stay in the house. I wired to my chief clerk, who is a good fellow, saying that I was unwell and asking him to come down to Westgate with me for two nights. While we were there, I was burgled. The loss was trifling, a suitcase, a suit of clothes, a shirt or two, sponge, pyjamas, in fact— except that I had taken my brushes with me—the things one usually packs for a weekend. But that's not all. I must tell you first that I purposely tested my condition while at Westgate. I took a longish walk by myself and I felt all right. The sea air did me good. I had intended to keep the door between

Sparling's room and mine open at night, but it was not necessary. I felt perfectly secure, and slept well. The next day I sent my second wire to you. I returned to London on Monday with Sparling, but I begged him to come back to Greenwich with me for the night, as I was not yet absolutely certain that I should be easy in my own home. The maids met us with the story of the senseless theft. They had found the drawers in my bedroom pulled out on Sunday morning, and they had reported the matter to the police. The policeman on duty that night was a new man on the beat; he said he had seen a man come out of the house with a suit-case about 10 PM, but had thought nothing of it. Now comes the extraordinary and disconcerting thing. The same constable came to see me to ask the necessary questions, and the moment he entered the room I saw him give a start of surprise. He recovered himself quickly and grinned in rather an insolent way. When I asked him point-blank what he meant by his behaviour, he put on a knowing air and said, "I expect *you* can clear this little matter up. It don't seem a case for the police." I again asked him to explain himself, and went to the sideboard to mix him a whisky and soda. It had the usual propitiatory effect, for he then said, rather apolo-getically: "Well, sir, the person I see coming out of that front door Saturday night was a gentleman as didn't walk quite easily." At this, my glass shook in my hand so that I had to put it down. I managed, however, to assert pretty emphati-cally that *I* was at Westgate with a friend that night. He noticed my agitation, and smiling with a cocksure benevo-lence terrible to me, he replied, "Gentlemen does sometimes find it handy to be in two places at once. Good evening, sir." I know I dropped into a chair like one stunned. How long I sat there I don't know. I cannot tell you now all the thoughts which rose in my mind in connection with what had happened. Had I better stay where I was, or fly? You will see from the address at the top of this letter that I decided to return to Westgate. I have not been followed. The bad moments I endure are those when I first come into the hotel from a walk. Among the luggage of new arrivals I am always terrified of seeing my lost suitcase. But I am afraid of becoming afraid again.

Robert, after our long estrangement, I cannot ask you to leave your work and join me, but if old days still mean anything to you, as, thank God, they seemed to when we met, do not desert me. It is not in the name of affection I ask you to hasten your return and come to me—I have no right to anyone's affection, let alone yours—but take pity on me, help me. Come. Wire that you will come. With you I am my better self, my *old* self; I feel it. Then I am safe.

I must tell you that I took a Shakespeare to Westgate. This morning I picked it up, thinking it might distract my mind. On the page I opened I found these lines marked:

> *It will be short: the interim is mine;*
> *And a man's life is no more than to say, one.*

I have not dared to look at anymore.

Below the signature of the letter was scrawled this PS: "I have not told you all."

On first reading this letter, Harby concluded that Pargiton was going off his head, but on second thoughts he was inclined to suspend judgement. He would, in any case, be returning shortly to England, so he decided to wire that he would join him at Westgate. He left for England the next day.

On the journey his thoughts were naturally much concerned with Pargiton, and he reread his letter several times in the train. It was clear that he imagined himself to be the victim of some kind of supernatural persecution. Of course, the most plausible explanation of the facts was that he was suffering from incipient persecution mania, which had been intensified by the odd coincidence of his house having been broken into by a man who was also as lame as himself. The marking of the books was certainly an odd feature of the case, but it was probably self-justificatory evidence forged by the unhappy man himself to account for terrors peculiar to his state of mind.

When Harby stepped off the steamer at Dover, almost the first person he noticed in the crowd was Pargiton, who raised his hand in a kind of solemn, Roman gesture of greeting. He wanted to return straight to London.

All attempts on the journey to talk of things in general broke down, and the presence of other people in the carriage prevented confidences. They dined in London, and Pargiton's spirits seemed slightly to revive, but he was not communicative. They drooped again on reaching Greenwich.

His house was, as he had said, a small one; a semi-detached villa standing back from a road shaded by tall old trees.

A short, paved path led from the little gate to its pillared but modest portico. Pargiton's sitting room on the ground floor struck Harby as a delightful room. It was lined with books, and a large square mirror over the mantelpiece reflected prettily the green trees outside. Pargiton threw himself into a chair with something like a sigh of relief.

"You're thinking I ought to be happy here. Well, I am—as long as you are with me. I wish, old fellow, we could live together as we used to in old days. Anyhow," he added, "don't leave me yet awhile."

"About your letter," Harby began ... but Pargiton seemed reluctant to discuss that and proposed a game of chess.

"Just like old times," he said, setting the men; "it is the best dope in the world," and for half an hour he appeared to find it so. Then he suddenly jumped up before the game was finished and said he must have a breath of fresh air before going to bed.

As soon as the small iron wicket had clicked behind them, and they found themselves in the road, Pargiton, taking his friend's arm, said, "You noticed my postscript? I think now I can tell you everything. I have what I want—now, yet it has come to me in a way which has robbed me of all power to enjoy it. You remember I was very set on getting on? I was reckless, unscrupulous; I was also a failure. Do you remember my brother? No, of course you don't, but you must remember my talking about him. It was his death that saved me. I never cared about him, but I wish he hadn't died." He stopped speaking, and for some time they walked on in silence up the road towards the open heights of Blackheath. "My trouble—my trouble, which I wrote to you about is, I'm certain ... and yet I am not ... My brother was drowned. Did you see anything about it in the papers? Skating on the lake at his place in the country. I was with him at the time. It was terrible."

They had now emerged from the avenue into the open moonlight and the road lay white before them. Harby's eyes had been for some time fixed on the ground, for he had been filled with that uneasy feeling which possesses us when a companion is endeavouring to speak openly and yet is obviously unable to do so. He could not meet Pargiton's eye, who was continually turning his head towards him, as though he hoped to see that he was conveying more than he had actually succeeded in saying.

"It was terrible," he began again. "The ice broke whenever he tried to hoist himself on to it."

But Harby, though he heard the words, hardly took in their meaning; his eyes were fixed on what was in front of him. He stopped in amazement: their united shadows had unmistakably three heads.

"It was my fault, too," Pargiton went on, still trying to read his face. "I challenged him to a race. If I had not fallen myself and broken my thigh, I should have been done for, too."

Part of the composite shadow slowly elongated itself, and a pair of shoulders appeared beneath the extra head. Harby felt a grip on his arm; Pargiton had jerked him round.

"Don't you understand?" he said, in a voice of extraordinary tension; "it was partly my fault, *my fault*. My God, man, what's the matter with you? Listen, you must listen; it seems to me now that it is possible that—I am tortured by the suspicion that I believe I *knew* the ice near the other side of the lake was unsound."

Harby again turned his eyes from the agitated man beside him to the road. He was about to point to the shadow, when a cloud covered the moon. Perhaps it had been fancy. Yet, at the back of his mind he still thought he had seen what he had seen. Anyhow, the cat was out of the bag; Pargiton had made his confession, or as complete a one as he could bring himself to make. They presently turned back and descended the avenue together.

It was not abhorrence that Harby felt for his companion; or, if it was, it was so mixed with pity that it amounted only to a neutral feeling of indifference; but the sensation of Pargiton's arm in his had become unpleasant, and he could hardly listen to what he was saying: Pargiton was talking volubly about his past life. He did not mention his brother again, but he began to pour out an account of all he had done and regretted in the past. The past was the past—that was the refrain. A man could make a fresh start, couldn't he? He, Pargiton, was certainly now a different man. Hadn't Harby himself noticed that? A man might be too hard on himself, mightn't he? Might fancy he had been baser than he had been, especially if there was really a lot of good in him? By the time they reached the house, Pargiton had talked himself into a sort of wild gaiety. When they parted on saying goodnight, he wrung Harby's hand with an earnest squeeze, which made him more anxious than ever to leave the next morning.

Pargiton was still standing in the hall. To feel those imploring eyes upon his back as he ascended the stairs was bad enough, to return their gaze impossible. He passed the landing corner without looking back. How—in what words—should he tell Pargiton in the morning that he could have nothing more to do with him, that he must leave him to his fate? Was it horror at his crime, he asked himself (Harby was quite certain he was guilty), or fear of having to share some horrible experience with him that lay behind his resolve to go? In his mind's eye he saw again that third shadow detach itself from their combined shadows upon the white road. Was it, then, merely fear? In that case, ought he to yield? Did he care for Pargiton? No: that was over long ago. Yet he had undoubtedly begun a kind of friendship with him again—at any rate, he had roused in the wretched man some hope that he would not be in the future left utterly alone. What was the decent thing to do? Of course, he could make work an excuse tomorrow, and the easiest way would be to say he must go up to London, then wire that he was detained. But Pargiton would guess; he would insist on coming with him. To be followed about by a haunted murderer was unbearable. Yet he could not blame Pargiton for clutching on to him. What *ought* he to do?

He remained awake for hours, so it seemed, his thoughts

revolving round and round the same problem, only sometimes interrupting them to strain his ears to catch some tiny noise or other in the dark. Once or twice, when his thoughts were busiest about his own predicament, he had been nearly certain that he had heard, not the dreaded creak of Pargiton's footsteps on the stairs, but a strange, low, ringing sound, and twice he had switched on the light; but when he concentrated upon listening, he could hear absolutely nothing.

At last, without knowing it, he must have fallen asleep. For he found himself standing on the edge of a sheet of black ice. The moon was up, yet daylight had not quite left the sky, and a white mist lay knee-high round the shores of a long lake. Someone was waiting there in a creeping agony of excitement, but Harby could not tell whether it was he himself or another who was experiencing this horrible sense of expectation, for he seemed to be both the man he saw and a disembodied percipient. Again, his listening attention caught faint, faint at first, that low, sweet, ringing sound. It was coming nearer now, growing louder, and mingled with it he could distinctly hear the hiss of skates. Presently, he, too, was moving, travelling with effortless rapidity over a hard slightly yielding surface. He felt the wind of his own speed against his face; he heard the bubbles run chirruping under the sweep of his strokes and tinkle against the frozen edges of the lake; he felt the ice elastic beneath him, and his chest oppressed by a difficulty in breathing which was also somehow indistinguishable from a glow of triumph. Suddenly from the mist in front of him, he heard a crash, a cry. The echo seemed to be still in the room, when with flying heart and shaking hand he touched the switch of his lamp.

His door had been thrown violently open, and in the doorway stood Pargiton.

He was still fully dressed, but Harby only noticed his face.

The stricken man stood with his mouth a little open, swaying slightly. Harby went up to him, took him by the hand, led him to the bed, and made him lie down, but neither spoke, till Harby tried to disengage his hand and said, "I'll go and fetch a doctor."

Pargiton, who was lying motionless with open mouth, staring at the ceiling, rocked his head twice upon the pillow, and without moving his lips, breathed out the words: "No use."

"What's your maid's name? I'll call her."

Harby felt the grasp upon his hand tighten.

"I mean I'll shout for her," he added, "and tell her to fetch some brandy from downstairs."

"She mustn't go into that room," Pargiton breathed again.

"All right, but what's her name?"

"Bertha."

Without changing his position by the bed, Harby began to shout her name. It required a considerable effort of courage to raise his voice, but presently two startled women with outdoor coats over their nightgowns appeared. Harby took the situation in hand.

"I want you both to dress at once and go together to the nearest doctor. Your master has been taken ill. And tell him it's a heart case. No; tell him the patient is in bad pain. Tell him anything, to come prepared for anything—restoratives, sedatives. Quick."

A few minutes later the closing of the front door sent a shiver through Pargiton, and the next half-hour was the most painful vigil in Harby's life. For some time, the sick man lay still; then he raised the forefinger of his disengaged hand as though he was listening, or bidding his companion listen, while his face became festered with terror. Presently he sat bolt upright, staring into the passage. Harby wrenched away his hand and jumped up to shut the door. As he crossed the room the thought leapt at him that it might not shut—not quite; so vividly had those staring eyes imprinted, even for him, upon the framed oblong darkness, the sense of something on the threshold. Terrified himself, he flung his shoulder at the door and slammed it with a crash that shook the house. Pargiton sank back in a state of collapse upon the pillow; he seemed to have lost consciousness, and Harby made no attempt to rouse him from that happy state. A little later the sound of the doctor's footsteps on the stairs, however, did so only too effectively; all four of them found themselves engaged in a struggle with a wildly delirious man. At last, they succeeded in holding him down while a strong morphia injection brought at last relief. The doctor remained until a trained nurse arrived, and the dusk of early morning had already begun to brighten into day when he left. The same day Pargiton was removed by two trained attendants to a home for mental cases.

It was an inexpressible relief to Harby to find himself again in his own rooms. He went straight to bed, utterly exhausted, and awoke from a short sleep with steadied nerves, though with a strong reluctance either to think over what he had been through or to be alone. He decided to wire to ask an old friend, who was married to a particularly sensible and cheerful wife and surrounded by children of all ages, to receive him for a few days. The suggestion was warmly accepted, and Harby caught a late train. His hosts were puzzled by his looks and the suddenness of his visit, but they were kind enough to ask no questions, and a few days in their company did much to restore his equanimity. The first report he received of Pargiton (he had left directions that he should be kept informed) told him little beyond the fact that the condition of the patient was considered grave; the second, that he had had no more violent attacks, but that his despondent condition required the constant presence of an attendant. His physical state was also alarmingly low. The third report enclosed a letter from Pargiton himself; it ran as follows:

My DEAR HARBY,

I have enjoyed today and yesterday a peace of mind such as I have not experienced for a long time. I know what is the matter with me, and you know, but those who are looking after me do not. I know, too, that my release is near, and I have an inward confidence that it will not come in too cruel a way. I have paid my awful debt—my death is but the small item which still remains due. The worst is over; but I should like at least one other human being to know how bad it has been, and, especially, that you, my old friend, should know what I have had to endure. It may help you to think more mercifully of one whom you have reason to number among the basest of men. Verbally incomplete as my confession was on our walk at Greenwich, you grasped the whole truth. I was aware of it, as I watched you go upstairs to bed that night; and when you did not turn to look back at me, I knew that I had lost even the little claim I had upon your sympathy.

I find some difficulty in describing my state of mind at that moment. My confession, shirking, halting—for it concealed from you my certainty of my own guilt—lying as it was, had brought me extraordinary relief, and my courage had been artificially heightened by the whisky I had just drunk. I saw that I was repulsive to you, but depression at that was quickly succeeded by hope. I went into my room and drank another whisky and sat down in that big chair which faces the looking glass over the fireplace. My thoughts were busy with all I intended to do to atone, with my plans for that boy and his mother—the woman my brother intended to marry—and for you. I have no doubt I was maudlin; but you cannot imagine how sweet it was, even for awhile, to feel that I was not a scoundrel. The persecution I have suffered has not come from my poor brother; I am certain. The very nature of it had from the start pointed to a very different origin, even if the revelation I am about to describe had not occurred. Had I been pursued by his revengeful spirit, believe me, I should not have suffered so much, for I am capable of feeling enough genuine remorse to have bowed my head with recognition of its justice. No: my persecutor has been a being so intimately identified with myself that escape from him, or it, has been impossible, and propitiation a contradiction in terms. I have been pursued and tortured by a being who has as good a claim to be myself as the Pargiton you know, but who is now utterly repellent to me, and to whom every attempt on my part to dissociate myself from him—can you imagine the horror of this to one who longs, as I do, to have done with the past?—gives an intensified power of independent action. After every attempt I made to make amends, I have felt his power grow stronger. It was not until I first tried to help mother and son that I was conscious of him at all. I think now that it was because in your company, I was a better man that he came so close to me after we parted. What followed my confession to you, which was the greatest effort I ever made to reconquer self-respect, you shall hear.

How long I had been sitting in my chair planning how I should give up my ill-gotten wealth and lead the life of service, pure devoted service, which seemed miraculously open to me, I do not know. Perhaps I fell asleep; my sleep has been very poor and thin for a long time, hardly filming over a riot of thoughts and consciously created images. My future life was unrolling before me in comforting colours when, suddenly, the series of pictures was shattered by the clash of the iron wicket in the front of the house. I did not start, my new-found happiness was too strong upon me, though the thought occurred to me that the hour was singularly late for anyone—and who could it be?—to come to see me. It was the next sound which set my heart thumping; someone was approaching up the stone path to the porch. Now a lame man learns to know well the rhythm of his own footfalls, especially if he walks alone as often as I do. A heavy step, the click of a stick, a scraping, light step and then a heavy one again—Harby, those approaching steps were my own! I heard the grate of my latchkey in the lock and the heavy breathing of a cripple pausing on the mat. Two lurching steps would bring him, I knew well, within reach of the handle of the study door and from it I could not take my eyes; I tried to cover them, but I could not move my hands. I heard a stumble, a fumble; the brass knob turned and the door began to open slowly—nothing came in!

There are moments of terror so dreadful that nature in man cries out, "This can't be true," and I pray for all men that our death may not be such a moment; but there is, believe me, a terror beyond that, one which carries with it a sensation of absolute certainty against which the brain can raise no protest of frantic disbelief. I spun round in the agony of one who, not finding his assailant in front, looks behind, and I saw a face, an awful face. It was mine. Oh! sweet relief, I knew in an instant it was my own reflection in the glass;

that wild white face was mine, those glaring eyes were mine. I was still alone.

But the profound relief of that moment of recognition did not last. While I was still staring at myself, holding myself at arms' length from the mantelpiece, I thought the lips of my reflection smiled. When I put one hand to my mouth to feel if I too were smiling, the gesture was not repeated by the figure in front of me! The next moment that ultimate terror was on me with the spring of a tiger; though both my hands were clutching the mantelpiece and I could swear to the chill of the stone beneath them, the hands in the mirror were slowly stretching out to reach me. I heard a crash; I must have fallen; I don't remember picking myself up. When consciousness returned, I was standing at your bedroom door. You know the rest.

I have only one more thing to tell you. Lying here in this place, where everyone is kind and no one understands, I have been thinking things out. Those hopes of a new life were all false dreams; I could never live such a life. I see what I must do: I understand now that to go on defying my Past Self, though every act of defiance intensifies his power to destroy me, *is* my proper expiation, and when I think of him in that light, I am no longer afraid. What is death without terror? Nothing—an event that isn't even part of life. Even my weakling's confession to you almost enabled him to get his hands upon my throat. I have written to my brother's wife—for so I always think of her—telling her how and why the idea entered my head of luring my brother on to ice I had tested and knew did not bear. I have not spared myself. I have, of course, left everything I possess to her and her boy. My end therefore is now certain. If you care to see me again, come, but don't think that I am asking for or depending upon support.

When Harby read this letter, he wired to say that he would be with him that afternoon, but a telegram, which crossed with his, informed him that Pargiton had died in his sleep the night before. What had been, Harby wondered, his last dream? In his coffin he looked stern and peaceful, but the faces of the dead tell us nothing.

PUBLISHER'S NOTE

This book was produced as part of the Publishing master's degree program at Western Colorado University, Graduate Program in Creative Writing. The students worked cooperatively to produce these fine new editions of worthy public-domain works. The intent is to bring literary classics to a new readership. For the enjoyment of a modern audience, some minor revisions to archaic terms or punctuation may have been made.

Because these works were written in a different time, some attitudes and phrasing may seem outdated to a modern audience. After careful consideration, rather than revising the author's work, we have chosen to preserve the original wording and intent.

ABOUT THE COMPILING EDITOR
LADY CYNTHIA ASQUITH

Born in Wiltshire, England on September 27, 1887, Lady Cynthia Asquith would become known for her diaries during World War I. In 1918 she would become the personal secretary to J.M. Barrie, author of *Peter Pan*. She stayed in this role until his death in 1937, after which she inherited a good portion of his estate. A writer in her own right, she published novels, biographies, screenplays, short story collections, and works for children.

A popular anthologist, Lady Asquith edited many collections for children. In 1926, Lady Asquith compiled what was widely considered the first literary attempt to collect non-traditional ghost stories in the twentieth-century and titled it *The Ghost Book*. She included authors who were friends, like D.H. Lawrence; literary stars, such as Algernon Blackwood; and included one of her own written under the pseudonym C.L. Ray. She would return to the series 25 years later to compile and edit *The Second Ghost Book* in 1952 and *The Third Ghost Book* in 1955. She would write and publish many other works of short fiction until her death on March 30, 1960.

ABOUT THE FOREWORD AUTHOR
KEVIN J. ANDERSON

Kevin J. Anderson has published more than 175 books, 58 of which have been national or international bestsellers. He has written numerous novels in the Star Wars, X-Files, and Dune universes, as well as a unique steampunk fantasy trilogy beginning with Clockwork Angels, written with legendary rock drummer Neil Peart. His original works include the Saga of Seven Suns series, the Wake the Dragon and Terra Incognita fantasy trilogies, the Saga of Shadows trilogy, and his humorous horror series featuring Dan Shamble, Zombie P.I. He has edited numerous anthologies, written comics and games, and the lyrics to two rock CDs. Anderson is the director of the graduate program in Publishing at Western Colorado University. Anderson and his wife Rebecca Moesta are the publishers of WordFire Press. His most recent novels are *Clockwork Destiny, Gods and Dragons, Dune: The Heir of Caladan (with Brian Herbert),* and *Double-Booked.*

ABOUT THE EDITOR
JESSICA GUERNSEY

Jessica Guernsey has over two decades of experience in editing her own works. With a degree from Brigham Young University in Journalism, she's worked in minor roles in print media. By day, she crushes dreams as a slush pile reader for a mid-level publisher. Freelance work includes developmental editing and manuscript evaluation. She has been an integral part of the editing team for WordFire Press over the last year, producing a novel and one full-length anthology.

After spending her teenage angst in Texas, she now lives on a mountain in Utah with her family and a co-dependent mini schnauzer. She often teaches at writing conferences and volunteers as a Municipal Liaison for National Novel Writing Month. Jessica will graduate with her Masters in Publishing from Western Colorado University in August 2023.

WORDFIRE CLASSICS

Mother of Frankenstein: Maria: or, The Wrongs of Woman &
Memoirs of the Author of A Vindication of the Rights of Woman
by Mary Wollstonecraft

We: The 100th Anniversary Edition
by Yevgeny Zamyatin

One Stormy Night : A Story Challenge That Created the Gothic
Horror Genre
by Lord Byron, Dr. John William Polidori, and Mary Shelley

HOLIDAY CLASSICS

The Ghost of Christmas Always
by Charles Dickens & Kevin J. Anderson

The Santa Claus Stories
by L. Frank Baum

Our list of other WordFire Press authors and titles is always
growing. To find out more and to shop our selection of titles,
visit us at:
wordfirepress.com

f facebook.com/WordfireIncWordfirePress
🐦 twitter.com/WordFirePress
📷 instagram.com/WordFirePress
BB bookbub.com/profile/4109784512